Christmas

THEN AND NOW

Stories of the Season

Dr. Jon R. Roebuck

This book is dedicated
to my family…

Linda, Andrew, Andrea, Katie Grace, Jason, Anna, & Rob

Their willingness to share their lives with me makes my "life story"
immeasurably full and overwhelmingly blessed.

Contents

CHRISTMAS NOW...

Preface

For those of us who climb into the pulpit week after week, month after month, and year after year, telling the story of Advent can be a little difficult for several reasons. First, there is the problem of repetition. Many of us lead churches that celebrate the four Sundays of Advent. Do that in the same setting over the course of several years, and suddenly the well can get a little dry. For example, I am well into my fifteenth year at my current pastorate. Do the math. That's sixty Advent messages to write. Sometimes fresh ideas can be difficult to find.

Second, there is the problem of familiarity. Without exception, everyone to whom we preach has heard the story of Mary, Joseph, and the child in the manger. Everyone. So how do we make the message of Christmas relevant, new, and exciting, season after season? I wondered if there was a way to tell the "old" story in a "new" way.

A few years back, I decided to try something a little different. I decided to write a story of Christmas, using both historical setting and pure imagination. I enjoyed the diversion from normal sermon writing. I also enjoyed the process of creating an original narrative to convey the message of Christmas. I first wrote a "period" piece set in the context of ancient Israel. I then tried my hand with a modern-day story. Both were well received by my listeners. Soon, the stories became a part of Christmas at Woodmont. What you hold in your hand is a collection of twenty-five stories that I have written over the past dozen or so years. Some are set centuries ago while others are drawn from modern life—thus the title, *Christmas: Then and Now*. It is my sincere hope that each of these stories will remind you of God's unfolding plan of redemption and grace offered through the child born at Christmas.

Christmas Then...

CHAPTER 1

Sneaky Grace

Isaiah 9:2; John 1:1-5a

His hands were old and gnarled, just like the pieces of knotty pine that had helped to make them that way. For a lifetime, Samuel had been a carpenter, like his father and grandfather before him. Shaping and carving wood was all he had ever known. It was all he had ever wanted to do. It was his passion; at times, it was his obsession. His earliest memories were bound to his father's shop. As a young boy it was his job to sweep the sawdust and the wood shavings out from under his father's feet. He learned early how to use a saw, how to sand, how to carve, and how to shape into form. By the time he was a teenager, he had already become one of the better carpenters in the whole village.

Through the years, his skills sharpened, as did his fame. His work was sought out by some of the finest families in town. They would come to his shop and describe the piece they desired. He would take their dream and turn it into reality—a chair, a table, a cabinet, whatever was needed. It seemed that he could do it all. He was a master carpenter whose skills were second to none.

Once, the local rabbi had commissioned him to carve new wooden spindles to hold the sacred scrolls of the prophets, which were read each Sabbath day. Such spindles are called in the Hebrew language *azei hayyim*, which means "Tree of Life." He labored for months over every intricate detail. The wood was polished to the point that it looked like marble. Carefully, he carved symbols of faith into each piece—a Star of David, a shepherd's staff, a sacrificial lamb. When the final product was presented, his heart filled with pride. Each week as the scrolls were unfurled, he felt a sense of justifiable accomplishment.

He worked with all kinds of wood, though cedar was his favorite. It was soft and easy to carve. Wood from the olive trees was by far the most durable, yet many saws had he dulled on its tough texture. He made furniture, wall hangings, and small carvings of various figures within the Old Testament stories. On each piece he would leave his mark. He took a branding iron and heated it in the fire until it was red hot. He would then sear his unique mark into the wood. As a master carpenter the brand carried weight. Any piece that bore that mark was valuable, well made by one of the best. But that was a long time ago.

Time had not been a friend to his craft. He had not aged well. His hair had turned gray, his eyes had become weak, and he carried a little weight around the middle. His back always hurt, and it was hard to stand without his knees screaming for some relief. Over the years his hands had begun to lose their skill. They were no longer steady as they had once been. They were now stiff, and the joints ached each time he gripped a hammer or attempted to hold a chisel. The demands for his work were all but gone. His time was spent mostly on repair jobs, fixing pieces made by other more skilled carpenters, which on occasion needed a repair. He made stools and simple chairs. Any young apprentice could have made the tables he now made. The masterpieces were just ordinary things, nothing of real value, nothing held in much demand by anyone. It had been years since he placed his mark on anything.

A year or so ago, a woman had stopped in the shop. Her mother had given her a beautiful table and chairs that he had once made. She needed another chair. "Can you make one to match the others?" she inquired. He offered her great assurance, but in his mind he had his doubts. He worked on it for nearly three months. He cut, and he carved, and he shaped. His hands ached, and his back screamed for relief. But over time and with great effort, the task was complete. He turned it over and burned his mark onto the bottom of the seat. He loaded it on his back and began the journey across town to where the affluent lived. He found the address and knocked at the back door. She let him inside and led him to the place where it was to sit. He unwrapped it carefully and sat it next to the others. She took one look and said, "I'm sorry, but it's not even close. I can't use it." He could not even muster up any anger, for he knew that she was right. It looked horrible in comparison. He tipped his hat and loaded it onto his back and began the long walk back home. It was twilight by the time he got to the shop. He set it in the middle of the floor. He thought of all the toil and effort, all the weeks spent working the wood. He picked up a small hatchet and smashed the chair into a thousand pieces. He spent the night watching each piece slowly burn in the fire. It was as though his very life was going up in smoke.

As the months progressed and his skills continued to diminish, he found himself slipping into a deep and dark depression. All that had once been his joy and passion was now a part of what pained him the most. He spent his days playing the part of a beggar. He was soon known and recognized by the people of Bethlehem for that role. Former friends would go out of their way to avoid him. During the day he would go from shop to shop, from stranger to stranger: "I'm just an old carpenter…could you help me out a little?"

Each day he would collect a little—a coin here, a few coins there. Not enough to live on, but enough to buy some sweet wine at a local tavern where he could drink away the pain of being too old, too useless, and too unimportant. Every night he would make his way to the tavern. He would sit in a corner, always alone, having conversations with himself. Sometimes the dialogue would become heated and angry. Sometimes he would cry. Sometimes he would curse his hands, which had once given him such status but now betrayed him over and over again. Each night he would quickly spend all of the day's collection. At closing time the owner, who treated him with patience, would help him to the door and would always wish him well as he walked away: "Shalom, Samuel."

Samuel learned how to survive. He would stumble his way down the narrow streets looking for a place to bed down for the night. Sometimes he found a quiet corner between a couple buildings. Sometimes it was a doorway that gave him shelter. Sometimes it was the soft ground beneath a shade tree. This night he lucked out. He wandered around the back of an old inn, where he discovered a stable. A young boy was pitching fresh straw among the animals. "Don't mind me, boy. I'm just an old carpenter looking for a place to sleep it off," he said. Then he found a quiet corner with plenty of soft hay, and within moments he went into a deep sleep.

He remembered stirring for a moment during the wee hours of the night. The same boy was moving among the stalls gathering up clean straw for some reason. He dismissed it and went back to sleep. Several hours later he awakened with a jolt. Though he had consumed enough to keep him groggy for hours, he found himself very much awake, with the realization that a number of people had crowded into the stable. He heard excited voices and shouts of praise. Hidden in the shadows, he moved a bit closer, where he could see the source of all the excitement and conversation. Though it was still well before sunrise, he could make out the features of at least ten people in the stable. Who, what, and why? He saw the young stable boy again, but there were others. They had the smell of shepherds. Some were still holding their staffs, but most were kneeling as though in prayer. One very excited young man was telling the story of all that he had seen and heard. He talked of angels in the night sky and of heavenly choruses singing praises to God. The angels had said, "For unto you is born this day in the city of David, a savior, who is Christ the Lord."

He moved closer and saw the object of their excitement. A young mother was holding a newborn child. The father stood close by. The mother's face was glowing like that of any new mother holding her child for the first time. She was excited to hear the words of the shepherds. She, too, had heard from angels concerning the birth of her son. She spoke of how the angel Gabriel himself had appeared to her, announcing that she would bear the Son of God! The shepherds hugged and wept and prayed and rejoiced. They seemed almost giddy with excitement. One of the younger shepherd boys asked, "What are you going to name him?"

The father of the baby said, "God has told us to name him Jesus, meaning, 'One who will save the people from their sins.'"

It had been a long time since Samuel had been in the synagogue on the Sabbath. He had drifted away from God in the midst of his frustration and anger. Yet, suddenly, the words of the prophet came to mind, words taken from the scroll of Isaiah, which had been rolled on the spindles he had once made. The words of the coming of the messiah raced across his mind with such clarity that he could almost see them: "For a child will be born to us, a son will be given to us; and the government will rest on his shoulders; and his name will be called Wonderful Counselor, Mighty God, Eternal Father, Prince of Peace." Could it be? Could the salvation of the world have come? Could this tiny child, born among the animals and common people of his day, be the son of the living God? Earlier, the father had mentioned that they were traveling because of the census. They were from Nazareth, of the house and lineage of David. It all fit—the angel's proclamation, the evidence of Scripture, the promises of God's coming messiah. It was happening in this place, on this night, in the presence of these people!

The baby drifted off to sleep again. The mother carefully wrapped him in a blanket and placed him in the animal's manger. It had been stuffed full with soft hay and seemed to make a wonderful crib for the newborn infant. After several final moments of praise and bowing before the manger, the shepherds quietly left the stable, not to awaken the child. Soon the mother drifted off to sleep, completely exhausted but completely filled with joy. The father, Joseph, placed his coat around her and sat nearby until exhaustion finally caught up with him as well.

It was already mid-morning by the time Samuel awoke. It took just a moment for him to get his bearings. As he was wiping the sleep from his eyes, he suddenly remembered all that his eyes had seen the night before. The young family was busy packing up their belongings. Their donkey was being loaded with their meager possessions—a few blankets, a cloth bag into which the mother had placed some bread and cheese. The baby was sleeping soundly in the manger. When everything was packed, she took him into her arms, and they walked out into the bright morning sun. As she passed by the manger, the fringe of her shawl caught momentarily on the corner. Without her knowledge, the small manger overturned and landed quietly in the soft hay.

Only after they were out of sight did Samuel move from his seclusion. He walked over to the manger and quietly set it on its feet again. Something caught his eye. It was a carpenter's mark, seared on the bottom of the manger. It was the distinct mark that he once seared into every piece he made. Could it be? Was this the product of his hands? The mark was undeniable. Somewhere long ago, he had fashioned this very manger, maybe as a young apprentice in his father's shop. And suddenly he realized that his skill had not been wasted, but used of God. Of all the masterpieces created in his life of carving and cutting, this had become his greatest work. This simple manger had become a crib for the newborn king. The Son of God had rested in a manger made by his hands!

He stood lost in his thoughts for a long time. Finally, he was interrupted by a young woman's voice. He turned to discover that it was the young mother with her child. "Are you the innkeeper?" she asked. "I wanted to say thank you."

"No, I'm not the innkeeper. You see, I'm just an old carpen… I mean, I'm a master carpenter. I have even made a crib for the king."

"You must be gifted by God," she said. "I hope someday I can see your fine work." She turned and walked away.

He would never be the same again. He noticed the sun seemed a bit brighter, the air more alive. The beauty of God's world was a bit more brilliant. He walked to the synagogue, a place he hadn't been in a long time. It was not the Sabbath, and only a few people were even around. He knelt down to offer his thanks to God, thinking of how much his outlook had changed just from seeing the child of Mary and Joseph and the hope his coming had promised. A young Levite student was reading aloud from a scroll, the spindles of which had been beautifully carved. He read from Isaiah, "The people who walk in darkness will see a great light. Those who live in a dark land, the light will shine on them."

Sometimes the grace of God sneaks up on us. Just when we feel forgotten, alone, depressed, and discouraged, the light of God's love reaches to lift us to life again. On our darkest days, when hope is gone and joy is drained away, still the angel's proclamation is meant for us: "Behold I bring you good news of a great joy which shall be for all the people. For unto you is born this day in the city of David, a savior, who is Christ the Lord."

Let's face it. We do live in a dark land. There is injustice, evil, hatred, and prejudice. There is greed and envy and jealousy. The darkness seems to close in around us, and sometimes we wonder, "Where is the hope? Where is the answer?" Look to the manger again and remember who the child in the hay turned out to be. John's Gospel describes him this way: "In the beginning was the Word, and the Word was with God, and the Word was God. He was in the beginning with God. All things came into being through him, and apart from him nothing came into being that has come into being. In him was life, and the life was the Light of men. The Light shines in the darkness."

This Christmas, allow God's grace to sneak up on you. I don't know all the circumstances of your life story this Christmas. Maybe this has been a difficult year. Maybe you lost a loved one. Maybe you lost your job. Maybe you lost your marriage. Perhaps your self-esteem has taken quite a beating. Maybe you have been lost in the darkness of sin and failure. The point of Christmas is that you do not have to stumble around in the dark any longer. Even now, God's grace is reaching out to your life and to your heart. He has not abandoned you, nor has he given up on you. You are his child. You are of great worth. He sent his son to earth just to remind you how much he loves you. Stand in wonder. Stand in awe. It's God's grace that fills your heart.

CHAPTER 2

Enduring Hope

Psalm 146:5-10; Luke 1:47-55

He was born to poor parents, "people of the earth," or so they were once called. People who came into the world with nothing and would one day leave it the same way. But like all parents, they held high hopes for their son that his life would be better than theirs. Invested in him were all their dreams and plans. They were honest people, simple people, hard-working people.

His father worked the vineyards and kept the livestock for an affluent family. Up before the sun each day, he would walk to work, pausing only for an hour or so in the middle of the day to eat his lunch, which he carried in a small burlap sack. Everything about his looks spoke of the hard life he lived. His clothes were always filthy; dirt was always under his nails. His face was tanned and bore deep wrinkles around the eyes from too many years of squinting in the bright sun. He was thirty-six years old, but he looked the part of someone twice that age. He was stooped and walked with the gait of someone who seemed to have been worn down by life.

Michael's mother was also working her way to an early grave. At home, she did all the normal chores in their one-room home. She was always the first to awaken each day. Long before Michael awoke, she had done a day's work. The fire in the earthen stove would be lit, and bread would be baking for the family's daily needs. She was also the last to lie down at night. If she had ever been sick a day in her life, Michael had never seen it. He would often hear her late at night offering her prayers. She would sometimes quote the psalmist: "How blessed is he whose help is the God of Jacob, whose hope is in the LORD his God, who made heaven and earth, the sea and all that is in them; who keeps faith forever; who executes justice for the oppressed; who gives food to the hungry." Sandwiched between the hours of toil and labor at home, she worked every day, all day, making cloth for a local merchant. She made wool blankets with intricate designs and patterns. She also made shawls and sometimes would sew together a new robe or cloak when the market called for such wares.

Michael seemed destined to follow in his father's footsteps, though his father wanted something more for his son. But from the time Michael could first walk, he followed his father to the fields. He would shadow his father's every move. And though he soon learned the workings of the farm—the tilling of soil, the pruning of vines, and the feeding of the sheep—he loved the horses most of all. He loved their beauty, their strength, their speed. By the time he turned ten, he had become a good farmhand and was a great help to the owner, who began to pay him a small wage. Michael didn't enjoy the long hours of tedious work in the vineyards, but he gladly spent those hours just to have a few moments each day with the horses. He dreamed of a day when he might have a horse of his own, but deep inside he knew caring for horses owned by other men would be the closest he would ever get to that dream.

The defining moment of his young life came at the age of eleven. The owner of the farm had purchased an Arabian stallion. It was bigger, stronger, and more beautiful than any other horse Michael had ever seen. His father had seen the gleam in his eye and could see the wheels turning in his mind. He knew of the potential for danger. "Don't ride the wild stallion," he warned. "It's not something that a boy can handle. Don't get on that horse. You hear me, son?" Michael nodded.

It was about a week later. The afternoon was late. His father had already begun the trek home. "I won't be long," said Michael. "I've just got a few things to finish up. I'll be along shortly." With bridle in hand, he walked into the corral with the stallion. He called it by name, and it quickly came to where he was standing. Very gently and very slowly, he slipped the bridle onto the horse's head. With one quick leap he was sitting atop the mighty animal. He patted the neck to ensure the horse was comfortable with the feel of his new rider. After a moment, Michael gently kicked his heels. In a flash, the horse went from a calm stand to a raging fury. Michael was bucked into the air and landed on the ground with a thud. A pain like he had never experienced shot through his left leg. The bone was shattered, broken in at least three places. He screamed at the top of his lungs, but no one was within earshot.

After what seemed like an eternity, he finally spotted another farm-hand way off in the distance. Again, he screamed, and soon the worker was kneeling at his side, surveying the damage. "It's broke bad," said the farm-hand. "It looks real bad." As he ran for help, all Michael could think of was his father's advice: "Don't ride the wild stallion; it's not something you can handle."

His life was never the same again. At first he was confined to his mat in the corner of his family's home. After a few months he was able to walk with a splint and a cane. In time the splint came off, but the cane remained for many months. He learned to adjust, and soon even the cane was put away, but he was left with a severe limp. It pained him to walk for very long. His days of working the fields were over. His employment soon ended, as did his future. He mostly stayed at home, never venturing far from the house. The boys his age soon began to make up nicknames. Each time he came outside, he heard the taunts and the ugly jeers. It's amazing how quickly people can ridicule those who are different from themselves.

To make matters worse, whispers and rumors among the people of the village began to spread like wildfire. "It's God punishment," they said. "It's obvious that he is paying for his sins or those of his father." Most believed that physical illness was a result of some spiritual transgression. Even his father gave in to their way of thinking. Mixed in with his anger was the disappointment he felt over a son who would never amount to anything. The broken leg meant broken dreams. The relationship became strained over the months and even verbally abusive at times. His father seemed mad at the world, mad at life, even mad at God. Armed with only the love of his mother and few meager possessions, at the age of fourteen, he walked out of his father's life and out of his house.

He went from door to door looking not for a handout, but for a place to work, a place where he might stay. He had inherited his parents' work ethic, and he was ready to do almost anything. After several days of sleeping on the ground and scrambling for food, he noticed an old inn at the end of a narrow street. What caught his attention was not the inn itself, but the unde-niable smells of a stable, which was located in the back. He walked around the back and noticed a couple donkeys and a cow penned up in the stable. He climbed up on the fence and gave the cow a soft pat between the eyes.

"What are you doing there, boy?" asked an old man. He was appar-ently the innkeeper, who looked somewhat awkward at tending to animals.

Michael could tell that this task was not a part of his normal routine. "Nothing, sir. I just thought I might look at the animals for a while."

The innkeeper raised an eyebrow. "You know much about animals?" he asked.

"Yes, sir, I do," he said. "I used to help tend to 'em all the time, that is, before I got hurt and had to quit."

The innkeeper saw a glimmer of hope from his tired back and blistered hands. "How about taking care of these animals for me tonight? I just lost my help a couple days ago. Come back tomorrow, and I'll pay you for your time, not much, mind you, just a few pennies if you do a good job."

That night, Michael slept on the soft hay right in the stall with the animals. The next morning, by the time the innkeeper got around to check on him, he had already filled the manger and the water trough, raked out the dirty straw, and brushed out the manes of both donkeys.

"What's your name, boy?" asked the innkeeper.

"It's Michael, sir," he replied.

"Well, Michael, this place hasn't looked this good in weeks. You're not interested in work, are you? With all these people traveling because of the census, I could use some help with the stable. People want a nice place for their animals, you know."

Michael couldn't believe his ears nor his good fortune. "I'd love to work here!" he blurted out. "I mean, I might be able to help out for a few weeks."

"Good! It's settled, then," said the innkeeper. "There's a small loft above the stable. You might make a place to stay if you want. I won't charge you anything for it. You just tend to the stable, and I'll let you keep all the tips."

Michael climbed the ladder to the loft. It was small and bare, but it was also away from the cold ground and near the animals. He could think of no better place to stay. There was a small table and a chair. It had obviously been the "home" of the former stable hand. Michael quickly began settling in. He unrolled his cot near the table. He brought up a little wooden chest from below, one that contained everything he owned. Inside was an oil lamp, which he took and placed on the table. It also contained his treasures—a good strong rope he had once used at the old farm, a little metal box in which he kept what little money he had, and his prized possession, a warm blanket that his mother had made. Along with the colorful designs, she had woven a horse design in the very middle. "It will help to keep me warm on cold nights," he thought to himself. His eyes misted as he thought of his mother. He missed her greatly. He missed his father too. He wondered if he could ever go home again.

The days passed quickly. It was an exciting life for Michael. Each day brought a different set of animals. He cared for them all—goats, donkeys, cattle, and even a horse every once in a while. He worked hard and befriended all the locals. They knew him by name, and they seemed to appreciate his hard work. The innkeeper would sometimes come out to share a conversation. In time, Michael told him his story, about the broken leg and all. He was treated fairly and made enough to live.

A second defining moment occurred a few months after he arrived. It was a busy night; the town was filled with travelers, and soon the little inn was filled. Business was good at the stable also. He worked late into the night, making sure that each animal was well cared for. Just about the time he was finishing up, he was startled by an old man who was snooping around. "I'm just an old carpenter, looking for a place to sleep it off," said the old man. He seemed harmless enough, and Michael knew what it was like to sleep on the street, so he gave the man a place to stay in "his" stable.

Much later, about the time Michael was reaching over to blow out his oil lamp, he heard the voice of the innkeeper. "Michael," he whispered, "you awake?"

"Yes, sir," he said. "What's wrong?"

"Nothing," he said. "There's a young couple at the door. They've been traveling all day. They look exhausted, and she is very pregnant. I was wondering if you could make a spot somewhere below for them to stay for the night? They'll take anything."

Michael thought of the old drunk already sleeping below. "Sure, why not?" The more, the merrier, he thought.

The innkeeper added, "They've got a donkey that needs tending to as well."

"Yes, sir, I'll get right to it," Michael promised.

Michael helped the young people. The innkeeper was right. They *were* exhausted, and she *was* very pregnant. They spread some blankets on the soft hay and watered down the animal. Michael noticed their kindness. They asked his name, and they thanked him for the help he offered. They even shared some bread and cheese they had brought with them. Before he could blow out his lamp, he could already hear the sounds of their deep slumber just below him. As soon as his eyes adjusted to the darkness, he noticed the stars outside his window seemed a bit more brilliant. He began to count them, and soon he, too, drifted off to sleep, grateful to have a full belly and a full stable of both people and livestock.

It was several hours later when Michael was jolted from his slumber. It was the husband, Joseph, whispering from the top of the ladder that led from the stable to the loft where Michael slept. "Michael, come quickly! I need your help. My wife has just given birth, and I need to make a soft bed for her to place our child. It's a boy! Can you help me?" He sounded desperate. Michael quickly lit his lamp and carried it with him below. He saw the young mother holding the child. She was beaming. Her face conveyed peace and joy. She no longer looked wearied, but aglow with life.

He quickly scanned the stable. "I know," he said to Joseph. "We can use the manger." He raked out all the old straw and quickly began gathering fresh, clean straw to fill the manger. Mary took her shawl from around her shoulders and carefully lined the makeshift crib.

"It's perfect, Michael," she said. "God has blessed us tonight by having you here to help us."

Joseph added his gratitude and then said, "Michael, we need some fresh water. Is there a well close by where I might draw some water for Mary?"

"I'll go!" Michael said. "You stay here with Mary, and I'll be right back." In a flash, Michael grabbed a wooden pail and limped off into the darkness.

By the time he returned to the stable, a group of boys and men had crowded into the entrance of the stable. He could tell they were shepherds, but he wondered why they had come. "I hope they are not bothering the young couple," he said to himself. He pushed his way to the front.

"This is Michael," Mary said to the shepherds as though she had known him for many years. "God also used him tonight to help us." She looked at Michael: "You must hear the story of the shepherds. You will understand why they have come."

Quickly, one of the older men began to retell the story. He told of the words of the angels and of the heavenly chorus that had offered such praises to God. "And listen to this, Michael," he said. "The angel told us that God would give us a special sign that would help us to identify the newborn savior. The angel said that the child would be lying in a manger." Michael's eyes widened. He felt a chill go down his spine.

"How could the angel know that?" Michael asked.

"Because," said Mary, "this is no ordinary child. Angels have also spoken to me and to Joseph as well. This child is the Son of God, the Promised One, sent to save the people from their sins. Michael, this child is the hope of the world."

He was dazed by it all. "Why here?" he wondered. "Why now? Why in this place—of all places?" It was more than his fourteen-year-old mind could even begin to comprehend. He looked around at the shepherds, who were kneeling before the child in the manger. He joined them as he wondered about all that he had heard and seen.

The next morning, the young family began packing their things to begin their journey home with their new child. Michael got to his chores with the animals but stopped every few minutes to see if he could help. Soon all was in order and carefully packed away. Mary took her shawl and wrapped it around her shoulders. She took one of the blankets they had brought with them and carefully wrapped up the infant. "Is that all you have to wrap up the baby?" Michael asked. "That old blanket is meant for horses, not for a baby. Wait here." He bolted up the ladder and threw open the little wooden chest at the foot of his pallet. He reached to the bottom and pulled out the soft blanket his mother had made for him, the one with the horse woven into the center. He quickly climbed down the ladder. "Here, take this. It's all I have, but it's soft. My mother made it. I want you to have it. I mean, I want the baby to have it."

A tear ran down Mary's cheek. "God bless you, Michael," she whispered.

Joseph added, "I'd like to meet your parents someday and tell them what a wonderful son they have—a son with so much to offer."

Michael skipped behind the donkey until they got to the edge of the village. As he walked back to the stable, you could hardly even notice his limp.

Christmas is all about hope. The story of Christmas reminds us that God not only cares for those who have been crippled by their mistakes; he also has a place for them, a place of acceptance and a place of service.

The Father said, "Thou shalt not worship false gods or use my name in vain. Honor your parents." He also said, "Don't murder; don't commit adultery; don't steal; don't lie; don't covet the things that belong to your neighbor." Michael's father had warned him, "Don't ride the wild stallion; it's more than you can handle." But sometimes we don't listen. Oh, we hear the words; we even nod our heads in agreement. We just don't obey. We've made a mistake or two, maybe a thousand. And so now we are crippled by our mistakes. We feel unworthy. We feel useless. We feel like our once bright future is now dim. We feel like the Father can't possibly love us anymore. And so we limp our way through life.

The gift of the Christ child changes all of that. The truth of the matter is this: God does still love you. He forgives you. He even wants to use you. Remember that Christmas is all about hope. Throw away your crutches and self-pity. I invite you to skip along after the Savior. You'll forget all about your limp.

CHAPTER 3

Distant Star

Matthew 2:1-12

Ever since the heavens were set in place and the moon and the stars were created, there have always been those who have spent their nights staring into the sky with fascination and wonder.

Omar, like his master, Balthasar, was one of those transfixed stargazers. He was seventeen-year-old and had served in the courts of one of Persia's highest officials since the day he turned twelve. His parents were poor and humble, nomadic mostly, selling and trading camels to those who dared to leave the region to explore the far reaches of the world. Omar had grown up like his father, knowing the business of camels. He could ride them, train them, feed them, and care for them. It was, in fact, the camels that were responsible for his introduction to Balthasar.

As a member of the elite ruling class of magi, Balthasar had numerous camels and servants. Omar's father often was called to the palace to tend to the needs of his rather large herd. Sometimes, when the workload was great, Omar would go with his father to help. Omar had a way with the animals. They seemed to be calmed by his gentle spirit. He brushed them, cared for their feet, drew water to satisfy the ever-present thirst caused by the dry and dusty desert land. His father was always pleased to have him along.

One afternoon as Omar joined his father in the palace stable, Balthasar was returning with a caravan of many camels, loaded down with all kinds of exotic fruits and fabrics and golden pots from a journey to places that Omar could only dream about. "These things must be quickly unloaded," Balthasar said. "Hey, you there, bring these two bags from my camel to my room immediately. Be careful not to drop them; they are fragile." He was speaking to Omar! Omar had never seen the magi before; he had only heard the stories his father had told of him. Somehow, in the confusion and congestion of the returning caravan, Balthasar had just assumed that Omar was one of the house servants.

Not to let an opportunity escape, Omar quickly unloaded the bags and followed Balthasar into the palace. He could hardly believe his eyes— such splendor, such luxury! "Just place them in my closet," Balthasar said, as he pointed to a door off of the main bedroom. Again, Omar couldn't believe his eyes. The closet was larger than his entire house! There were ornate hats and long robes; there were pointed-toe shoes and a dozen different sandals. Everywhere there were bright colors and shiny things, silks and linens and beautifully woven blankets. Omar's eyes were filled with wonder. He gently set the bags on the floor and turned to find his way out. "You must be new," Balthasar said. "Your face is not familiar. I have such a hard time keeping up with all the new servants. It seems each time I'm away, my wife hires and fires the whole staff."

"A thousand pardons, sir," Omar begged. "I am not a servant here. I work with my father sometimes in caring for the camels."

Balthasar replied, "It is I, then, who owe you a thousand pardons. I have treated you as a servant when, in fact, you are a guest. Tell me your name."

"It is Omar, sir." And with that conversation, the friendship began.

Omar's parents considered it the greatest honor when their son was asked to join the palace staff. It was such an honor to serve in the courts of the magi, the learned men of the land, wise men, priests, astrologers, those who could interpret others' dreams. One could only hope for such good fortune. Most commoners would never see the inside of the palace; now their son would be known by all those who dwelled there. He was only twelve when he went to live in the servant quarters. He was still just a boy in the eyes of his mother, but now he was a chosen servant of Balthasar.

In the early days, Omar was nothing more than one of the many household servants. He spent most of his days as you would guess, tending to the needs of the camels. It was really all he had ever known. But in time his duties began to broaden. There were days he was assigned to the kitchen to serve the cooks as they prepared lavish meals for visiting dignitaries. He learned the ways of proper serving etiquette. He soon became acutely aware of the details that needed attention whenever important guests were at the table. Other days he was assigned to the garden, some days to the house. Balthasar was pleased to see how quickly he adapted to each new role.

Omar's gentle spirit made him popular among the servants of the household and trusted by the family. With age he became among the most trusted and dependable of all the servants. He found favor in the eyes of Balthasar and was promoted to Balthasar's chief servant. With the learned man, Omar traveled to distant cities, ate exquisite food, and learned politics.

It was the daily contact with his master that taught Omar a love of the stars. Many nights, Omar would join him, along with the court astrologers, out on the portico of the royal palace. They would gaze into the night sky, counting the stars of each constellation, carefully charting the movements of each planet.

It was late in the year. A visiting sultan had joined the regulars at the palace. A banquet meal of epic proportions had been carried out with the greatest of pomp and circumstance. The food was delicious. There were delicacies from all around the world—sweet fruits, oranges, and dates. The meal also included every kind of meat imaginable, all cooked to perfection. Breads and pastries were placed on every table. Omar had overseen the entire affair. It was a resounding success. After dinner, the group made its way out onto the portico to enjoy the cool of the night air.

The winds were calm, and the temperature was pleasant. The guests sat on pillows and gazed up at the night sky. The stars were brilliant—a million of them splattered across the night sky. Omar took note of the familiar patterns, the shapes and designs of the stars. Another magi, Melchior, was the first to notice it, off in the eastern sky. It was a star that no one had ever noticed before, which was strange because it was as bright as any star in the sky, and yet it hung just over the horizon. "There is something different about that star," Omar said.

Balthasar added, "Oh, yes, something different indeed. It's a special star. It's a sign of some type—a sign of hope, maybe, a sign of mystery, perhaps a sign of a rising king in the east. It is maybe a sign sent from God himself."

For the next several nights the magi gathered on the porch. Each night, the star would again appear on the eastern horizon, more brilliant than before, each night brighter than the last. Conversations about the star began to buzz in every household. All the scholars of the kingdom gathered to discuss its meaning. Some were at first fearful of what it could mean. Others saw in the star great promise and hope. All seemed to agree that it was a special sign from God.

"We must go," said Balthasar. "The star is calling to us. We must seek its meaning and worship its king. Omar, prepare for the journey. We will need much because the distance will be great. Prepare gifts appropriate to celebrate a new king's rise to power."

"How far, master? How long?" Omar asked.

Balthasar replied, "We will travel well beyond the river, far beyond the desert. You must prepare well; the journey will be longer than any you have ever made. I fear it will be longer than any of the journeys *I* have ever made."

Omar responded, "Master, the cost could be staggering. What is it that you hope to gain from the journey?"

"I don't know," Balthasar said, "but I can promise the worth of the journey will far exceed the cost."

The Persian Empire was the greatest the world had ever known. The far-flung empire was divided into twenty city-states, all joined by an excellent system of roads. Trade routes extended from border to border. It would be possible for Omar's journey to begin with known territory, a friendly language, and good travel. It was what lay beyond the borders of the kingdom that troubled Omar. What would the journey hold? Who would they encounter? Would they be accepted in a strange land, or would they be captured and even killed? The uncertainty was troubling, but the intrigue was intoxicating. It was a journey they could not avoid. It was to be the journey of a lifetime.

It took weeks to prepare for the journey. Omar's list of things to pack was longer than any he had ever prepared. "We will need the finest gifts that Persia has to offer," Balthasar stated. "It is a king we seek, so we must offer him our best. Go to my vaults and draw out gold and silver. Pack fragrances and food and fine linens."

"I will make it so," Omar declared, and he began the process of gathering all that such a journey would require.

He began with the herd, naturally. Forty of the strongest, sturdiest camels were chosen. He then began to gather provisions. First, the food was organized. He packed load after load of wheat and barley. He gathered nuts and fruits of various varieties. He picked servants from the magi's kitchen and told them of the long journey to chase the star. "The magi must eat well," he declared. "You must bake bread each day and prepare meat each evening."

Next, he turned his attention to those things that would give the travelers rest at night. He packed tents and blankets and pillows. More servants would be needed to set up the tents at each resting point along the way. They were given the specific charge of caring for the tents and all that was needed to set the tent up properly. Other servants were selected to pack the magi's wardrobe. Omar advised, "You must pack a little of everything. We do not know that climate of the distant land. It may be cool; it may be wet; it may be hot and arid. We must keep the master as comfortable as we can."

The final step was that of packing the gifts for the new king. They were to be chosen with care. Omar left this task to himself. He chose two gifts that were native to the region—silver and gold. Coins minted from each were placed in small leather bags that Omar vowed would never leave his presence. He packed jewels and rare spices and even some silk and linens. The master wanted to offer his best, and Omar made sure that he would be pleased.

No one could have imagined the length of the journey. It would span a thousand miles, countless horizons, various cultures, dusty deserts, and fertile valleys. They would travel to places where the roads of Persia were no longer to be found. At times they would laugh at their good fortune, while at other times they would fear for their lives. It would be a journey measured in months, not days. All the while, they were led by the distant star. Each night, it seemed to glow more brightly than the night before. And as its glow grew more intense, so did the excitement and the anticipation.

The journey was not without its problems. Three camels had not survived the first month. Some of the wheat was lost to insects. Good water was not always easily found. A number of servants grew sick from a rancid well, and the whole caravan stood still for nearly a week.

Once, the journey was halted because of a swollen river. There was no way to get that many camels and that many people and that many supplies safely across. A search party of ten was dispatched to follow the river to the north in order to find a place to ford the river. Bandits attacked the group; a life was lost, and much of the equipment was taken. The survivors had to return to the caravan for more supplies and better protection. This time they headed south, and after only a three-day journey they found a shallow spot where the crossing could occur.

For Omar it was a journey of great excitement and grief. The servant who had been lost in the raid had been a longtime friend and a trusted companion. He had taken young Omar under his wing years earlier when he arrived at the palace and had offered much counsel through the years. When news of his death reached Omar's ears, he tore his clothing and wailed in his sorrow. He cursed the place and those who had brought about the death of his friend.

There were also, however, many good days. Omar treasured the evening hours. In the twilight they would gather just beyond the tents to gaze at that star—always brighter, always more brilliant. They would often gather in the magi's tent and talk and laugh the night away.

Omar also enjoyed the adventure of traveling through the unfamiliar regions. He often thought of his father, who had never been more than a few miles from home. He wished he could take the adventure home to his father. He promised himself that he would remember every detail and share the stories with his parents as soon as he returned. He decided that he would attempt to take something with him from every new place he traveled. With each passing group of traders and from every village marketplace, he would barter for a tangible reminder of his adventure. Sometimes he traded gold, sometimes a bag of wheat, sometimes a woven blanket. The collection grew. He had leather clothing, strange musical instruments, ivory figurines, blown glass, precious stones, colored beads, and ornate pottery. He treasured each item and longed to tell his family all about the journey.

Gaspar, the wisest of the magi, discerned from the star's position that the journey would end in the region of Palestine, not far from the coast of the Great Sea. Though no one in the group had ever set foot on this foreign soil, the learned men knew of its existence. They had often heard from traders, who traveled the trade routes of the world, that it was a land fertile and mighty, a land that clearly had the mark of God upon it.

A caravan of such proportions seldom went undetected as it crossed the borders of a new land. So as the magi entered the land of Israel, word quickly spread about the foreign visitors who were now in their midst. The magi learned from the locals all they needed to know to make the proper diplomatic gestures. Out of respect to King Herod, the delegation made its way to Jerusalem to the palace of the king. All the proper etiquette was followed. As ambassadors from Persia, the group was warmly received. The magi praised Herod for his fine palace and stable rule and provided him with many gifts from their faraway kingdom.

It was what happened next that sent shock waves through the palace. It was their question—right question, just the wrong person to ask. "Where is he who has been born king of the Jews? For we saw his star in the east, and we have come to worship him!"

Herod must have thought, "What is this talk of a new king? There is no king but Herod. I must find this king and kill him and squelch all this idle chatter. I will help these foreigners find him and let them lead me to his bed."

The chief priests and scribes offered their counsel: "Search in Bethlehem, for so the prophets have spoken."

As soon as they left the presence of King Herod, they once again looked to the skies and to the star. It only confirmed what the chief priests had spoken. It led them to the village of Bethlehem. There was great joy in their hearts as they entered the outskirts of the town. The journey was near its end. The long arduous days, the cold nights, the strange land, the unusual food, the insects, the sickness, the toil, the days away from home and family, all the miles, all the difficulties, all the pain—it all seemed to vanish. There was nothing but joy as they entered Bethlehem. Their steps seemed light; their hearts rejoiced. They talked with laughter, their eyes wide with excitement. It was the right place all right; the star was transfixed above the little town.

The star led them onward, until they reached the house of Mary and Joseph. And with their own eyes, they beheld the new king—just a child and yet a king. It was hard for them to describe, but there was just a feeling in his presence, a sense of peace, a sense of holiness. It was evident to all that they were kneeling in the presence of one who would rise to greatness unknown by the rulers of this world. And so they bowed and presented their gifts, gifts that were rare and valuable and beyond worth. It was in that place that they worshiped him and the God by whose grace they had been led.

Omar spoke to the child's father, who he had learned was named Joseph. Their conversation was carried out in a back room. The others did not even notice they were gone for a moment. Omar emerged with yet another souvenir of his travels. This time it was just a small wood carving of a lamb, fashioned by the hands of a Judean carpenter. He told Joseph that he wanted to remember the very place where he had knelt in the presence of the new king. It was no longer the journey that he longed to describe to his family, but the story of the new king. Sometimes the cost of the journey is far exceeded by its worth.

The journey of faith is like that. It always costs. Discipleship means paying a price. It means sacrifice. It means discipline. It means denying self. It means leaving everything behind. It's a lot to consider, this journey of following Christ. And sometimes in our weaker moments, we wonder if the journey is worth the cost. And then we remember that the same king who was found at the end of the wise men's journey will be found at the end of ours. And we realize that no cost is too great, no sacrifice too lavish, for it's Jesus we celebrate and eternal life we find.

And Jesus said to them, "Truly I say to you, there is no one who has left house or wife or brothers or parents or children, for the sake of the kingdom of God, who shall not receive many times as much at this time and in the age to come, eternal life" (Lk 18:29-30).

"For we saw His star in the east, and have come to worship Him" (Matt 2:2). It is a journey I pray we are willing to take...regardless of the cost.

CHAPTER 4

We'll Leave the Light On

Luke 2:1-7

Josiah was well known throughout the city of Hebron. It was there that he had made his home, raised his family, and earned his living. He was fortunate. He had been very successful. Through the generations, his family had pieced together a rather large tract of land just south of town. On that land, hundreds, maybe thousands, of olive trees had been planted. The rich soil of the region and the abundant water supply provided just the right ingredients for the trees to produce well. The family not only harvested the olives each season, but they produced the byproducts that were much in demand. Some olives were taken straight to market to be sold for food, but most of them were taken to the stone olive presses so the oil could be extracted. The real money was in the oil. It was sold as a fuel, as a medicine, and as a cooking agent. Even the older trees became a part of the profitable business. The wood of the olive tree was sought out because of its durability. Rough-hewn timbers were used all throughout the region in the construction of buildings and homes.

When his father died, the estate had fallen into Josiah's hands because he was the eldest son. His younger brother and his two sisters lived on the land and worked in the family trade. But it was Josiah who ran the estate, made all the decisions, and counted all the money. All the siblings enjoyed a good life, but Josiah enjoyed the best life. He and his wife, Rebekah, lived in a large home with their four children. It was Rebekah's task to raise the children and manage the household. This she did quite well, with the help of several house servants who aided in raising the children and preparing the meals. In addition to the olives, they owned horses, cattle, and sheep. The estate was large, so many caretakers were hired to keep things running smoothly.

Business was Josiah's passion. During the warmer months of the year, he traveled frequently throughout Judea, seeking out new markets and new customers. The town of Hebron was ideally located. It was nineteen miles south of Jerusalem, fifteen miles west of the Dead Sea. Roads were good, so travel and commerce were easy for Josiah. From his collection of horses, Josiah had several favorites. His prized horse was a black stallion with a streak of white down the nose. It was this horse that Josiah often rode as he made his way throughout the region to do business. Usually his trips could be completed in a day. Sometimes, however, when he rode to distant cities like Joppa or Caesarea, his journey would last for several days. And like most travelers who make frequent journeys, he had his favorite spots to eat and stay.

The day had started early. Business was to take Josiah to Jerusalem and back. It was a trip he made often, so he knew the roads well. Up before the sun, he packed a bag with fresh bread and water, placed some coins in his pocket, and collected some parchments and placed them into a leather pouch. He kissed Rebekah goodbye and promised to be home long before dark. He mounted his favorite black horse and began a slow trot down the lane that headed to the north. As he rode between the rows of olive trees, he watched the morning sun peek above the eastern horizon. The skies were clear, and the temperature was pleasant. "Should be a good day to travel," he thought to himself. "I'll be home in no time."

It was late morning when he arrived in Jerusalem. He left his horse in the charge of a local stable. He knew the stable hand well and felt comfortable in leaving his horse with him. "I should be back within a couple hours," Josiah said. "Make sure my horse gets food and water, but not too much water."

"I'll take care of everything," the stable hand answered. "He'll be ready when you come for him."

Josiah made his way to the open-air market that dominated the center of town, just a short distance from the temple mound. As always, the market was teeming with life. Vendors from all around the area had gathered for another busy day. There were tables and booths set up along several streets. Fresh fruit and fish, grains and wheat, brightly colored linens—all for sale. There were shiny pots and pans and pottery vases and plates in several spots. Some merchants sold beads while others traded in leather and some in livestock. There was the smell of grilled meat in the air and freshly baked bread. Josiah listened as different merchants argued over prices, realizing that in a few moments he would contribute his voice to the conversations of commerce.

He stopped long enough to buy some dates and honey to eat with the bread he had packed earlier that morning. After browsing briefly, he arrived at his destination, a booth where olive oil was sold. "And how is my old friend Jacob this day?" he asked.

An older gentleman with tanned skin and gray hair looked up from behind the small counter and flashed a grin at Josiah. "It is good to see you, my friend. I hope your family is well."

They talked for a few moments. The two men did a lot of business together. Jacob had traded with Josiah's father years earlier when he would travel to the market to sell his oil. They talked of business, supply and demand, and the cost of the olive oil. Commitments were made, and with a handshake the deal was struck. Both seemed pleased.

"I'll have the bottles to you in less than a week," Josiah promised. "I'll bring a hundred on my next trip and the rest the following week." He loved this part of his life, the trading and making deals. He knew Rebekah would be excited about the news, and he longed to get home and tell her all about his day.

He found a spot away from the busy marketplace, not far from the stable where he had left his horse. Resting under the shade of a tree, he took out his water and bread and the fruit he had purchased earlier. He didn't know if he was just really hungry or if the food was especially good, but either way he gobbled up his food in minutes. He ate every last morsel and stretched out on the ground for a short rest before the long ride back home.

He was awakened by a group of young boys playing nearby. The sounds of their laughter and play reminded him of his own children. "I better be going," he thought to himself. "It's getting a little later than I had thought." He gathered his belongings and headed toward the stable. He paid the stable boy and thanked him for the special treatment. He loaded his things, and within a few minutes he was passing through the southwestern gate of the city, sometimes called the Gennath Gate. The trip was all rather uneventful as he made his way to the outskirts of Bethlehem. He could tell he was near the town as he passed pasture after pasture filled with sheep and the ever-vigilant shepherds.

The roads were filled with travelers, much more so than usual, due to the Roman census that was being taken. The government wanted an accurate count of the people so its oppressive taxation could continue. Josiah had already been enrolled a week or so earlier in his hometown of Hebron. A prosperous estate like his would surely take a hard hit at the hands of the Romans. The closer he got to town, the greater the congestion. All those claiming to be of the lineage of David had to make their way to Bethlehem, and it seemed to Josiah that everyone had waited until the last minute to make the trek. The road was crowded with carts and horses and donkeys and people. Josiah couldn't get over all the travelers. The roadway seemed flooded with people the way a river sometimes overflows its banks. It soon became apparent that he would not be able to get home before darkness set in.

Even though Bethlehem was only about fourteen miles from Hebron, Josiah rarely stayed there overnight. In fact, he could only recall about three times he had ever spent the night in the small town. "Better start looking for a place to stay," he thought to himself. "Rooms will be few and far between. Besides, what does this little village even have to offer? I'll bet it will be hard to find any place to stay." He was right. Bethlehem was overflowing. All the usual spots were filling up quickly. Josiah noticed that a few people were spreading blankets under some shade trees, obviously preparing to spend the night out in the elements. "I'll find a spot," he thought to himself. "Money always talks, and I'll offer a little extra to some innkeeper." He was surprised by the reaction he encountered. He stopped in three places before he finally discovered an innkeeper who would be glad to make room for him.

"I'll need a place for my horse," Josiah said. "I need a safe place and someone to care for him. I'll gladly pay a little extra for his care."

The innkeeper's eyes lit up with the thought of making yet a little more profit off the traveler. "No problem," he said. "I just happen to have a stable out back. It will be warm and clean for your horse. In fact, I just hired a new stable boy. He's young but very good with the animals, especially horses. I'll make sure that he takes good care of your horse."

Josiah was, of course, a little skeptical. "Why didn't I leave Jerusalem a bit earlier?" he thought to himself. "I could have been home by now and sleeping in my own bed tonight." Speaking to the innkeeper, he said, "Sounds good to me. Mind if I take a look for myself? I'd like to talk to your stable boy."

"No problem," the innkeeper said for the second time. He led Josiah around back to his stable. In his mind the innkeeper was really thankful that he had recently hired young Michael to care for his stable. He was a good kid, and the place looked better than it had in months.

"Michael, come here for a minute," he shouted. Michael, who walked with a limp, quickly made his way to where the two men were standing. His eyes immediately focused on the beautiful black horse. "He needs you to care for his horse tonight."

"Yes, sir," Michael quickly replied. "It's a beautiful horse. I'll see to it that he gets the best stall, and I'll bring him plenty of fresh straw. I'll be glad to brush him out if you want me to. I've got a good brush."

Josiah was pleased with the enthusiasm of this young boy, who was not much older than his own son. A quick glance at the stable assured him that all would be well. "Thank you, Michael," Josiah said. "I'll reward you first thing in the morning." The innkeeper caught Michael's eye and gave him a wink.

Josiah was not nearly as impressed with the inn as he had been with the stable. "You call this an inn?" he thought to himself. "I wouldn't let my family stay in a place like this." It was not an inn like you might imagine. It was really just a large room that had been divided into sections by blankets that had been strung up from the ceiling. It looked as though the innkeeper was trying to squeeze in everyone he could.

"This is your spot," the innkeeper said to Josiah. "I've put you here in the corner. Should be quiet, no one stepping over you during the night. Let me spread out your pallet." The innkeeper unrolled several blankets on the floor and smoothed them over. "There. You'll be nice and warm and comfortable."

Josiah thought, "You and I have different definitions of 'nice and warm and comfortable,'" but he held his tongue. At least he had a place to stay, and by daylight he would be well on his way to Hebron. Rebekah would be worried by now.

"Any place around here to get a bite to eat?" Josiah asked.

"Sure," said the innkeeper. "But there is none better than what my wife can offer." Again, the wheels of further profit turned over in the innkeeper's head. "She is already preparing stew for some of the other travelers; she'll be glad to have you join us." In his mind the innkeeper thought, "Just water down the stew a little bit, and there will be plenty."

"Thanks," Josiah replied, "but I think I'll just try my luck in one of the local spots." The thought of stew in the innkeeper's home was not his idea of fine dining.

Back out in the street, Josiah wandered his way through the small village of Bethlehem. Because of the crowds, it was a busy and noisy evening. People were everywhere. He listened to the conversations all around him. Some spoke of the Roman census; others talked of the weather and the star-filled skies. Still others talked of tomorrow's plans. He found a small tavern and went inside. The food didn't smell all that bad; surely it would be better than homemade stew. It wasn't. The meat was tough, and the bread was stale. The wine was watered down. "Deliver me from this godforsaken wilderness," he thought.

Josiah noticed an old bum making his way around the tables. He wondered why the owner didn't throw him out. He approached Josiah's table. "I'm just an old carpenter. Could you help me out a little?"

The tavern owner shouted, "Leave him alone, Samuel. You'd better be on your way; it's getting late." It became obvious that this "Samuel" was a regular and that the owner at least tolerated his begging.

It was late by the time Josiah got back to the dimly lit inn. Several of the patrons had already settled in for the night. Josiah carefully worked his way around to his "corner," stretching out on his pallet and covering himself with a blanket. He could already tell that it was going to be a long night. He really didn't feel all that well. Lousy food and watered-down drinks made his stomach hurt. The bed was lumpy and hard, the street outside the inn still noisy with people. He worried about his horse and was especially worried about his wife and family.

Sometime later, he finally dropped off to sleep, only to be awakened by a loud knock on the door. The innkeeper stumbled his way over several sleepy guests and cursed when he stubbed his toe on someone's wooden trunk. Josiah could overhear the conversation at the door. It seemed a young couple was still looking for a place to stay the night. He heard the husband explain that his wife was pregnant and in need of rest. "I've got no room," the innkeeper explained. Still, the wheels of profit turned over in his mind. "But I could probably make you a comfortable place to stay out in my stable."

Josiah thought to himself, "You'd better be careful of his definition of 'comfortable.'"

"I won't charge you very much," the innkeeper promised, "and you can let your donkey stay for free."

"They better not mess with my horse," Josiah thought. A few minutes later, he heard the innkeeper stumble his way back into the inn. "I guess they got settled," Josiah thought. "Maybe now we can all get a little rest."

Hours later, sometime in the wee hours of the morning, Josiah heard voices outside—a lot of voices. "Who would still be out at this hour? Who is even awake this time of night?" he wondered. Except for shepherds, who would stay awake all night to protect their flocks, Josiah could think of no "normal" people who should be out celebrating at this hour of the night. It was still too dark to get up for the day, so he tried to ignore the disturbance and eek out a few more hours of sleep.

With the first rays of sunlight, Josiah was up and going. He collected his things, paid the innkeeper for a wonderful night's stay, and headed out to the stable to collect his horse. Michael, the stable boy, was already up and hard at work. "Good boy," he thought. "Your hard work will pay off someday."

"Hey, mister, did you hear what happened last night?" asked Michael with excitement in his voice.

"No, son, I didn't. Tell me what happened."

Michael recounted the night's events: "A lady had a baby, born right here in this stable. You just missed them. Her name was Mary, and you should have seen the baby, a boy! Mary said he would be a special child and that he was sent from God to save the people from their sins. And then, later, some shepherds came to worship the child. They said they had been told by angels to come here to the stable."

"Sounds exciting," Josiah said. "I'm sorry I missed it." He marveled at the child's imaginative story. He quickly saddled his horse, loaded his possessions, and flipped Michael a silver coin.

"Thanks, mister!" Michael said.

As he quietly rode to the edge of town, Josiah thought about how good it was to finally be on his way home again. He thought of the night he had just spent. "Lousy food, bad drinks, lumpy bed, busy town, noisy shepherds. What a godforsaken place to spend the night."

Josiah missed it. It was the most important birth in all of human history, and he missed it. He would go back to Hebron, live his life, sell his oil, and raise his family. He would soon forget all about the tale that Michael had told him about the baby born in Bethlehem. In fact, he would soon forget Michael. With luck he would even forget the miserable night he had spent there. How tragic—to be that close to Christmas and yet miss it.

The real tragedy is that there will be many this year who will also miss Christmas. Some of us who are believers will miss it. We'll miss it because of the hectic pace of the holidays. We'll attempt to squeeze too much life into too little time, and before we know it Christmas will have come and gone. It's odd how we can attend every school play and hear every choir concert and even drop our coins in the Salvation Army bucket and still miss Christmas. Through bleary eyes many of us will make the family listen to a reading of

Luke 2 on Christmas morning, as if two minutes can magically put us in the Christmas spirit. Christmas is not something we can package at the mall. It is not a feeling we can unpack with ornaments in the attic. Christmas is about celebrating the most important birth in human history, the birth of God's only begotten Son. It is all about celebrating the glory of God's love. And yet it sometimes gets lost in the shuffle of the season.

And if believers can miss it, so can the rest of the world. Non-Christians will get up on Christmas morning, and they will give gifts and eat lavish meals and hug their children and decorate the tree. But they will go to bed Christmas night just as empty on the inside as ever. Why? Because they missed Christmas. No, they didn't miss the season; they missed its significance. When all is said and done, it really is a baby's birth we celebrate, the most important birth in all of human history. Don't come so close and still miss it.

CHAPTER 5

Benjamin's Lamb

Revelation 5:11-13

Though he was only seven, Benjamin's future occupation was set. He would be a shepherd, like his father, his grandfather, and his grandfather's father had been. It was the family business, a way of life, really a way of poverty. The cycle would no doubt continue through endless generations of Benjamin's family. Shepherds were very low on the social ladder. In fact, they were rock bottom. They were a part of the culture known as the *am ha aretes*, or "people of the earth." The work was not glamorous by any stretch of the imagination; in fact, it was just the opposite. Shepherds were dirty, gritty, uneducated, and distant. Their hair was matted, their nails dark, and their beards long. They always smelled of the animals they kept and the fields they roamed. For obvious reasons they never ventured very far into other social circles. And so young Benjamin was destined to be a shepherd for life.

The family farm was rather meager. Benjamin's father and uncle, along with his grandfather, owned a small portion of hillside on which they could manage a flock of around fifty sheep. The members of the family all lived under the same roof, huddled together around a small courtyard with half a dozen rooms. A stone oven sat in the middle of the courtyard. It was there that Benjamin's mother and aunt did most of the cooking for the clan. In summer the men and boys stayed gone for weeks at a time, driving the flock in constant search for more grass and water. Young boys like Benjamin were dispatched almost daily to bring food and wine to the men working in the fields. Shepherding was not easy, but it carried enough profit to provide for the family. Sheep gave milk to drink and wool to wear. After they were slaughtered, the hide was used to make clothing, and the meat would feed the family for days.

The family always did well around Jewish feast days, especially Passover. The choicest animals were used as part of the sacrificial system in the temple. Worshipers would slaughter a lamb in order to atone for their sins. The old saying among the shepherds was, "The darker the sin, the whiter the lamb." Every shepherd knew the better sheep would always bring the higher price. Those without spot or blemish were always sure to be sold and used for sacrifice.

Benjamin had been working the sheep as long as he could remember. It was the only life he knew, and he could not remember his life prior to walking and working in the fields. Still, at the age of seven, his work ethic was not well defined. He played more than he worked. He loved to explore and climb the hillsides near Bethlehem. One of his favorite ways to spend time was climbing to the top of a hill that overlooked the marketplace of Bethlehem. On market day he loved to watch the merchants set up their wares and see the people as they bargained for the best deals. Every once in a while his father would take him into town, usually to sell a lamb or maybe two. He was fascinated by the sights and the sounds and the smells. He loved the smell of fresh dates and figs when they were in season. He was also fascinated by the beauty of the cloth that the weavers sold and the wonderfully crafted furniture sold by the carpenters.

Some days Benjamin enjoyed exploring the hillsides. His mother used to always shout after him, "Be careful, son. Not too far, understand?"

"Of course, Mother," he would say. "Besides, I've got my slingshot with me." Benjamin had grown up hearing the stories of King David. Bethlehem was, after all, his birthplace. Benjamin's father had been careful to tell him of King David's mighty armies and all their victories. But, of course, no story carried any greater weight than that of shepherd boy David and giant Goliath. Benjamin kept a shepherd's bag slung across his chest. He kept it stocked with bread and occasionally some olives. But always he carried in it his slingshot. And just like his hero David, he always kept five smooth stones with him, just in case he might meet up with a giant. With the imagination only a child can possess, Benjamin would go out, and in a day's time he would kill countless giants with each sling of a stone. He actually grew to have a pretty good aim, and apparently the giants heard about it, because they seemed to stay away.

One evening, while gathered around the table at home, Benjamin's father announced, "God has blessed us yet again. Two new lambs were born last night. One is a ewe, the other a male." He had chosen the word "blessed" because he knew that each lamb would one day produce a profit. Benjamin noticed how his father always seemed to be in a good mood when the flock was increased.

"Can I see them, Father?" asked Benjamin.

"Of course, my son," he replied. "We'll go in the morning."

Benjamin woke early the next morning and quickly dressed. His father had already been up for some time tending to chores. They quickly ate their breakfast, and then the two made their way out to the stable where Benjamin's father had penned up the new mother with her two little lambs. Both seemed healthy and strong, although the male was a little small.

"This female will certainly make a difference in the flock. I'm not so sure about the little one; I hope he makes it, but I've got my doubts."

"Sure, he'll make it," declared Benjamin. "All he needs is a little attention." And then came the question that all parents have heard from their children at such a moment: "Can I keep him, Father? Can I, please?"

"What would you do with a lamb like that?" asked his father.

"I'll feed him and brush out his coat. I'll give him plenty of water, and I can protect him with my slingshot!"

"Well, we'll see. I'd better talk to your mother before I make any promises. Besides, he'll have to stick close to his mother for a while. We've got plenty of time to decide." Benjamin's dad figured that after a couple weeks, Benjamin would move on to something else. The little lamb would be forgotten.

As the days passed, however, Benjamin did anything but forget. In fact, each day brought the same question: "Daddy, can I keep him?"

His mother, starting to show signs of caving in, said, "And what would you call him? He has to have a name, you know."

Without hesitating for a moment, Benjamin said, "I'll name him Amos, after the great prophet. He was a shepherd, you know."

"Yes, son, I know," said his father. "I'm not sure the rabbi will think all that highly about the name; it sounds a bit disrespectful, but why not? Amos it is. You can keep the lamb for now. Just don't get too attached. He may be needed as a sacrifice in the temple one day. The day may come when you have to let him go."

Benjamin didn't hear anything after "You can keep the lamb." He jumped for joy and said, "You're the best parents in the whole wide world!" Within moments he was at the pen, talking to his new possession, Amos the lamb.

Benjamin was true to his word. He cared for the lamb just like he had promised. He fed him, brushed him, and gave him plenty of water. A bond developed between the two over the months that followed. At first Amos would only eat the food that Benjamin would place on the ground, but in time Benjamin taught Amos to eat out of his hand. Soon, Benjamin would call Amos by name, and the little lamb would come running, following Benjamin all around the yard. He even got to the point that he would join Benjamin on his long hikes. Wherever you saw one, you saw the other. Benjamin took an old blanket and made a special bed for Amos in the stable. The whole family would laugh at the spectacle of it all—"slingshot-totin' Benjamin and his sidekick Amos," they called them.

Benjamin's mother noticed that Benjamin started wearing his shepherd's pouch to dinner at night. It wasn't big enough to sneak Amos in, but it was certainly big enough to sneak a little food out. More than once, Benjamin's mother saw him grab an extra piece of bread and stuff it into the pouch. "My, your appetite is getting bigger by the day," she would say. "I know I just put bread on your plate a minute ago."

"Just hungry I guess," said Benjamin. "It's not easy hunting for giants, you know."

There were days when Benjamin's father worried a little about his son and his lamb. From time to time, he would offer the reminder, "Don't get too attached; one day he may have a greater role to fulfill."

This was not the message Benjamin wanted to hear. Just to be sure that his dad didn't get any wild ideas, Benjamin would take a piece of charcoal and rub it on Amos's right hind leg, leaving a big, black spot. "That ought to do it," he said to himself. "The darker the sin, the whiter the lamb, but the darker the lamb, the better for me!" It was Benjamin's little insurance policy that Amos would never be considered for a sacrificial offering.

Late one afternoon, Benjamin and Amos were returning home from a day of exploring when Benjamin noticed the local rabbi talking to his father. After putting Amos in his pen, he found his mother and asked the reason for the rabbi's visit.

"Rabbi Simon is here to negotiate a price with your father for five of the sheep. He is here to handpick the five best in the flock to be used for the feast celebration."

"Which five will he pick?" asked Benjamin.

"Your father said that Rabbi Simon could pick any that he wanted, any from the entire flock. They are to be used for sacrifice to atone for the sins of the people. Your father said it would be an honor to have any of his sheep used for such an important purpose."

Terrified over the possibilities, Benjamin asked, "When is he going to choose?"

"As soon as they set the price," his mother answered.

There was no time to waste. In an instant Benjamin bolted for the door and ran out to the pen where Amos was being kept with the other sheep. He grabbed his trusty charcoal and went to work. He drew spots all over Amos's body. And for good measure he smashed mud all over his head, caking it into his wool. By the time Benjamin was finished, Amos looked more like a mangy old dog than a beautiful lamb. The rabbi was afraid to even get close to him while he made his selections. Benjamin's father shot him one of those "boy-are-you-going-to-get-it-later" kind of looks. Benjamin didn't care. All he cared about was saving the life of his lamb, which he had done.

After supper, Benjamin cleaned Amos from top to bottom. He brushed out the mud and washed away the charcoal. His father came out to the pen.

"I told you not to get too attached to that lamb, Benjamin. That was some trick you pulled today. It was not right for you to deceive Rabbi Simon."

Benjamin looked at his father and asked, "Would you have sold Amos today? Would you really let the rabbi take him away?"

His father took a deep breath and collected his thoughts before he said. "Benjamin, you know I love you with all my heart. You are my only son. I would never want to hurt you. In fact, I'm sort of attached to Amos myself. But if Rabbi Simon had said that Amos was needed to atone for someone's sin, then we would have to sell him. What's more important—the life of one lamb or someone's freedom from sin?"

Benjamin responded, "I still don't understand why finding peace with God must come at the cost of a precious lamb."

"Someday you will, my son, someday," his father replied.

Then, Benjamin's father got around to his punishment: "Benjamin, tonight you will go with me to tend the flocks in the field. You'll miss your warm bed and your mother's lullaby. You will sleep on the ground with me as we protect the flock as they graze."

Benjamin hated night duty. He had only gone with his father a couple times. He was still frightened by the dark. There were too many strange sounds and too many pairs of eyes peering in the darkness.

"Can I bring Amos?" he asked.

His father nodded.

"At least he will keep me company," thought Benjamin.

It was well past midnight when one of the other shepherds first saw a blinding light shooting straight out of the heavens. The men cried out in terror, and the sheep scattered in all directions. Little Amos cowered behind the shaking legs of Benjamin, who was cowering behind the legs of his father. They were afraid to look and afraid not to look. Suddenly, a voice shouted from the heavens, "Do not be afraid, for I bring you good news of great joy, which shall be for all the people, for unto you is born this day in the city of David, a savior, who is Christ the Lord." The angel went on to say the newborn would be found wrapped in cloths and lying in a manger of all things. The whole sky was filled with a thousand angels praising God and celebrating the birth of the child. And then, as quickly as it had started, it was over. The night grew dark again, and the voices drifted away into the heavens.

The shepherds stood speechless. "What does all this mean?" whispered Benjamin to his father.

"It means we're going into town; that's what it means! We must see this child whom the Lord has revealed to us."

"What is so important about the baby in Bethlehem?" asked Benjamin.

"He is the promised messiah, the savior who will rescue the people from their sins. It is the child who has been promised by the prophets of God."

"Can I go with you to Bethlehem?" asked Benjamin.

"Yes," said his father. "This is a night you will never forget."

Quickly, the shepherds secured the flocks and raced toward the town of Bethlehem. Benjamin was tagging along the heels of his father, with Amos tagging along at his heels.

It took only a few minutes for them to find the stable behind the inn. And there in the quiet stillness of the night, the shepherds found themselves in the presence of the newborn king. All were hushed in reverence. Several knelt before the manger. Some whispered psalms of praise to God. Benjamin's father stepped forward and knelt near the manger. He motioned for Benjamin to do the same. As Benjamin knelt, he felt the cold, wet nose of Amos against his cheek. Amos stood motionless, as though he somehow sensed the reverence of the moment. After a minute Amos stepped toward the manger and gently sniffed the child wrapped in all the swaddling cloths. Joseph, the child's father, looked at Benjamin and said, "That's quite a sight, two little innocent lambs."

Later, as they made their way back to the Judean hillside country, Benjamin was talkative and curious about all that he had just seen: "He didn't look like a king to me. He's just a baby. How could he be the savior? How is a little baby going to save the people from their sins? No one is going to sacrifice him like a lamb, are they?"

The question just sort of hung in the air unanswered. Benjamin's father recalled the words of their earlier conversation: "What's more important—the life of one lamb or someone's freedom from sin?"

It is a little hard to grasp. The child of Bethlehem became the savior at Calvary. Why did it take the death of God's only begotten Son to give us eternal life? Because the darker the sin, the whiter the lamb. Only a perfect and complete sacrifice could remove the stains of our sins. We needed a savior. We needed Christ. And God was willing to give.

We join our hearts together at Christmas to celebrate not just Jesus' birth, but also his victory over sin and death. In Christ alone we have life. In Christ alone do we find peace with God. In Christ alone can we stand before the Father. This Christmas, all of creation should shout, "Worthy is the Lamb, who was slain to receive power and wealth and wisdom and strength and honor and glory and praise!" (Rev 5:12 NIV). Worthy is the Lamb! Worthy is the Lamb! Worthy is the Lamb!

CHAPTER 6

The Light of the World

Isaiah 9:2

Aaron had been successful enough to own his own shop. It was small, mind you, but it was his livelihood and his life. It was all he had ever known and really all he ever aspired to do. He was a potter by trade. For most of his life, he had spun the potter's wheel and watched pieces of raw clay become shaped into form by his hands. He was in his late thirties but looked at least a decade older. His head was balding, his beard was gray, and his belly a little larger than most. His hands were a distinguishing feature. They were stained a deep red from all the years with the clay. His shop was located on the main road that led from Bethlehem to Jerusalem, a really good location. He was a fixture in the small village, known by nearly everyone. Through the years his pottery had gained some notoriety because of its color and strength. There were few homes in the village that didn't have at least one or two items made by Aaron's hands.

Aaron had little family to speak of. He had never found the right girl to settle down with. He had moments of loneliness, like anyone would, but whenever he felt the pain of being by himself, he would just dive into his next creation. He had friends. He had money. He had some status. He did have a nephew, Timothy, with whom he was close. Timothy's parents lived in the area, so Timothy had always spent a lot of time in the shop, especially as a child. He adored his uncle as a child and would often sit and watch Aaron as he shaped the clay. Timothy was now an adolescent. Other interests had caught his attention, but he managed a visit from time to time. In fact, when business was good or when Aaron had to be away, Timothy would even manage the shop for his uncle.

Aaron made all kinds of things on his potter's wheel—cups, saucers, plates, bowls, pitchers, and an occasional vase. Behind the shop was an odd-shaped oven that Aaron used to "fire" the pieces he made, to give them strength and to dry the clay. Next to the oven was a curious mound covered by a tarp. It was where Aaron kept his special clay for making pots, the real secret of his success. The tarp was needed to keep the clay from drying out, while also keeping it from becoming too wet. The shop itself was only one room, about twenty cubits by twenty cubits. One corner was dominated by the potter's wheel, and the rest was filled with shelves and benches, all covered with various pieces of pottery. A counter near the door had a small uncluttered spot where the money would change hands when a purchase was made. A small staircase led to an upper room above the shop where Aaron slept on a bed made of straw and a few wool blankets.

Aaron, or so it was said of him, was rather particular about his clay. And there was a difference. The color was different, as was the texture, and some even said the pots he made were stronger than those made by others. Aaron often said, "To make the best pottery, you must have the best clay." Years earlier, Aaron had discovered clay unique to a little spot where the Jordan River emptied into the Salt Sea. Maybe it was the purity of the Jordan or the silt that it carried or the salt content of the surrounding area, but something made the clay a bit different. Aaron tested it out and discovered its unique abilities. Twice each year Aaron would hitch his donkey to an old wooden cart and make the arduous twenty-mile trek to that little spot on the riverbank where he had discovered the special clay. His nephew would always join him for the trip. It was always an adventure, and young Timothy always returned with a rich repertoire of stories. Aaron would load all the clay the little cart would hold. Once back at home, he would unload it behind his shop and cover it with the tarp.

And so it went, season after season, year after year. Aaron would turn the soft clay into useful pieces of pottery. Whenever he worked the clay, Aaron was careful not to ever waste even the smallest amounts of the leftover clay. During the day he would collect bits and scraps in a small bowl. Then, when all the plates were made and put into the oven to cure, Aaron would take the lump of leftover clay and carefully shape it into a small oil lamp. He usually made a couple at the end of each day. They were oblong, with a hole into which the olive oil would be placed, and then another hole on the end where Aaron would place a small piece of twisted flax that he would use for a wick. There were always a dozen or so of the small clay lamps resting on a shelf near the door of the shop. Each one was just like the next. The only thing that made them unique was a special design that he stamped onto the side when the clay was still soft. Only about the size of a fist, he always sold a few each week.

For nearly a month business had been unusually brisk. Because of a Roman decree that everyone had to return to his or her ancestral home for a census count, the road to Jerusalem was filled with travelers. Anyone claiming to be from the line of King David had to return to Bethlehem to be counted. It seemed people were constantly in his shop. Some stopped to ask directions, others seeking advice about where to stay or where to find food. Some actually bought a thing or two. Aaron was putting in some long days. For hours he sat at the potter's wheel, spinning the clay into creations. There was a constant fire burning in the drying oven out back. He replenished the shelves daily. He even thought to himself, "If this keeps up for very long, I'll have to make another run to the river for more clay."

In the midst of the hustle and bustle, Aaron noticed a young couple who walked past the shop late one afternoon. They were traveling from the north. As he stopped to look up from his work, he saw the husband gently leading a donkey upon which his pregnant wife was riding. Obviously they were from out of town, and obviously they were weary, as though the trip had been a long one. Aaron would never have thought of the couple again, if not for the visit later that night.

It was well past dark; in fact, it was late into the night. Aaron had already cleaned off the potter's wheel, covered the clay, doused the fire in the oven, and eaten a bite for supper. He was in the process of sweeping out the shop when a stranger walked through the door. He remembered the face. It was the man he had seen earlier in the day leading the donkey along the road.

"Can I help you?" asked Aaron.

"I hope so," said the stranger. "I saw your shop earlier in the day. I was hoping that you had a couple oil lamps I could buy pretty cheap."

Aaron pointed to the shelf near the counter. "I've got plenty, made from the best clay, you know."

The stranger walked over to the shelf and began to examine one a little more closely.

"It's kind of late to be shopping for a lamp, isn't it?" asked Aaron.

"I guess it does seem a little odd," answered the stranger. "It's been a long day. My wife and I have traveled all this week from Nazareth. We're in town to register for the census. I never imagined that all the inns around here would be filled. We couldn't find a place anywhere. Finally, one innkeeper offered us a spot in his stable. It's not ideal, but it's better than nothing. It's fine for me, but I'm worried about my wife. You see, she's expecting a child any day now. I'm afraid she's not very comfortable, especially after the long trip."

"I'd hate to be in your place," said Aaron. "It must be hard being this far from home. Anyway, why do you need a lamp?"

"It's for the stable," the stranger replied. "It's pretty dark in there. Mary's a little scared of the dark. She worries about spiders and any other creature that might come walking in during the night. I just figured maybe a lamp could give off enough light to make a difference in the dark. I would have brought one from home, but I just never guessed I'd be in the spot I am tonight."

Aaron watched as the stranger carefully examined a couple of the small clay lamps.

"How much?" asked the stranger.

"They're a drachma each," replied Aaron.

He noticed the stranger looked a little apprehensive. "I don't guess you'd be willing to trade for it, would you?" asked the stranger.

"Trade? What would you have to trade?"

"Well, I'm a carpenter back home. I have a small wooden bowl that I made. It's good for holding bread or maybe some stew." He pulled the bowl out from underneath his robe. Aaron looked it over for a moment.

"Bowls I have," said Aaron. "I really just need the money. But I'll tell you what; I'll give it to you for half the price." The stranger smiled and thanked Aaron for his generosity. "I'll even fill it with oil if that will help."

"Thanks," said the stranger. He quickly took the clay lamp and headed out the door into the dark night.

"Go with God!" called Aaron after the stranger.

The stranger called back over his shoulder, "Shalom!"

Aaron closed the door to the shop, blew out the lamps that were burning, and made his way up the stairs to fall into bed. Joseph, on the other hand, quickly made his way along the streets of Bethlehem to the stable where Mary was anxiously awaiting his return. "Joseph, why have you been gone so long?" she asked. "I was starting to get really worried."

"Sorry, I meant to be back sooner, but I got you a little present," he replied.

"A present? Joseph, you know we don't have any extra money for presents, especially with the baby due any day now."

"Don't worry; it's nothing extravagant, just something to help you get through this night in the barn." Mary looked puzzled. From underneath his cloak Joseph produced the tiny oil lamp. "Here it is. It's just an oil lamp to give us a little light during the night. Maybe it will chase away all the spiders," he joked.

He walked out to the courtyard in front of the barn where a young stable boy had built a small fire. He reached down and removed a small stick and lit the wick on the oil lamp. Shielding it with his hand, he walked back to the barn, where he placed it on top of a ledge that divided some of the stalls. Immediately, the glow of the light seemed to chase all of the darkness from the small stable. Dark corners were filled with light. Scary shadows became recognized shapes. Strange creatures turned out to be a colt, a donkey, and a lamb. "It's not so scary anymore, is it?" asked Joseph.

"Not at all," said Mary. "It's really surprising what a difference a tiny light will make in the midst of all the darkness."

With plenty of light with which to see, Joseph busied himself with making a comfortable place to rest for the night. He gathered some straw and spread some blankets over the top. Mary carefully unpacked a small bag she had brought along on the trip. It contained some bread, some dried meat, and some fruit. She spread it out across the blankets that Joseph had placed on the straw. The two of them sat down to eat before calling it a night. As they prayed over their meager meal, Joseph was careful to thank God for the simple things that had made a difference. He thanked God for the gift of light that seemed to make their little corner of the world a little brighter. He thanked God for Aaron, the shopkeeper he had met, who had given him a special price when he bought the lamp. He thanked God for the food they were about to eat, for the donkey that had carried Mary safely along the journey.

As they finished their meal, Mary and Joseph noticed that the stars had come out in the evening sky. They were as brilliant and bright as the two of them could ever remember. One star in particular seemed to outshine the others. "Maybe it's a sign of good things to come," remarked Joseph. "Even the sky is filled with light tonight." The two settled down for a few hours of rest. Joseph went to sleep quickly, but Mary had trouble getting comfortable. At first she didn't know if her supper wasn't sitting well or if it was the strange surroundings, but something certainly had her mind racing and her stomach twisting. It wasn't long until she figured it all out. The pain in her belly was intense at times, and then it subsided, intense again, and then relief.

There was a definite pattern to it all. A thrill, a worry, a joy, and a fear all shot through her mind at the same time. The baby! The baby was on its way!

She shook Joseph from his slumber. He was a bit groggy at first, but as soon as his mind comprehended her message, he became fully awake. "The baby? Here? Tonight? In this place?" She quietly nodded her head. To be honest, looking back, Joseph didn't remember much about what all took place over the next couple hours. He just knew that he had become a father and that now he had a son. As Mary was holding the baby, Joseph reached up and took the small oil lamp in his hand and held it close to Mary. The light from the candle was reflected in Mary's soft eyes. For the first time he was able to see clearly the face of his newborn son. The light of the lamp seemed to bounce off the face of Jesus. There was a brilliance and radiance. Joseph was caught up in the moment, and his mind raced a dozen different directions. "What now, God? Where does the story go from here? Who is this child? How will he save the people from their sins?" Even though he still had dozens of unanswered questions, his heart was warm, and his mind was at peace. He couldn't explain it all, but he just knew that somehow he was watching the unfolding plan of almighty God, right in front of his very eyes.

Again, Joseph was struck with the intensity of the light that was reflected in the face of his newborn son. He remembered what Mary had said earlier in the night: "What a difference a little light can make." If his mind had been clear and his thoughts more focused, he might have even recalled the words of the prophet Isaiah: "The people who walk in darkness will see a great light; those who live in a dark land, the light will shine on them."

It's true that we never know what difference a little light can make. But we can speak with certainty about the light Jesus brought to our world. Since his arrival on that first Christmas, the "Light of the World" has continued to spread. In Christ there is hope. In Christ there is life. In Christ there is forgiveness. In Christ there is grace. When the true Light shone, all the dark corners were filled with light. Scary shadows became recognized shapes. Strange creatures turn out to be a colt, a donkey, and a lamb. It's not so scary anymore, is it? No. Not since the Light has come.

CHAPTER 7

Looking for Jesus

Matthew 2:13-17

Marcus was born to be a soldier and nothing else. From the time he arrived in the world, his parents had dreams of his military career. They dreamed of the day when he would lead the mighty armies of Rome. They dreamed of the day when he would parade the streets of Rome as a hero returned home from a victorious battlefield. They dreamed of the day when he would be mentioned in the same breath as the other great soldiers of the empire. They had the vision and the means to make it all happen.

Marcus's family lived on the outskirts of Rome, the eternal city. Their home was near the banks of the Tiber River, in an affluent part of town. His father had done well, first as a merchant and then as a respected member of the Roman senate. The family name was well known and well respected. It seemed apparent that young Marcus would rise to greatness as his parents had dreamed. He was educated in the finest schools of Rome. He learned languages, histories, dramas, and math. He excelled in his studies and grew strong physically as well. After a time he was sent to be trained in the Roman military. There, too, he did well. He learned battle strategies and studied the history of famous leaders. He learned of leadership and power. He also became adept at using a sword. He had the makings of a fine soldier, destined to attempt great things for the cause of Rome. At the age of twenty-one, he received his first commission. He was named a centurion, quite a feat for someone so young. Centurions, as the name implies, led groups of one hundred soldiers.

In those days, Caesar Augustus was the emperor. For over forty years, he ruled the world, bringing both stability and advances. Roads were built, cities were established, laws were enacted, and peace was maintained. In order to rule such a broad empire, kingdoms were established all across the land. It was in Palestine that Herod the Great came to power. For thirty-three years he would do in Palestine what Augustus had done in Rome. New buildings were built, new roads established, and Roman culture and thought would be imposed upon the kingdom. Maintaining peace on the local level was not as easily accomplished.

There were many in Israel who did not like the oppression of the Roman government. The Israelites were a proud people with a strong heritage. They, too, had military leaders who had led them to prominence. Joshua had led them in conquest of the whole land of Canaan. King David had established a strong nation and had put the Philistine threat to rest. Even though they would later be defeated by the Babylonians and their cities destroyed, they never forgot their sense of national pride. When they came back to their homeland after the exile, many of them were hungry to be independent again, to be strong again, to throw off those who would attempt to oppress them.

There were even groups committed to that end. There were pockets of resistance scattered throughout Herod's kingdom. One group, the Zealots, continued to attempt undermining the authority of the Romans. There were constant threats of overthrow and assassination. Things got so bad, in fact, that word reached Rome that trouble was brewing in Palestine. In response, Augustus decided to send a few more troops. Word was dispatched to a general, who sent word to a major, who sent word to a captain to coordinate the effort of sending reinforcements to King Herod. It was decided that a legion of men would suffice. Ten centurions were to be selected with their men and sent to Palestine. "I have just the man," declared one military official. "He's young, bright, and eager to see action. He's the kind of guy who wants to make a name for himself." Marcus spoke with great excitement when he told his parents that he had been chosen to represent Rome in the distant country of Israel. They, too, were filled with excitement and pride.

It was early spring, just after the harsh storms of winter were past, when Marcus and his men left from the seaport of Anzio en route to the western Israeli seaport of Caesarea. The trip was long but adventurous. Many of the soldiers, like Marcus, had never traveled far from Rome. It was their chance to see the world, to explore new horizons. Many battled seasickness during the first few days of the voyage before settling in to life on the seas. Along the way they anchored in places like Crete, Rhodes, and Malta. Each stop allowed the men a chance to sample other cultures, other food, and other ways of doing things. Because they sailed under the banner of the Roman government, they were afforded nice lodging and good food. The only skirmishes they faced were at the hands of one another as an occasional political debate got a little too heated.

It was well into the summer when they arrived in Caesarea. They were met at the port by one of Herod's generals. It was immediately apparent that they were a long way from home and from the splendor of Rome. The language was different. The food was different. The people were different. The attitude was different. It was clear to them that not all the citizens of Palestine welcomed their arrival. In fact, Marcus felt an immediate sense of tension between the Romans and the locals. "Better guard your back at all times," he warned his men. "I'm not sure everyone respects the authority of Rome as much as they should."

It had been decided that Marcus's troops would be assigned to Jerusalem. To those who did not know him, Marcus looked a little young and a little inexperienced, so it seemed wise to send his group to Jerusalem, where the Roman presence was strong and Herod's power well secured. After a couple days of rest from their journey across the Mediterranean, Marcus and his men began what would be a five-day, fifty-mile trek toward Jerusalem. They camped along the way and ate rations that had been provided by local merchants who had forcibly "volunteered" to help. Marcus was visibly excited when he led his men into the walled city of Jerusalem for the first time. He felt both a sense of pride and accomplishment in what he was doing and in where he was doing it. He thought of his parents and how much they would have enjoyed this moment.

Conditions in Jerusalem were better than they had been along the way to Jerusalem. Herod had built a complex of barracks not far from his palace. The walls were thick to give protection. The rooms were designed so that each soldier would have a bed of his own. There were places to store weapons and armor. There were places to bathe and places to repair equipment. There were also places for the men to eat. "Could be a lot worse," Marcus thought to himself. "At least I'm not out sleeping in a tent, fighting bugs, and fearing the locals."

One military commander gave a briefing and made the assignments, advising, "Rule of thumb around here is to do your job and avoid the locals."

Marcus and a few of his men had been assigned the duty of guarding the stable in which Herod's horses were kept. It was not the glamorous and exciting duty for which he had hoped. He didn't like the smell, the boredom, or the constant jokes that the other soldiers made about the "mighty defenders of the barn." He longed for the day when he could see "real action." He complained to himself that in the months since he left Rome, his sword had not been out of its sheath a single time, except to clean it. Marcus had decided to keep a journal of his exploits. He noticed how so many of the daily entries read the same: "Reported for duty. Secured the stables. Walked around town."

Many of the soldiers found their way to the local watering holes at night to drown their homesickness and to talk of their daily routines. Some would talk of being in the outlying areas, where occasional skirmishes would occur between the locals and the Romans. Those on the front lines would always talk of adventure and experiences that Marcus would never live as long as he was confined to guarding the stables. His only real brush with the locals came one night at the tavern where he often gathered with some of his men.

A group of locals was there, and they seemed more agitated than usual. As the night wore on and the wine took its effect, verbal exchanges were traded among the soldiers and the locals. Marcus offered a few disparaging remarks about the Israelis. The verbal barbs turned into ugly insults. Tensions mounted. One of Marcus's men noticed a tattoo in the shape of a palm branch on one of the locals. "He's a Zealot," whispered the soldier. "I think we've been set up!" In a flash, the group of Zealots sprang to their feet and produced daggers from their clothing. The soldiers drew their swords. For the first time, Marcus felt the steel of his sword collide with the steel of the Zealot's dagger. The skirmish lasted only for a brief moment. Neither side had a clear advantage. One of the soldiers was badly wounded, and two of the locals had to be carried away.

The next day, Marcus received quite a "dressing down" from his superior. His commander was angered at his willingness to put himself and his men in harm's way. He was angered that one of the soldiers was injured. He was angered that the Romans were blamed for starting the ruckus. "You have been warned not to deal with the Zealots. You could have lost your life!" he shouted. "Couldn't you keep your mouth shut? Better for you to stay in the barn for a few more months. Maybe then you'll learn to control yourself!" The incident was recorded, if not in the pages of a journal, at least in the mind of the commander who thought less and less of young Marcus and his ability to lead anything.

The only positive thing about guarding the stable was getting to meet dignitaries who made their way to Jerusalem to gain an audience with King Herod. Marcus would never forget the day when magi from Persia came waltzing into the city. Marcus had never seen anything like it before. He described the visit in his journal: "I am told that the magi are astrologers, stargazers who search the heavens and study the arrangements of the stars in order to gain messages from God. This group had the appearance of royalty. They arrived on camels with many other servants and still other camels loaded with supplies for their journey. Their clothing was silk, and their beards were long. They wore purple, deep blues, and green. Their clothing was accented in gold, and incense seemed to swirl around the entire caravan. They were people of worth; there is no doubt of that in my mind."

When they arrived at the palace, the magi had simply announced that they had come on a most urgent visit. Their study of the stars had revealed a most important discovery. In the king's private chamber they told the reason for the visit. According to some of the fellow soldiers who were with the king at the time, these wise men had come to find the new king of Israel. "We have seen his star rising in the east, and we have come to worship him," they said.

If Herod was shaken by the news, he certainly didn't play his hand. Feigning an air of camaraderie, he said to them, "Quickly, go search for the child, and when you have found him, report back to me that I might worship him as well. Find out where he was born and when."

The news of their visit and the subject of their search soon spread like wildfire across Jerusalem. For those clinging to the hope of a promised messiah, the news was received with great joy. God had not forgotten. But for most the news was troubling. Who was this new king? How would he come to power? Would there be an overthrow? Would there be rebellion? Would bloodshed come? Would their land once again be torn and their cities left in ruin?

The royal caravan only enjoyed the splendor of the palace and the warmth of Herod's hospitality for a few days. They were anxious to find their way to Bethlehem, to see the child, to worship him, and to offer to him their gifts. The star led them to the house where the young family was now living. They presented their gifts and offered their praises, and after being warned in a dream not to return to King Herod, they made their way back toward their homeland.

When it became apparent that the wise men had chosen not to return to Herod to make their report, the king became angered, maybe even a bit panicked and paranoid. Troops were called up to go to Bethlehem to secure the area. They were simply told to look for the new king. None of them could imagine that within days, the desperate king would order the slaughter of all the boys two years of age and younger, rationalizing, "Better to kill a child than to lose the kingdom."

When the king ordered troops to Bethlehem, the commanding officer began to think about which men should go. "I have just the perfect man in mind," he thought to himself. "I'll send Marcus to Bethlehem. Maybe a little time in the Judean hill country will straighten out his attitude."

Marcus was thrilled with the prospect of a new assignment. "I'll be out from the stables," he thought. "Maybe now I'll see some real action."

But just when Marcus thought things couldn't get worse than guarding a stable, he discovered what life was like in Bethlehem for a young Roman solider. He was assigned to the Gaza road, which led out of town to the south toward Egypt. His duty was to set up a checkpoint, watching all those leaving town. He was told, "You are to look for the new king. If you find him, detain him. King Herod himself wants to come and worship."

On the outskirts of the sleepy town of Bethlehem, there were no barracks, no taverns, no shelters—just hillsides and sheep. The only locals were shepherds and poor farmers, none of whom spoke any language Marcus could understand. He found himself sleeping in a tent, fighting bugs, and fearing the locals. He was glad his parents weren't around to see him now. Here he was, the pride of Rome, a young and promising centurion, living on the backside of an obscure little Judean village. And now he was to spend his days looking for the new king, as if any king could possibly be born in a place like this.

For hours a day he and another soldier would stop every traveler who headed down the desert road. "Have you seen the king?" they would ask. It bordered on the absurd.

"Haven't seen any kings around here lately, have you?" the soldiers would ask in jest.

Once, they even stopped a young couple with a small boy. Their donkey was heavily packed. They were obviously at the start of a long journey. Marcus thought, "Some threat to the empire this is—a young mother, a little boy, and a carpenter father." "Have you seen him?" Marcus asked.

"Seen whom?" was the reply.

"Have you seen the new king of Israel? We're looking for him."

The father replied, "What would we know of kings and kingdoms? We're just simple folks."

That night in his journal Marcus wrote, "I've spent the last eight days on the Gaza road. No sign yet of any king."

Could someone really be that close to the child of Christmas and completely miss him? Yes. Millions do everywhere. Oh, they search for Jesus. They check in every package they open. They look in every nativity scene they find. They hope to hear him in the carols that are played over the radio. They come close but never find him because they haven't looked in the right place, for the Christ child resides in every human heart. Some of us need to displace all the distractions of Christmas long enough to have a quiet moment to ourselves where we can find his voice deep within us. And in the solitude of our hearts, we should worship. Some of us need to look into the hearts of others this season—the lonely, the scared, the depressed, the fearful—because he can be found in those places as well. It may be in the giving of your time that you will find him. He wants to be seen. In fact, Jesus longs to be discovered.

God himself said, "You will find me when you search for me with all your heart."

Have *you* seen the king? Good question. I hope you will.

CHAPTER 8

The Census Taker

Luke 2:1-7

The declaration made by Caesar Augustus instantly brought a flurry of activity throughout the empire. A census was to be taken of the entire earth—every single inhabitant. Every person in every village, town, and city was to be counted and their names carefully recorded. Information about ethnic origin, place of birth, nationality, occupation—all the vital statistics were to be gleaned. The task of counting the entire Roman Empire was a daunting task in every way. How to organize? Who to do the counting? How to keep the records? It seemed an impossible undertaking, but when Caesar made a decree, such questions were not asked. The command was simply followed.

It was decided that every person living in any country within the empire would have to return to his or her place of birth in order to be enrolled. That way, family units could be tabulated and recorded. Offspring could be traced and the genealogies written down. It was also decided that in order to keep the process from dragging out for years to come, all of the tabulation needed to happen within a very brief period of time. From the time that the decree was issued, every family had only months to accomplish whatever journey was needed in order to obey the decree. As soon as word about the census began to spread, people began making their plans. Some would have to travel only across town, while others would have to travel for days and even weeks to visit their ancestral homes. Roads became crowded, merchants became busy, and people became weary.

Governor Quirinius of Syria quickly moved the people of his administration into action. Wanting to impress those who might be looking from

Rome, Quirinius began setting up an organization that could function well and accurately count those under his rule. Every village and town that had at least fifty men would be required to set up a centralized place within the city where those being enrolled would have to go to register. The "census office" was to be situated in a prominent place, either along the main road leading into town or within the city gate through which people would pass in the case of those towns that were fortified by a city wall. Quirinius also began a process of recruiting young but well-educated men to staff the various registration places. In the case of cities where synagogues were built, Quirinius's staff worked with the local religious scribes to build a list of names of young men who could read and write and keep meticulous records. He also set a good wage for those who might be interested in the short-term job. It was hoped that many would respond. And they did. However, others needed a little extra prodding by the Romans before deciding to "volunteer."

In the northern town of Capernaum, the name of a young seventeen-year-old was given by a rabbi to the leader of the Roman garrison. His name was Matthew, the son of Alphaeus. Matthew had been raised in the synagogue school and was well educated by the rabbis. He was fluent in Greek, Aramaic, and of course Hebrew. He was also single and ready to venture out from under the control of his father. He was asked if he was interested in being a census taker in a different city from his own. There were needs in some of the larger towns to the south. "Why not?" he thought. Within a few weeks he was assigned duty in the city of Bethlehem. He was promised a place to stay while he worked and given some money for travel.

Matthew's father vehemently opposed the idea. He didn't like the fact that his son was moving away, and he especially didn't like the fact that his son would be working closely with the Romans, warning Matthew, "My son, if you play with dogs, soon you will smell like a dog. People will have difficulty telling the two of you apart. Today you're a census taker, tomorrow a tax collector."

Matthew responded, "Father, I would never betray my own people for the sake of collecting money. This is just a short job with good pay. I will return soon, before the season even changes."

His father said, "Don't be so sure, and don't be so naïve, my son. Power and wealth have distorted many lives."

"I'll be home soon; you'll see," Matthew promised. And with those words, Matthew headed south on the back of a wooden cart pulled by Roman horses.

The census taker's booth in Bethlehem was located within the city gate. Typically, the city gate contained more than just the huge doors to be closed at night. Within the walls of the gate were rooms and chambers where the business of the city was conducted. Government leaders were stationed there. Commerce was conducted and deeds registered. Taxes were paid, and judges ruled on certain matters in that spot. Sometimes garrisons of troops were also housed at the city gate. Matthew was given a small room in which to do his work of recording the census. The back wall was covered floor to ceiling with a grid of vertical and horizontal boards that made a number of small cubicles. Each cubicle contained four or five scrolls of parchment. The parchments were arranged by lineage and family names. There were hundreds of scrolls, each containing dozens of names. Matthew had done an exceptional job in meticulously arranging the scrolls. He seemed to know the exact place to look as each new head of household entered the room.

His desk sat in the middle of the room. It was large, solid, and strong. On the desktop were a couple of oil lamps that were continually lit. There were also a number of quills and a few small clay pots filled with ink. Matthew kept a blotter on the desk as well, careful not to smudge any entry that he made. There were also bits and pieces of parchment on which Matthew would scribble the occasional note or try out a quill before setting it to the census parchment. Behind the desk sat a sturdy chair. Matthew had covered it with several wool blankets to make it soft during the long and tedious hours he spent recording all the census information. There were windows along both side walls, which were helpful in letting in both a breeze and sunlight. To the right of the desk, along the wall under the window, was a simple wooden bench. It was always occupied by two Roman soldiers who were sent there each day to watch over the process, making sure that every name was recorded and every head counted. They had been given orders: "No one is to be left out or skipped." It was never said, but they assumed that taxes were coming from these records, thus the importance of the careful recordings.

The opposite wall also contained a long bench, just to the right of the doorway as one entered the room. It was the place where family members could sit while the head of the household was being interviewed by the census taker. The soldiers thought it best only to let one family in at a time. The father of each family was told to sit in a chair just in front of the desk. Matthew would ask a number of questions and carefully record the responses. It was the same with each family: "What is your date of birth? What is your father's name and his father's name? Are there siblings? How many children do you have, and what are the names? What is the name of your wife? What is your occupation? Where is your residence?"

On and on the process went. For days on end, Matthew sat at his desk asking the same questions. His eyes grew weak in the dim light. His hand quickly tired from all the writing. His head hurt, and even his ears grew weary of listening to all the stories and all the complaints. It was a laborious process that took weeks and weeks to complete. There was an endless line at the door. People were there when the day began, and they were there when the time came to close each night. Rarely did he get a day off. At least he was given the Sabbath, a concession given by the Romans but not appreciated by them.

It was late one afternoon when a husband and wife were allowed to enter. The husband was told to sit in the chair, and the woman was directed to the wooden bench to the right. Both seemed grateful to have a place to sit. Like all the others, they had been standing for hours outside. They were weary and hungry and frustrated at the whole census-taking process. The young woman all but collapsed on the bench. She was obviously very preg-nant. She tried to sit one way and then the next, but it was apparent to Matthew that she was well beyond the point of being comfortable again until the child was born. Not unsympathetic to her plight, he offered one of the blankets on which he was seated. She gladly took it and thanked him for his kindness. Matthew looked at the man seated before him; he looked a few years older. Matthew could see that the husband had slept very little in the past few days. His eyes were bleary, and his voice was scratchy.

"Hopefully this won't take too long," said Matthew. "But there are questions that I must ask. The first concerns your lineage. Tell me your name, the name of your father, and the name of his father."

Joseph quickly replied, "My name is Joseph, son of Jacob, son of Matthan, son of Eleazar."

Matthew leaned back in his chair and stroked his beard for a moment as though lost in deep thought. He then got up from his chair, turned to the wall behind him, and started shuffling through several scrolls. "Ah, yes, here it is," he declared. He then stretched out the parchment across the top of the desk. With the use of the ink and the quill, he quickly began drawing lines and writing names. He then began his litany of usual questions. He soon learned that the young couple was from Nazareth. The husband was a carpenter. There were other brothers and sisters. His father had died, and his mother was aging. They had traveled for a number of days. They owned their own shop, along with a few goats and sheep and a donkey, which they had secured just outside the door. Matthew also discovered that this soon-to-be-born child would be the first born to the young couple.

Matthew said, "Of course you know that if the child who is born is a son, you will have to return to this office so that his name will be recorded here in this spot, just below that of your own."

"Oh, it's going to be a boy," declared Joseph. "You can go ahead and write it down if you would like. I can even give you the name if that will help."

Matthew held up his hand as if to stop the enthusiasm of the husband: "Joseph, let's not become too anxious. Surely every Jewish father longs for a son, but you must wait and see. The child is not yet born! Only then can I record the name. Mistakes are not tolerated. Besides, what makes you so sure that you will have a son? Can you see through flesh? Can you see into the womb of your wife? Are you a prophet?"

Joseph leaned back in his chair and stroked his beard, wondering how much to share publicly. He proceeded, "I know that he will be a son because it has been revealed to me. The angel Gabriel appeared to me in a dream and told me of this child—and the angel appeared not only to me, but to my wife Mary, who received the same message."

Matthew looked toward Mary, who simply nodded, as though such things were commonplace. Matthew thought to himself, "These two are either more foolish or more faithful than most. Maybe they are just hopeful."

Joseph continued, the excitement growing in his voice, "The angel announced that Mary would conceive as the result of God's Spirit working in her life. She is to have a son. He will be the fulfillment of prophecy! He will save the people from their sins. The angel has told us this news!"

Again, Matthew stopped him mid-sentence: "Oy! All this talk of angels and deliverers—Joseph, do you really think that God would visit such a place as this with such a son of promise? This is surely not the place or time. Are you greater than our forefathers, Abraham, Isaac, and Jacob, to whom his promise was given? Do you think God would fulfill his work through your child? Do you really think God is in the habit of speaking to peasant carpenters and young women? What would you have God do next—put a star in the sky or fill the air with more angels? I think you are too weary, my friend. Your dreams have chased away your common sense. You should go now. I have all that I need for the census. Go your way and find rest and food and shelter. And settle your wife. She has that look about her. I fear that you won't wait long to meet your child."

Matthew shook his head in amazement as the two left his presence. He carefully rolled up the parchment on which he had written Joseph's records. He stood from his desk and placed the scroll into the cubical, muttering under his breath, "Can you just imagine it? God's chosen born to a carpenter and his wife? How do people come up with some of the stuff they do?" He turned and gave the soldiers a nod. One of them walked to the door and called for the next family waiting in line. Matthew reclaimed his blanket, padded his chair, and sat down again, picking up both the quill and the next conversation.

Two weeks later, Matthew had all but forgotten the young couple and the extraordinary stories they had told. He was working away on some documents that he was required to submit to the Roman authorities. His concentration was broken by the sound of a baby's cry. He looked up from his work and gave himself a moment to allow his eyes to adjust to the noonday sun that came pouring through the doorway. At first all he could make out was the silhouette of a man and woman, but as they walked toward his desk, he could see their features clearly. It took him but a moment to place the two who were standing before him. It was the young couple from Nazareth who had talked of the angels and about the son who would be born to them. In her arms, Mary cradled a child.

"Can I help you?" Matthew asked.

"Yes," said Joseph. "We are here to register our child, our son. You told me he should be added to your records."

"So you were right. It *is* a son, as you predicted—excuse me, as the angel had predicted," said Matthew. He reached for the parchment, remembering the precise spot where it had been placed. Drawing a line for the name, he looked at Joseph and asked, "And what is his name; what shall I write?"

Joseph said, "His name is Jesus."

"Jesus?" asked Matthew. "There is no such name in your family. I have over five generations of your family recorded in front of me, and not one member of your family bears such a name. Why would you not honor your heritage? Why would you give him that name? What does it mean, anyway?"

Joseph responded, "The name was not chosen by us, but by God. We are only doing as God has commanded. His name is a testimony to what God will do. It simply means, 'The one who saves the people from their sins.'"

Matthew had trouble sorting it all out, asking, "Save the people from their sins? How? Is he like a lamb to be slaughtered, a sacrifice to be offered? He is a boy and nothing more. Let me see the child who bears such a name." Mary unfolded the blanket in which Jesus was wrapped. Matthew held the lamp close to his face to see him clearly. At first he thought, "This is a child just like any other child. You've seen one; you've seen a thousand." But an odd feeling came over him that he couldn't really explain. He felt drawn to the child, as if there was some special quality. He felt intrigued, gladdened, almost hopeful. Maybe it was just wishful thinking to imagine that this child was special. Maybe he was just tired and the stories Joseph and Mary had told were starting to chase away his good sense. As he wrote the name Jesus on the parchment, he also made a note about the meaning of the name—"the one who saves the people from their sins." He wondered if he would ever write that name again or hear it mentioned or even think of the name once the young family left his presence.

In fact, Matthew *would* see the child again, some thirty years later. He would record the meeting this way: "And as Jesus passed on from there, he saw a man, called Matthew, sitting in the tax office; and he said to him, 'Follow me!' And he rose, and followed him" (Matt 9:9). It's interesting that when he would later write the whole story of Jesus, Matthew not only included the precise genealogy, but he even told the story of how the angel Gabriel had visited his father Joseph.

Be careful when you read the story of Christmas for yourself. You may begin as a skeptic but leave as a follower. You see, there really was a child born to Mary and Joseph whose name was Jesus. The name really does mean "the one who saves the people from their sins." He really was conceived by the Holy Spirit. He really was slain on a cross to atone for the sins of the world. And if, in faith, you trust in him and claim him as Lord, your life will never be the same again. You will be joined to him eternally and welcomed into his royal family. Joy to the world! He comes as a child, yet he comes as king!

CHAPTER 9

Living Water

John 7:38

"He who believes in me, as the Scripture said, 'From his innermost being shall flow rivers of living water.'"—John 7:38

Jude was often described as being "wiry." Some would call him downright skinny, although it was apparent that he possessed a great deal of physical strength, resulting from many years of hard work. His skin had a dark olive hue and resembled leather that had been exposed to the sun for too many years. He had dark eyes, gray hair, and a short-cropped beard. Though no longer a young man, he could still work for long hours, and he still had the agility of someone much younger. He was well known around Bethlehem for many reasons. Some thought him to be eccentric, or even a little odd. He was known to have long conversations with himself. He would sing his way down the street and do a little dance as he went from place to place. He seemed happy, and most people in the community seemed to know him and accept him. He was good-natured and well liked. He was also good at what he did.

Some said Jude had a special gift—an unusual talent, a strange skill, a unique ability. Some suggested he was possessed of a demon, and others just thought he was a little crazy. But he could find water. Not like stumbling across a hidden pond or discovering a creek that few people knew about. No, this gift was different. He could discern when there was water underground. He could feel it in his bones. Some call it "witching for water," or "dowsing," but the truth of the matter was that Jude could take a tender, freshly cut willow branch in the shape of a "Y," peel away the bark, and hold it in his hands in just a certain way. He had an amazing accuracy in finding the location of an underground spring or water table. He called the underground water "living water." He said, "It's down there all right, just waiting to be born." He would walk across a plot of land, pause when the stick started to point downward, and simply say, "Here. Let's dig the well in just this spot." It was rare when he wasn't dead-on accurate.

Jude's skills were much in demand. He lived and worked out of a small shop on the edge of the community. It was a simple place, containing only two rooms. The front room served as the place where he did business. There, he kept his records on parchment, along with the tools of his trade. Scattered about the room in no particularly organized way were shovels, picks, a hatchet or two, and a few sharp knives. He also had a pushcart with wooden wheels that he used to haul away dirt when he was in the process of digging a well. The back room served as his living quarters. It was fairly sparse. There was a small cot on which he slept. There was a stool and table where he would eat his meals. There was also a wooden chest where he kept his blankets and a few articles of clothing. He also kept a couple pairs of sturdy leather shoes next to his cot. The corner of the room contained an earthen stove on which he occasionally cooked and from which the room could be warmed in the winter months. There were windows that faced to the south and east. He loved to keep them open as much as possible. He loved working and being outside as much as possible. Just outside the back door was a small stairway that led to the roof. He loved to climb the stairs at night and stretch out on the roof. He loved to smell the distinctive smells. Some nights he could smell the incense from the synagogue a few blocks away. Some nights he could smell meat that was being grilled at a nearby home. Some nights the smell of fresh bread hung in the air. He also loved staring into the night sky. He would count the stars and wonder at the magnitude of the heavens.

There was always a need for his gift. In the arid, dry regions of Palestine, water was scarce, wells were few and far between, and only an occasional oasis dotted the landscape. Some areas of Israel were fertile and green, but as one heads toward the east, much of it grows pretty barren. Word of his fame spread far beyond Bethlehem, in places like Tekoa, Bethany, Jericho, and a lot of other little spots toward the east where the soil was dryer, the land rockier, and the sun hotter.

Bethlehem itself had a few wells scattered about. The largest and most public well was the one in the middle of town. People would trek to the middle of town each morning to drink from the cool, refreshing waters.

Women would draw enough in the early hours to use in their homes for cooking and cleaning and even some for the livestock. Only the foolish or marginalized would dare to go in the heat of the day when mostly men gathered around such places. King David, who of course grew up in Bethlehem, knew of the well. The Scriptures tell the story of David and his men, who were once separated from the city by the Philistine army. From their vantage point in the surrounding hills, they could see into the center of town and even see the well. When King David spoke of how much he desired a drink from the well, three of his bravest men stealthily made their way through the Philistine camp and into the city, just to bring him some of that water.

Though Jude was wiry, he was amazingly strong. He had broad shoulders and a muscular back from where he had spent so many endless hours digging into the earth to find the "living water." Sometimes the work was easy and smooth when the water was near the surface. At other times it was extremely hard, and the wells had to be very deep. His clothes were always caked with sweat stains, moist dirt, and a little blood from his blistered hands or an occasional scrape.

Jude eked out a living digging wells—at least he made enough to get by. He was never wealthy, but he had more than a lot of folks who worked with their hands. He could afford to buy fruit and vegetables from the local markets and a little meat on occasion. He usually bought a little fresh bread from a small place a few doors down from his shop.

He claimed to be a God-follower. He knew the Torah. He read the prophets and writings and yet was not always present for Sabbath worship. He and the local rabbi had reached a friendly understanding in their discussion of such things. Jude agreed never to work on the Sabbath nor to allow anyone working for him to do the same. He would come to the synagogue during the major feasts events, and he would ensure that the springs that fed water to the purification basins stayed clean and flowing. In exchange, the rabbi gave him relative peace and would only ask him about his tithing disciplines on rare occasions.

Jude had just returned to Bethlehem after digging a well in a nearby small town just a few miles to the south. As he had traveled and worked, he had been interested in all of the talk he had heard about the Roman census. People were freely giving their opinions about Roman taxation, travel, and interruptions to their lives. Jude noticed that the roads were already getting crowded and inns were filling up with travelers even though the deadline to register was still over a month away. He also noticed how small roadside stands were sprouting up all over the place, where merchants were selling fresh fruits and bread to those traveling. "I'll be glad when this is all over," he said to himself. "I'm ready for things to get back to normal." Still, in his mind he knew that it would be weeks or maybe months until all the talk and travel of the census would subside.

The morning after he returned, he was startled from his slumber by a sharp knock on the door to his shop. He opened it to discover a young boy who had been sent to ask him about a business proposal. The stable boy, Michael, worked for an innkeeper whose inn was on the main road out of town, just on the outskirts of the community. The innkeeper had a business proposition, so Michael was told to please bring him to the inn.

"I can't go yet," replied Jude. "Haven't eaten. You can't expect me to deal on an empty stomach. We will go, but first we will eat."

"Did you say 'we'?" asked Michael.

Jude noticed a spark of excitement in the young boy's eyes. "Yes, *we*," Jude replied. "That is, if you can join me this morning." That's all it took, and a new friendship was forged.

The two had quite a feast in the back room of Jude's shop. Jude had apples and oranges that he had bought from one of the roadside vendors the day before. He also had some cheese and bread. The two of them enjoyed the meal while they talked of horses and hay, water and wells. Within the hour the two of them stepped out onto the street, where Michael led them to the inn to meet with the innkeeper. When they arrived, Michael made the introductions, and the two men shook hands.

It seemed that the innkeeper was in need of water, or at least access to it. For years, water for the inn had been carried by hand from some distance away. Several trips were required early each morning to get enough to meet the needs for the day. Michael had been good about going since coming to work in the stable, but in his youthful exuberance he tended to spill more than he returned with in his bucket. Besides that, with all the traveling families, more and more water was needed at the end of the day to drink, to cook with, to bathe. It made it harder and harder to keep enough on hand at the inn, so the innkeeper was hoping to have a well of his own. It would be great for his business. "So, Jude, is there water in this place? Can a well be dug? And how soon can you start? Things are only getting busier. I'd like to have a well, if there is water to be found. I hear you have a knack for finding it."

"Not so fast, my new friend," said Jude. "Yes, I can dig a well. I have dug many in the past. And yes, I can start very soon. But is there living water in this place? Who's to say? Pray, my friend, and maybe tomorrow we can know."

Jude promised to return at daybreak the next morning. He bid fare-well to his new young friend Michael and to his new enterprising employer. He spent the rest of the day walking among the willows that grew along a creek on the road that led toward Jerusalem. He found three of the special Y-shaped branches that he thought might work. He carefully cut them, stripped away the bark, and turned them over in his hands to see which had just the right "feel." Confident that he had found such a branch, he headed home to an early slumber so that he and his skills would be sharp and keen in the morning.

He arrived at the inn just as the sun was peeking over the horizon. Michael had already been up a while anticipating his arrival. He had already tended to the animals and made the trips to the well in the center of town for water. Soon, the innkeeper stumbled his way out of the back door of the inn and walked over to the spot to where Jude and Michael were standing. "So are you well this day?" asked the innkeeper.

"Quite so," said Jude.

The two spoke briefly, and then Jude began his work while Michael and the innkeeper watched. He first walked around the perimeter of the prop-erty. He made careful measurements and stepped off the length and width of the lot. He then asked Michael to clear away as much clutter as possible so he could walk freely about. He then reached into his burlap pouch that had been slung across his shoulder and drew out one of the willow branches that he had cut the previous afternoon. After closing his eyes and whispering to himself, perhaps a quiet prayer for wisdom, thought Michael, he care-fully took the willow branch in his hands, holding the two ends of the "Y" in each hand, twisting it so his palms were face up and the single end of the branch faced forward. He began to walk aimlessly around the lot with his eyes closed. He quietly took a few steps this way and then that way. He would pause for a moment, twist his head as though he was listening to an inaudible voice, and then he would walk some more.

This process went on for quite a long time. Michael watched intently. The innkeeper watched skeptically. Then it happened. Suddenly, the front of the branch began to point downward. The branch seemed to twist in his hands! Jude took one additional small step forward before he opened his eyes and declared, "Here! There is living water in this spot! Mark it, Michael. We will dig in this place."

"Are you sure?" asked the innkeeper. "Are you certain there is water below our feet?"

Jude replied, "We can never know for certain until we dig, but I'm confident that this is the place."

"And do you know the depth of the well and the time it will take to dig?" asked the innkeeper with growing enthusiasm.

"I'm not a prophet," Jude said. "Just a man with a helpful skill. We'll reach water when we reach water. Only then can I tell you how deep is the well. Surely my back and your purse both hope that the task will not be a lengthy one."

By late that afternoon, Jude had begun quite a hole. It was a circle that measured about five feet across. At the end of the day, the hole was almost waist deep, and the pile of dirt in the courtyard started to increase with size. Several days later the top of Jude's head could no longer be seen flush with the ground. By the second week, Jude was using a crudely constructed ladder to climb down into the hole. He had built a pulley with a crank above the hole. A rope was tied to a large bucket, and every once in a while, Jude would yell to Michael to pull up the rope. Michael would grab the rope and pull it over his shoulder so he could use his legs to strain against the load. He would tie it off around a tree. Jude would climb out of the hole and empty the bucket onto the ever-growing pile of dirt. He would then lower the bucket back to the ground and climb back into the depths of the hole.

The hole grew deeper, the pile grew larger, and the innkeeper grew more skeptical as the days passed. Jude estimated, by the length of the rope, that he was probably about thirty-five feet down by the end of the second full week of digging. It was on the morning of the fourth day of the third week that he noticed that the dirt began to change over to soft mud. He raced out of the hole and showed his find to the innkeeper and to Michael. "This is very good!" he declared. "There is moisture in the soil. Soon, the living water will come." All three brightened with the hope of success.

For the next two days, Michael noticed that each time Jude descended into the well, he tied a rope around his waist. He finally had to ask, so Jude told him that sometimes with just the right stroke of the shovel, the water would come rushing in. The dirt on which he was standing could wash out very quickly, and he could become stuck in the soft mud. "It's just for my protection. Who knows? You may have to haul *me* out instead of mud!" He laughed as though what he had said was no big deal. Michael thought it all sounded a little scary.

At the end of each day, Jude would drag his exhausted body back to his shop. After his evening meal he would climb to the rooftop and catch the cool evening breeze. His body relaxed, and he would often drift off to sleep.

He had noticed something a little strange over the past few nights. It seemed to him as though one of the stars in the sky had become much brighter. "Maybe I am just dreaming," he thought. He dismissed what he had seen by claiming he had been spending too much time below ground.

It was early in the afternoon when it finally happened. Jude noticed that he was suddenly standing in about six inches of water. Within moments it reached his knees. He quickly grabbed his pick and shovel and climbed his way up the ladder and out of the hole. He called Michael over, and the two of them watched as the afternoon sun reflected off the pool of water that was beginning to emerge at the bottom of the well. "The living water!" shouted Jude. "It has come!" He began to dance around like a man released from a prison cell. Michael ran to get the innkeeper. He ran to the hole and joined in the excitement of the great blessing.

"It's not a bit too soon," he declared. "You notice how full the inn has been these past few weeks? Tonight will be no exception; already, my place is almost filled. I have run myself ragged."

Michael thought to himself, "Who's been run ragged? I'm the one who has been making all the trips to the well in the center of town!"

Jude began the work of changing over the equipment used for hauling up the dirt to that which could be used for water. He fashioned a hand crank to a log and cut it to fit some upright posts he had dug into the ground. He took a fresh piece of rope and tied it to a new wooden bucket. He began raising and lowering the bucket into the water below. At first the water was muddy and filled with silt. But by nightfall each bucket was filled with nothing but cool, clean water.

As he had worked, Jude barely noticed how crowded the inn had become. Apparently it had been filled to capacity. Michael had been running around all afternoon. The stable was filled with a number of animals. He had pitchforked a lot of fresh straw and hay and had swept out the stalls several times. The two had barely spoken except for the brief moments when he came to draw water from the well to water down the livestock.

It was late in the night by the time Jude had finished all of his tasks. He was seated on the ground, leaning back against the huge mound of dirt he had created, almost drifting off to sleep when he noticed the innkeeper leading a young couple and their donkey out to the stable. Was he actually going to let them sleep in the stable? "Got to do what you got to do," he told himself. He must have drifted off to sleep for a few hours before Michael was suddenly shaking him awake. Startled, he asked, "What is it, Michael? What's the matter?"

Michael could hardly get the words out of his mouth: "I need water—quick! A baby has been born in the stable. It's a boy. We had to use a manger for a crib. The father said to get him water."

Jude jumped to his feet and quickly shook the cobwebs from his mind. "Don't worry about the water, Michael. Go help the young couple and find out what else they need. I'll draw all the water they need. Now, go!"

Jude felt like he had cranked the bucket up and down a hundred times before the night was over. What he heard and saw was more mysterious than even the strange star he had seen above his roof. There had been stories told of angels in the sky. Shepherds had been drawn in from their fields. Joseph and Mary told of their conversations with the archangel Gabriel. The child born that night was declared to be the "son of promise," the messiah who would come to change the world and save the people from their sins. But in such a place? On such a night? Is this really how God works?

Jude thought of the living water he had brought up from the well. He wondered at the timing of it all. It had quenched the thirst of the father, Joseph, and cooled the brow of the mother, Mary. It had bathed the child, Jesus. It had satisfied the weary shepherds and restored energy and life to the listless livestock. Was God doing something in their midst? Could it really be that this child was the savior of the world? Could it really be that God had ordained the events of this one, single night? Could it really be that even an old well digger had been gifted with a talent just to bring glory *to* God by being used *by* God?

It's all a little hard to take in. Not just the timing of the event, or the setting for the birth, or the details that surround it. What's hard to take in is the fact that God has chosen to call each of us to life through Jesus. We celebrate Jesus' birth, our hope, and the world's salvation. Once, when Jesus spoke to a woman at a well, he said, "If you knew the gift of God, and who it is who says to you, 'Give me a drink,' you would have asked him, and he would have given you living water" (Jn 4:10). I invite you to take a long drink. There is life in the Water.

CHAPTER 10

A Donkey Named Caleb

Luke 2:1-7

Although donkeys are mentioned numerous times in the Scriptures, rarely do they have a chance to tell their story. In fact, only once in all of the Bible does a donkey actually get to talk. You remember the story of Balaam's donkey? Balaam was on his way to curse the king of Israel one day when suddenly his donkey began acting rather strangely. The donkey could see things the prophet could not, namely, the angel of God standing in the road, holding a mighty sword. When the prophet and the donkey finally got to the point where they could see things eye to eye, the donkey started talking. With perfect diction and inflection, the old donkey pretty much told Balaam off.

It's funny with animals—sometimes they hear noises that humans can't hear. Maybe they sense things that humans can't sense. They seem to know a lot, and it would be great to hear their story. But rarely do they talk. This story tells of a gentle gray donkey. He's not a talking donkey. He doesn't see visions of angels or speak words of prophecy. But he is part of the greatest story ever told. As you hear his story, hopefully you will be reminded of that great story.

It all began late one afternoon when Joseph came bursting through the front door with great excitement in his eyes. Mary was startled at his presence because he typically stayed at the carpenter's shop until late. "Mary, I have a surprise for you!" he declared. "Go look out back!" With a little bewilderment and uncertainty, Mary rose from the table and peered out the back window of their small home. She looked left and then right and then looked again, not really knowing what to expect.

"I don't really see anything," she said. "Just someone's little gray donkey tied up at the back fence."

"That's it, Mary! That's the surprise—the donkey! I bought him for you earlier this morning," Joseph shouted.

"You bought me a donkey?" she asked. "I'm not sure I was looking to own a donkey."

"Sure, Mary," Joseph replied. "It's for the trip. I mean, it's a long way to travel at anytime, but especially while you are expecting. The donkey will keep you from having to walk so much. Besides, there is a lot of stuff we will have to take along that we can't possibly carry on our backs."

"That's great, Joseph. I would love for us to have a donkey, but can we afford one? How did you find the money to pay for him?" Mary knew that things were tight and would only get tighter once the baby was born. Carpenter work was good, fairly steady work, but it was not the kind of job that made anyone rich. Mary was just starting to let it all get to her—this whole life to which she had been called. It was one thing to care for the two of them, but a new baby would mean more expenses and more stress.

"Nothing to worry about, Mary," declared Joseph. "It's all been taken care of. You know Simeon, up the lane? He needed a couple chairs and a table, and I happened to have some in the shop. I also promised to fix his fence later this year. So we just worked out a little deal, and I came home with the donkey. His name is Caleb. Simeon named him after his own brother— thought that would be funny. And he's young, Mary, only about three years old. I'll be an old man long before he's gone." (The conversation reminded Mary of a young boy asking his mother if he could keep the puppy that followed him home.)

Mary and Joseph walked out the back of the lot so Mary could meet Caleb. She took one look into those big, soft eyes, and suddenly she was a believer. "Well, he seems gentle enough," said Mary.

"Oh, he is," Joseph quickly replied. "He's been pampered since birth, and he just loves to be around people. He even knows his name." Joseph called out Caleb's name, and within seconds the little gray donkey walked over to Joseph and started nuzzling his nose into Joseph's chest. "I think he likes me," Joseph said. "And he loves it when I brush him down."

Mary turned and asked, "I thought you just got him today. When did you have time to brush him down?"

Joseph looked down like a guilty little boy. "Well, maybe I've been thinking about this for a while."

"I see," said Mary.

As it turns out, the donkey really would be of great help. He seemed surefooted, strong, and sturdy. He also seemed to be very protective of Mary. Never once did he buck when Joseph set Mary on his back, and never once did he try to bite. They made quite a team, the three of them. And anytime Joseph or Mary walked into the yard, Caleb always sauntered up and waited for someone to pet his long nose.

Joseph busied himself over the course of the next few weeks in planning for the trip to Bethlehem. It would not be an easy journey. As the crow flies, it's a distance of only thirty to forty miles, but the roads and the hills would make it much longer. Joseph knew they would have to travel to the south by going east of the Jordan. There was no way they could travel through Samaria. The discord between the Jews and the Samaritans would have made such travel extremely dangerous. So Joseph planned a route to the east, which included fording the Jordan River at the shallows just north of the Jabbock River. From there they would travel the road to the south that went past Alexandruim, Archelais, and eventually Jericho. This route was nearly eighty treacherous miles in length. There would be rivers to cross, deep ravines to negotiate, and mountains to climb. At best, thought Joseph, it would take a couple weeks, maybe a little less if the weather was good. Joseph hoped they could travel about eight miles a day. They would have to rest and, of course, give the donkey time to graze and recover. Seldom would they be alone, however. Due to the Roman census, they would soon find other family groups or caravans with whom they could travel for some of the journey.

Joseph tried to make a list of all the supplies they would need. He packed some blankets and pieces of canvas, knowing they would spend many nights under the open sky. He took along a leather pouch in which he would carry as much money as he could scrape together for the trip. He also gathered some dates and oranges, along with several loaves of bread and some cheese. He also tried to anticipate whatever else they might need. He packed a few of his carpenter tools, thinking he might need to repair something for someone along the way or set up a little business on the side of the road if they needed some money on the return trip. He really didn't know what to pack for Mary. He knew it was a possibility that she could give birth along the way. He just prayed that God's timing would cause it to happen at a moment when he could find help and shelter. Surely the God who had *promised* the birth would *provide* for it.

It was a bright, clear morning on the day that Joseph, Mary, and Caleb took the first steps of the journey. They had awakened before dawn, eaten breakfast, and headed out. Mary sat on a blanket while riding on Caleb's back. Joseph held a staff in one hand and the rope that led to Caleb's bridle in the other. Slowly but surely, they walked down the very familiar streets of Nazareth, making their way to the road that led to the south. The day went according to plan with little deviation. Caleb had responded well, and Mary had ridden somewhat comfortably most of the way.

Toward late afternoon they searched for a good spot to spend the evening. Joseph got busy doing the things that would become part of his daily routine. First, he would unpack Caleb and let him graze on the nearby hillsides. His next order of business would be to find water. He brought along a wooden pail, and after making sure that Caleb had a good drink, he would get more and pour it into a wooden bowl to be used for cooking or drinking. He would build a small fire and roll out the canvas, using a few sticks to make a simple lean-to. After supper, once Mary seemed settled and comfortable, Joseph would take a brush and methodically brush down Caleb and pat him gently.

Toward the end of the first week, an unusual event happened late one night. The caravan of three had stopped on the outskirts of a small village. Joseph and Mary were sleeping soundly when all of a sudden Caleb started braying loudly and stomping his feet. Joseph jumped to his feet and shouted, "Caleb, hush! You'll wake the whole town! What's the matter with you?" It was only then that Joseph saw a wolf sneaking around the campsite. He quickly grabbed his staff in one hand and a few smooth stones in the other. He threw a few rocks in the direction of the wolf and banged his staff on a tree limb, and soon the wolf was out of sight. Joseph looked at Caleb, who was suddenly quiet and serene. For a moment he could have sworn that the little gray donkey nodded his head as if to say, "You're welcome."

Crossing the Jordan also proved to be quite an adventure. The place where the road led into the water was nice and smooth. Joseph waded out into the river and discovered that at the deepest spot, it was only about four feet deep, and the bottom seemed fairly smooth. He made a couple trips across, holding the family possessions high above his head so they wouldn't get wet. The third trip involved taking Mary by the hand and slowly but carefully guiding her over to the other side. All that was left was to "encourage" Caleb to walk through the river. Things went well until the two of them made it about halfway across. It was at that spot that Caleb decided he had gone far enough, and he dug his four hooves into the soft riverbed. First, Joseph tried to sweet-talk him into moving. He talked about how pleasant it was on the other side and about all the sweet things to eat and how much

Mary wanted him to come on over. That, of course, got him nowhere. Then he thought he could maybe push him along. He moved around behind and tried to nudge him the rest of the way—again to no avail. His last resort was to grab the rope to his bridle and try to pull him across. Joseph was pulling one way and Caleb the opposite way. Suddenly, the rope slipped off of Caleb's head, and Joseph fell backward, completely submerging himself in the cold water of the river. He jumped up coughing and spewing water in every direction. Mary was on the riverbank laughing so hard that she nearly went into labor. And while Joseph stood there drenching wet, holding the end of the rope in his hands, Caleb slowly and carefully marched his way to the other side where Mary was standing. Suffice it to say that Caleb didn't get his usual loving attention that night.

There were several times along the two-week trek that Mary and Joseph walked in the company of fellow travelers. There were always the usual conversations about family, hometowns, and occupations. And, of course, because of Mary's very obvious pregnancy, the conversations inevitably turned toward talk of the baby. Mary and Joseph didn't always know how to respond. How do you tell a complete stranger that you've been visited by angels and that you have been promised by the Almighty that the child you carry will be the long-awaited messiah? How do you explain the nontraditional name of "Jesus"? It's not that they didn't want to tell the story; it's just that they feared their words might seem blasphemous to some and worrisome to others.

Often, Mary and Joseph talked among themselves about the coming of the child. They wondered what the future would hold and how their lives would change. They wondered about their acceptance in the community and if God would reveal this special birth to anyone but them. "No matter what," Joseph would say, "we still have to be ready." And they would talk about the practical matters of raising a son: Where would he sleep? When would he first talk, and what would he say? Are we ready? Do we have the patience we need and the wisdom that is required? And what about the child—does he know the destiny into which he is about to be born?

The days grew long. Money was low, the food was stale, and most of the fruit was gone. It was late in the day when they finally arrived on the outskirts of the sleepy little town of Bethlehem. They were weary but joyful in the fact that their adventurous trip was drawing to a close. The little town was filled with people, mostly because of the Roman census. Local taverns were doing a brisk business. Various shops were still open, and many people were coming and going. The air was filled with the scent of various foods cooking on fires and in ovens all across the village. The sounds of people talking and laughing in the distance could be heard. Caleb's eyes opened wide, and his nose lifted high in the air when he caught a whiff of bread baking somewhere nearby. Joseph and Mary felt a sense of relief in knowing that they were finally back in civilization, surrounded by people once again. Joseph stopped at two different inns to see about a place to stay. He got the same response at each place: "Sorry, but we're full. Try down the street a ways." When he got to the third place, he knew the answer before he even asked.

Joseph was starting to worry because he felt that Mary was starting to worry. He explained his situation to the innkeeper. The innkeeper shook his head and said, "I'm truly sorry, but there is just no more room." As Joseph turned to walk away, the innkeeper called him back and said, "Listen, I'll tell you what I can do. I have a place out back for the animals. It's not much, but there is enough straw to make a bed. It's warm, and it's out of the weather. It's not fancy, but you are welcome to stay there. I'll have my stable boy bring some fresh water for you and your donkey."

Joseph was glad for the generosity. He thought to himself, "We've spent the past two weeks sleeping outside with a donkey. What could one more night hurt? At least we will finally get a good night's rest."

Joseph busied himself with making a comfortable pallet on which Mary could sleep. He could tell that she was getting more uncomfortable by the day. She was tired, her feet were swollen, her back ached, and she was just starting to have some really different aches and pains. The innkeeper sent out some leftover stew that his wife had prepared. Mary and Joseph were grateful for the warm meal, and Caleb was pleased by the fresh straw and grass that the stable boy had brought. It was late when Joseph blew out the little oil lamp that had provided some light as they got ready for bed. Mary fell asleep quickly. A small shaft of moonlight poured through the roof and illumined Mary's face while she slept. Joseph just sat for a while watching her sleep. She had the face of an angel, and Joseph could think of no other place on earth he would rather be than by her side. Finally, his eyes grew tired, and he drifted off to sleep.

The next thing he remembered was Mary's voice whispering into his ear. "Joseph, it's time! The baby is coming!" Joseph sprang to his feet, running around wildly in the dark. He bumped into Caleb, kicked over a bucket of water, and hit his head on a rafter. Finally, he was able to relight the lamp and get his bearings. He awakened the stable boy and told him to go for help. It wasn't long before the child was born. The child was perfect, and Mary was safe. The little baby boy started to cry as Mary held him in her arms. Caleb had never heard such a thing. He started braying with long and loud sounds. His braying, of course, startled the other animals. Soon a horse started to whinny and stomp its feet. In the distance a dog barked, a cow mooed, a cat meowed, and a rooster crowed!

Joseph started laughing with delight. It was as if the whole world was celebrating the birth of his son. And maybe it was. It's funny with animals—sometimes they hear noises that humans can't hear. Maybe they sense things that humans can't sense. Maybe Caleb's bray was more than just the sound of a startled donkey. Maybe it was the beginning of all creation's glorious praise that the savior had come.

The average lifespan of a donkey is more than thirty years. It's possible that this little gray donkey watched Jesus grow as a child and become a young man. Maybe he made the trip with Mary and Joseph years later when they traveled to the temple when Jesus was just twelve. Is it even possible that when Jesus sent the disciples to untie the donkey on which he would ride triumphantly into Jerusalem that, once again, this same donkey would carry Mary's child? That's probably a little too far-fetched.

The donkey is not the connecting point between the birth and the cross of Jesus. But don't miss the fact that the events are indeed connected. Without Bethlehem there would be no Calvary. Without Jesus' birth we could not be born again. Surely Christmas Day is worth a celebration. In fact, all of creation should echo the sound that the angels and the animals once proclaimed—that Jesus Christ is born.

CHAPTER 11

Josiah's Song

Matthew 1:18-25

Things are done a little differently up in heaven than you might imagine. Not all angels are the same. There are various classifications, duties, and responsibilities. There is a degree of seniority, and it can take quite some time to move from the bottom to the top in terms of angelic hierarchy.

At the top, of course, are the archangels, including Gabriel, Michael, and Raphael. They have the joy of standing in the very presence of God. They dialogue with him face to face. They serve him faithfully and carry out his most important assignments. They are clearly in the position of greatest authority, power, and rank in the angel world. Standing just one step below the archangels are the angels of wrath and war. Avoid these guys at all costs, and pray that they never have to visit your town. Just ask the ancient Egyptians. Remember when the death angel passed over the nation at the time of the exodus? He was in this classification. The name says it all. They disperse God's wrath and anger to those who have practiced remarkable disobedience. Two of them were once sent to Sodom and Gomorrah. Another was sent to Balaam while he was on his way to curse the Israelites. The angel spared his life but definitely offered the seer a little attitude adjustment. Walk softly when you tread in their presence.

Moving slightly down the order of the angels is the next group, the administrative angels, or charge angels, as those under their authority like to refer to them. They are definitely "in charge." Their task is that of making assignments for all the angels and evaluating the level of success attained. When reports come from all over the world about the need for angelic help, the charge angels select just the right angel for each particular task. It could be sending an important message, preventing a catastrophe, or helping a farmer's crops to grow. Imagine the worldwide need each day for a little angelic involvement. The charge angels plan, send, and evaluate by the thousands. They make the assignments, check the wing conditions, and evaluate how well each angel performed.

Under the charge angels are two separate but equal classes of angels: the messenger angels and the guardian angels. The messenger angels do exactly what you would expect; they deliver important messages. Sometimes their messages contain words of hope and promise, sometimes words of correction, sometimes words of warning and rebuke. At times they get to use their audible voices. At other times they train a person's eyes to see just the right words on a page or point an ear to hear just the right voice. They can even remind a person to pray for a certain need or help a person know of a potentially bad decision.

The guardian angels get a lot of press down here on earth. But in heaven they stay frustrated most of the time. A lot of their good work gets credited to coincidence or luck. They really do some extraordinary work, but most people miss the point. They keep people from dangerous places and harmful situations. They move people and objects into the right spot to protect and bless.

And then there is an entirely separate class of angels: angels in training, known to most as JGs, or "junior grades." Most angels start out at such a level. They train. They learn to fly. They learn how to avoid detection. As their skills grow, so does their ranking. Those who work hard can transfer to guardian or messenger status in just a few short decades. But some, especially the younger ones, tend to stay in training for a very long time.

Our story today focuses on two young JGs, John Michael and Josiah. The two of them were childhood friends and remain best buddies in the heavenly realms. They are young, a little rowdy, sometimes disruptive, excitable, and maybe even a little mischievous. Their charge angel, Teresa, had her hands full with this young pair. She had caught them on more than one occasion acting, shall we say, a little unangelic. Once, they bounced a little too hard on some thunderclouds and made it rain on a poor girl's wedding. On another occasion they made a wagon wheel fall off a cart, sending the occupants into a muddy pond alongside the road. Once, they even tickled a young boy who was attending synagogue with his parents. He started laughing with one of those "church laughs" that can't be extinguished. He later got a whipping for misbehaving during worship. Angel Teresa didn't think it was all that funny. Neither did John Michael and Josiah after she put them in charge of protecting a newborn nest of birds for a few weeks. Keeping a certain cat away was quite a task.

Through the years, Teresa had attempted to help them grow and mature. She had given each an assignment that both had carried out with relative success. John Michael had been sent to protect a family from some poisonous stew. His job was simply to fly down and spill the pot, which he did. The family was spared from illness, but in the process of tipping the pot, John Michael tripped over a flaming log and sent it rolling into the side of their canvas tent. The tent caught fire, and two more guardian angels were sent in to blow enough wind to extinguish the flame before it got out of hand. Josiah had been sent one day to keep a young boy from riding his horse too quickly. All he was supposed to do was make the horse slow down a bit. Rather than simply whisper into the horse's ear, Josiah took a more novel approach. He rattled the bushes along the side of the road to force a large snake to wriggle out onto the road, just in front of the horse. The horse stopped but threw its rider in the process. The young boy Josiah was sent to protect landed with a thud, resulting in a cracked rib and a broken collarbone. When Teresa heard the report, she just rolled her eyes.

One afternoon, John Michael and Josiah were sitting on a cloud somewhere over the Mediterranean, enjoying snickerdoodle cookies and some vanilla ice cream. (What else would you eat in heaven?) John Michael leaned back, put his hands behind his head, and said, "He's up to something, you know."

"Who's up to something?" asked Josiah.

"He" was the only response.

Josiah's eyes grew large. "You mean the big He?"

John Michael nodded and said, "Yep, that right."

"How do you know?" asked Josiah.

John Michael shouted out, "How could you *not* know? Everyone's been talking about it. Man, open up your eyes, and get the feathers out of your ears!"

His curiosity piqued, Josiah had to know all about it. And John Michael was more than pleased to give him all the details, as though he were an expert on the whole situation. He began telling Josiah how some pretty important messenger angels had been sent on a mission. "Rumor has it," said John Michael, "that their assigned task was to turn on a particularly bright star and give some wise men in Persia an unexpected and irresistible urge to travel to Israel with gifts fit for a king."

"Are you serious?" asked Josiah.

"Yeah," John Michael continued, "and that's not all. Apparently another angel was sent to a man named Joseph in Nazareth—a visible, audible message, mind you—and told him not to be afraid to take Mary for his wife even though she's about to turn up pregnant."

"Wow," said Josiah as his wings fluttered with excitement.

"And that's not all." John Michael looked both ways, making sure no one was within earshot before whispering, "Gabriel himself has gone down twice to earth."

"Gabriel?" blurted out Josiah. "Mr. Archangel himself?"

John Michael put his finger to his mouth. "Quiet! Don't you know that Teresa would clip our wings if she knew we were talking about such things?"

But the conversation was too addictive and too riveting for either JG to stop talking. "Tell me all you know," demanded Josiah.

John Michael gladly obliged: "Well, first he went to Zacharias and told him all about how his barren old wife would have a son and that he would grow up to be the forerunner of the messiah! And when Zacharias wouldn't believe him at first, Gabriel took away his speech for a while." Josiah just sat with his mouth hanging open. John Michael continued, "And then Gabriel went to Mary—you know, the one engaged to Joseph—and told her everything. He actually sat and talked with her, even answered her questions!"

Josiah asked, "What all did he say?"

"No one knows for sure," said John Michael, "but you know it's really, really important stuff."

Josiah nodded his head, "You're right. He's up to something really big."

About two months later, John Michael and Josiah were summoned to Teresa's desk. As soon as they stepped into her presence, they knew the conversation was a serious one. Josiah thought to himself, "I bet she found out about how we scared that group of cows the other day when no one was looking. That was so funny."

Teresa began to speak very carefully and deliberately: "The two of you may have heard that something really big is about to unfold. I'm not allowed to give you any of the details, but let's just say there's an opportunity waiting for the two of you to finally make it to full angel status if you do a good job." Both stood a little taller and tried to act as seriously as they could.

Josiah was the first to speak: "We'll do whatever you ask us to do. We won't let you down; I promise."

Teresa replied, "There is no room for mischief. The two of you have to be on your best behavior. You will have to follow my instructions exactly." Both nodded and affirmed their commitment to do a really good job. "Report back to me tonight," she continued, "exactly two hours after the sun sets in Israel. Be ready to go. Look your best. Have your faces washed, your wings pressed, and wear your best robes. And don't forget to shine your halos."

The two of them could hardly contain themselves for the rest of the afternoon. They were dying to tell all the other JGs about it, but Teresa had sworn them to silence. The hours seemed to drag on forever. They watched eagerly as the shadow of night began to make its way from east to west. Slowly, it covered Asia Minor and finally the Middle East. They watched as the lamps and lanterns were lit all across Israel as nightfall began to cover the land. At the appointed time the two quickly made their way to Teresa's desk, where they awaited their orders.

Her instructions were clear: "You are to fly down to the city of Bethlehem. From there you are to head to the east for a couple miles. You will find a group of shepherds who will be working their flocks. The hour will be late. Most of the men will be asleep. Stay out of sight, and be very quiet until you get the signal."

"What signal?" asked Josiah.

"Not to worry," said Teresa. "You will know when the time is right. You will be appearing visibly, and others will join you there." They couldn't believe their ears. And then she added, "When the shepherds are good and awake, you will need to sing at the top of your voices."

"That's it?" thought Josiah. "That's the big secret? We are going to Bethlehem to wake up a few drowsy shepherds and sing a few praise choruses?"

Teresa read their thoughts and responded, "That's exactly what you are to do. Do it well, and you will be rewarded. I promise."

When they got to the spot, they discovered that they were not alone. There were thousands of other angels, older messenger angels, who were all floating around, waiting for the big moment to unfold. In the twinkling of an eye, it happened. One of the most important messenger angels in heaven suddenly appeared. Josiah and John Michael were surprised to see the brilliant light that filled the night sky. It was the kind of light you see in heaven all the time, but never on earth. The angel's voice was strong, clear, joyful, not a hint of anger or wrath evident. The words were well chosen: "Don't be afraid." Josiah could tell the shepherds were shaking in their sandals. The angel then announced good news of great joy: "For unto you is born this day, in the city of David, a savior, who is Christ the Lord!" Not only were the shepherds stunned by the news, but Josiah and John Michael could hardly take it in as well. God's Son—the promised one, the light of the world, the hope of the nations, the savior of humanity, the messiah who had been proclaimed for a thousand years—had just been born two miles away!

Before the two JGs could even process the news and make sense of its importance, they were hurried into place by a messenger angel who specialized in choral music. The heavens were suddenly splashed with light, and the voices of a thousand angels began to sing, "Glory to God in the highest, and on earth, peace, goodwill to men." They sang the chorus over and over, with each refrain growing more pronounced and more powerful. It seemed to Josiah and John Michael that the very earth would explode with the incredible sound.

Then it all stopped as quickly as it had started. The night sky faded back to normal, and Josiah and John Michael were directed back to the heavens with all the others. When they arrived, they discovered that all of creation's glory was exploding with the exciting news. There was joy, laughter, and gladness. The two young angels had a sense that nothing would ever be the same again. When they finally made it back to their "resting cloud," they were greeted by a note from Teresa. It read, "The Father is most pleased by your efforts. Congratulations to heaven's newest messenger angels."

The word "angel" comes from the Greek word *angelos*, which means "messenger." Messengers deliver the words of God himself. The day will come when all of us will join those above. We may get our wings and live on a cloud and spend centuries protecting the unsuspecting. But until that day comes, we have been appointed on earth as his angels. We are called to share the words of God with his broken planet.

The world needs to hear from us. The world needs a word of hope and promise, a word of faith and glory, a word of victory and celebration. The world needs to once again hear the story of the Christ child, who came to earth so the world would never be the same again. Who will tell the story, if not us? Go and please the Father. Tell the story of God's Son.

CHAPTER 12

The Scandal of Christmas

Luke 1:26-38

It was their place, their own tiny little corner of the world where they could unwind, retreat, and escape. For years, Joachim and Anna sat on the back porch of their modest dwelling, taking in a thousand sunsets. It was more than a porch; it was more like a veranda surrounded by trees. It's the place where they had laughed, prayed, cried, talked, and dreamed for nearly two decades. The rear of their home faced the western horizon. The back door emptied out onto a patio that would catch the afternoon breezes that blew up from the valley below. As daylight turned to darkness, the glorious colors of a Mediterranean sunset were displayed before them like a masterpiece from some great artist. It was in this spot that they had dreamed their dreams, planned their lives, and discussed both blessings and hardships. It was where they had watched their little girl, Mary, grow into a young woman. The years had passed far too quickly. To Joachim and Anna the sixteen years that Mary had been a part of their lives seemed more like sixteen months. It seemed like yesterday that she wore a little sundress and played among the flowers that surrounded the back porch. It seemed like only a moment ago that she played with dolls and skipped along the path in front of the house with her friends. They could still remember the sweet laughter that seemed to constantly flow from her heart. They remembered her boundless energy and her kind smile. Where had the years gone? Now she was all grown up and engaged to be married. Before the next summer she would be a wife.

It was a quiet and pleasant evening. Joachim and Anna sat on the back porch as the last little sliver of orange sun seeped below the horizon. Mary was away for the evening. She and Joseph were working on some things at their future home. Joseph was adding on a room to his father's house, and he wanted to show Mary his handiwork and ask for her advice on where to put the window. After a few moments of quiet end-of-the-day reflection, Joachim broke the silence by saying, "You know, I really like that Joseph. He's a good man. He comes from a good family. He is a skilled craftsman, and he has a steady job. We are blessed that the two of them are promised to each other."

"And," Anna added, "he loves our little girl. He'll be good to her and will protect her." The two of them sat in the evening silence for quite a while, mulling over the blessings they enjoyed and the promises the future offered to their family.

The next several months seemed to race by. Mary and her mother stayed busy. There were plans to make, skills to teach, cloth to sew, dresses to craft, and dreams to discuss. Mary had been such a happy, obedient, and gracious little girl. She had grown up far too quickly. Now she had become a beautiful, intelligent, responsible young woman. Anna was proud of her daughter and of her eagerness to plan well for her marriage. Mary sought all kinds of wisdom and counsel from her mother. She had listened carefully and challenged herself to be the best wife she could be to Joseph. All the plans seemed to be falling into place. The dream of living a happy, long married life seemed to be only months away.

It was one of those conversations that changes the course of a family's life. It seemed to erupt like a sudden thunderstorm on a calm summer's night. Joachim and Anna had found their way out to their usual spot on the back veranda. They were relaxing after a meal of stewed goat, boiled potatoes, and warm bread. The evening was quiet, peaceful, and calm. Mary came out of the house to join them. She seemed a bit nervous, maybe preoccupied, as though her thoughts were a million miles away. "Mary, come and sit a while," invited her father. "You seem a bit tense. Is everything all right?"

Mary had trouble making eye contact with her father. Her lower lip quivered, and her hands were shaking. She gathered her breath and her resolve, walked over to where her parents were seated, and said, "We need to talk. I have some news to share with you, and I think it may be hard for you to hear—and even harder to believe."

Mary sat on a long wooden bench that faced the two rocking chairs in which her parents were seated. Both leaned forward and sat on the edge of their chairs as they listened to the words that came from Mary's mouth. The two of them could tell Mary had some rather ominous and troubling words to share. She fidgeted before them. She cleared her throat half a dozen times. She would almost speak, and then she would turn toward the horizon. Joachim knew his daughter well, so he said, "Mary, just spit it out. What do you need to tell us? We can take it; just tell us what is going on."

She began to stammer her way through her first sentence. It was a big one. "You're going to find out soon enough," she said, "so here goes. I'm pregnant."

The words hung in the air for several seconds. Both of her parents were stunned. She could tell that neither knew what to say for a moment but that both of them would soon have plenty to say. It was her mother who spoke first. "Mary, are you sure? Are you certain that a child is on the way?"

Mary nodded and said, "Oh, I'm sure."

A moment later Joachim exploded, shouting, "How could this happen, Mary? How could you and Joseph have allowed yourself to get into such a situation? You know that sexual relations are forbidden during the time of betrothal. How could the two of you have betrayed your vows? What were you thinking? And what will the community say? Our family will be disgraced. Joseph's family will be dishonored. I can't believe we have to deal with such a mess!" He stood to his feet and stomped around the patio. His face was red, and his heart was racing.

Finally, Anna spoke to her daughter again. "What did Joseph say about all of this? What was his reaction when he found out?"

Mary whispered, "He doesn't know yet."

"What do you mean, Mary? Why haven't you told him? He needs to know," said Anna.

"It's not his child," Mary responded.

"Mary!" shouted Anna. "What do you mean it's not his child?"

Mary said, "He's not the father. We have never been together. Joseph has never even hinted at being unfaithful to the promises we have made."

Joachim stood beside Anna and with a slow and forceful tone said, "Then who is the father? Who is the scum who has done this to you? Who's the man who has destroyed your life and your future? I will hunt him down; you can count on that. And we are going to have a little meeting. He needs to pay for his sins!"

Mary was trembling in the presence of her father. She had never seen him so angry, so hurt, so vengeful. "It's not like you think, father," she replied. "I don't blame you for being angry, but there is not another man to blame."

There was a moment of silence. "What do you mean there is no other man to blame!" shouted Joachim. "You are certainly carrying *someone's* child. I want to know who's at fault! I want answers, and I want them now!"

Mary asked her parents to be seated. "This is going to seem very strange, but I swear it is the truth. You have to believe me," she began. "About a month ago it all started. Late one night while I was asleep, an angel of the Lord awakened me. He called me by name and told me not to be afraid. He told me that I had been chosen by God, that the Lord had found favor with me. He told me that I would conceive a son and that his name would be 'Jesus.' The angel said that he would be the Son of God and would reign over the house of King David forever. I couldn't believe what I was hearing. It all seemed so strange, so mysterious. I asked the angel how all of this could even happen because I didn't have a husband yet. The angel explained that the child would be the work of the Holy Spirit, that God's own Spirit would place the child in my womb. I know that sounds crazy and hard to believe, but it happened just like the angel said. I can now feel this child inside of me, and yet I have never been with a man. I promise you. You have to believe me!"

Both Joachim and Anna sat in disbelief. Their mouths hung open. It was Joachim who responded first. He looked deeply into the eyes of his daughter. "Mary, look at me. Are you really telling me the truth? You really talked with an angel, and you have never been with a man?"

"Yes, father," she replied. "I promise that it all happened just the way the angel said."

Joachim sat back in his chair and looked beyond Mary. He looked out at the distant valley and the stars that were beginning to appear above the horizon. He stroked his long beard and mumbled a prayer under his breath. Finally, with tears in his eyes, he looked back at Mary and said, "I don't know if I believe all of your story, Mary, but I do believe in you. And if you say God spoke to you in a special way, then who am I to question the ways of God?" He reached out and hugged his daughter. The two of them stood in a silent embrace for several moments.

Anna was the first to bring up the other very difficult conversation. "How will you tell Joseph—and when? It's not the kind of thing you will be able to keep from him for very long. He deserves to know. And we need to be ready for his reaction. It may mean the end of your relationship. He may not believe you. He may even divorce you. Have you thought about that, Mary?"

"Of course, I have," she replied, "a thousand times a day. I want to tell him, but I don't know how. I love him. I don't want to lose him. I don't want to raise this baby alone."

"You won't raise him alone, Mary," said Anna. "You always have a home here. Even if Joseph should break your betrothal, we will be here to help."

For the next several days Mary was an emotional wreck. First, there was the morning sickness that came calling each day. She was having trouble eating and resting. Second, there was the question of how to tell Joseph. Mary didn't know how or when, but she knew she couldn't endure the anxiety very much longer. It was finally decided that it would be best to tell Joseph at the house, with her parents close by in case Joseph flew into some uncontrollable rage. Mary didn't think that he would get physical with her, but she still thought she could use the emotional support that her parents could lend. And so Joseph was invited over for a meal. Anna spent the day preparing a very nice dinner, and Joachim made sure he got home early, just so he was there before Joseph arrived.

The evening seemed to go according to plan. After a pleasant meal the four of them moved out onto the veranda. They chatted about the weather and the latest gossip of the community. Finally, it was time for Mary to unload her story and her burden. Taking his hands into hers, Mary said simply, "Joseph, I have something to tell you. It's a lot to take in, but I need you to listen and try to understand."

Joseph looked perplexed, maybe even a little frightened. "What is it, Mary? What's so important?"

Tears streamed down her face, and her voice broke as she told her story. "I love you, Joseph. You know that. And I want nothing more than to be your wife and grow old with you. But there is something you need to know. Joseph, I'm pregnant. I'm going to have a baby."

It took a moment for the words to sink in. And when they did, they hit Joseph like a ton of bricks. He felt betrayal, anger, hurt, and pain all in the same moment. "What do you mean you're having a baby?" shouted Joseph. "How could you have done this to me? How could you do something like that behind my back? How long has this been going on? I will be a disgrace to the community. We're done, Mary. This is just too much to bear. I don't want to have anything to do with someone like you!"

She tried to explain about the angel and the Holy Spirit and all that she had heard. But he rushed out of the house as though he could attempt to outrun the pain. She even ran after him, but he pushed her away and raced down the path that led from her house.

It had to be one of the longest and worst nights of Joseph's life. He wept bitterly as he roamed the streets of Nazareth. He walked for hours, trying to make sense of it all. How could Mary have betrayed him? How could she have thrown away the promise of their lives together? It hurt so deeply. The pain was the worst he had ever endured. He questioned everything—his life, his faith, his destiny. He finally wound his way back home and decided he would dissolve their relationship quickly and quietly. He would let her go and try to move on with his life. It was well into the wee hours of the morning by the time his head hit the pillow. It took him a long time to drift off to sleep.

And then it happened. His slumber evolved into a vivid dream. An angel of the Lord appeared to him and said just as plain as day, "Don't be afraid to take Mary as your wife, for that which has been conceived in her is of the Holy Spirit." The angel went on to tell the rest of the story. He spoke of the pregnancy and of the role Mary would play in bringing about this child who would save people from their sins. It slowly began to dawn on Joseph—all that Mary had struggled to say was true! What Mary had claimed had been confirmed by the angel of the Lord himself! Mary had not been unfaithful; she had not broken her vows. Her love had not wavered! She had been chosen by God for a special role, a unique destiny.

Joseph awoke from his dream and bolted from the bed, his thoughts racing. "I must get to Mary! I must tell her what the angel said. I must tell her that I believe her and that I believe *in* her!" He grabbed his robe and slid on his sandals. Stumbling over a stool and a chair, he groped his way across his dark room. He finally found the door and went tearing off into the night. He ran like a man possessed through the streets and then down the lane toward Mary's house. The darkness was just starting to turn to dawn by the time he got there. He started beating on the door and screaming to be let in.

The noise shook the household. Joachim and Anna bolted upright in their bed. Joachim grabbed his robe and the old stick he kept under his bed for protection. He ran to the door and shouted, "Who is it? What's the matter?"

"It's me, Joseph! I've got to talk to Mary. I've got to ask for her forgiveness. Let me in, and I will explain everything!"

By this time, Mary and her mother had joined Joachim in the front room. Joachim shouted, "I will not let you in until you calm down! You're acting like a crazy man!"

Joseph quickly responded, "No need to worry. I'm not crazy; I've just got some glorious news to share. Please let me in so I can explain."

Joachim opened the door, and Joseph came rushing in, instructing them, "Sit down, everyone! Let me tell you what happened to me!" Joseph told them all about the angel's visit and the words of encouragement and comfort the angel had offered. He looked at Mary and said, "Mary, I'm so sorry. I was wrong to doubt you and treat you the way I did. I am so sorry for the words I said. Can you ever forgive me?" Within seconds there were hugs and tears of joy and excited laughter. "Mary, we are going to have a baby!" The four of them held hands and danced around the room, giddy with joy. Though they headed into a very uncertain future, they did so with the knowledge that they had been chosen and blessed by God.

It really is scandalous, isn't it? Who would have thought that the King of Kings and Lord of Lords would be born to an unwed teenager living in a tiny town? Who would believe such a story? Who can believe in a virgin birth, or an angel's message, or a sudden bright star in the sky? Surely it was hard to believe back then, and for some it may still be a little far-fetched today. But isn't that the essence of faith—to believe in the unseen and to marvel in the story of God's unmerited grace?

There really was a town called Nazareth. And there really were two people named Mary and Joseph. And a tiny baby named Jesus really was born. What you choose to do with the story is up to you, but to believe in the child of Christmas, to believe in that scandalous message, is to find hope, peace, joy, and eternal life.

CHAPTER 13

The Stable of Christmas

Luke 1:26-38

Some babies are born in the safe and sterile confines of a hospital, where there are nurses and doctors and specialists to attend to every need and any possible complication. Sometimes babies are born on the way to the hospital, in the back seat of the family car or even in a taxi. Sometimes babies are even born at home, with an anxious father and a skilled midwife to help with the delivery. And sometimes babies are born in the oddest of places, maybe even in a stable.

His name was Joash, meaning "one whom God helps." Through the years he had developed quite a reputation around the small village of Bethlehem for the quality of his work. He was a common laborer and an honest man who had developed a skill set around building barns and stables. The quality of his work was well known, and he was certainly the man to call upon when a family needed a strong shelter for their livestock or even a small addition to their home. Joash had eked out a meager living and had known the joy of having a wife and raising their son, Timothy. Naturally, Timothy had grown up working alongside his father. And now that Joash was well past middle age, his son did more and more of the heavy lifting. The father had the brains, but the son had the brawn. Together, they made a good team. Joash would draw up the plans and take the measurements, and Timothy would do much of the hauling of materials and all of the roof work on any structure they built.

It had been several years earlier when the owner of a local inn had asked Joash to draw up plans for a new stable for his establishment. He explained to Joash that as his business had slowly increased, the need for a stable had also increased. Travelers in that region of the world would often travel by donkey or horse, maybe an occasional camel, and so to attract a little more business, the innkeeper thought it might be wise to add a building out back to take care of the animals whenever the need arose. Joash drew up some plans, made some measurements, and estimated the materials needed. He and the innkeeper wrangled for several weeks over a price, but finally the deal was struck, and the stable was begun.

Joash was a stickler for even the smallest of details. Each board had to fit perfectly. Every post had to be exactly the right length. Even the stones for the foundation had to be carefully selected. Finding stones around Bethlehem was not a problem, but finding the *right* stone sometimes was. Legend has it that when God created the world, he gave an angel two large sacks of stone to scatter over all the earth. When the angel flew over Israel, one of the sacks tore, and many stones fell to the ground. Whether or not the legend is true, Joash and his son never had difficulty finding stones among the hills and pastures of the region. Joash was particular about each rock, to the frustration of young Timothy. Joash would painstakingly measure the stone, examine its color and shape, and decide if it was right for the job. The process took a lot longer than it should, at least in Timothy's mind. He was always anxious to get back to the building site to start putting boards and planks together. But his father was slow and meticulous, and surprisingly right about most things. Sometimes right in the middle of some project, Joash would pick up a stone, or a certain branch, or even a leaf and say to Timothy, "Look at how God made this," as though he was learning even more insight into his world and how things ought to fit together. Not only did he instill an attention to detail into the mind of his son, but he also instilled values and a sense of respect for God. In fact, he had a life mantra that he often repeated to his son: "Honor God with the work of your hands and with the devotion of your heart." Occasionally, when the work got hard or when a hammer's blow would find a finger and not a peg, Joash would simply remind his son of those words of wisdom.

The foundation for the innkeeper's stable was carefully laid out. Stones were placed one at a time and carefully mortared together. Though it took nearly a month and a half, the completed foundation was solid and level and would provide the strength needed to support the stable for years to come. The rest of the stable would be well built from the right stuff. Every aspect would be well thought out. Joash liked to use hardwood trees for the posts and studs of the walls. Though working the tough wood always proved to be a time-consuming job, Joash would carefully shape and measure and cut each piece, ensuring that each piece fit exactly into place. Timothy was always amazed at his father's skill and his ability to plan every cut and every placement of each post. A different wood was used for the planking around the walls and for the planking that covered the roof trusses. Joash preferred the light, soft texture of the local cedar trees. He also thought the smell of the wood gave a pleasant aroma to the overall structure.

The design of the stable was rather detailed and somewhat intricate. Joash had designed the front of the stable to face the east in order to catch the morning sun. He liked the idea that sunlight would flood the stable early each morning, warming up the interior from the early morning chill. He also preferred the back of the stable to face the setting sun to block out most of the direct rays of the hot afternoon sun. The front of the stable had two large, wide doors that could be propped open. He also fashioned the doors to split in half about four feet up so the animals could be kept inside while still having an open and breezy entrance to the stable. To the right and to the left of the front doors were windows with shutters that could be closed or opened according to the temperature. Similar windows were placed along each side wall.

Joash had also constructed a stone fireplace and chimney along the left wall. In the cold of winter, a fire could be safely lit, and the warmth of the flames could travel throughout most of the stable. Again, he had chosen just the right stones and carefully placed them together to help anchor and support the entire structure. He had designed a gabled roof, which left enough room for a small loft above the interior of the stable. The loft could be used for dry storage or even as a small room for a stable boy if needed. From the loft a small hinged opening was created to vent heat out of the stable when necessary. The rest of the stable was thoughtfully crafted to maximize the space. There was a large bin for hay, three or four individual stalls for animals, some large enough for at least three or four goats or maybe a couple cows. There was also a work area that contained a table, a stool or two, and a workbench. Along the walls, Joash strategically placed pegs on which tools could be stored, or saddles placed, or coats and tunics hung up when not in use. He also built a few storage bins and feeding troughs, and on every post he built a small shelf to hold oil lamps to give light at night. The roof was made of sturdy planks, sealed with pitch and covered with cedar shingles. When completed, it really was quite a building. In fact, after a few years, the stable seemed to be in better shape than the inn itself, weathering the strong storms of spring and summer and the harsh cold of the winter. Occasionally, Joash would walk past the inn and steal a glance or two at his handiwork. From time to time, he even walked in and around it, just to make sure things were holding up well.

Joash had always had a funny feeling about the stable. He couldn't quite put his finger on it, but he felt that it was in some way more special than all the other barns he had built, like it was waiting to be used for a special purpose. He couldn't really explain his suspicion. He just had a special pride in this stable's construction, and it gave him a sense of satisfaction each time he walked past it. He remembered the days that he and his son had spent, side by side, working on it. When walking past, he would sometimes catch himself whispering, "Honor God with the work of your hands and with the devotion of your heart." He hoped that he had done both.

It was a few years later when the innkeeper once again called on Joash and his son. Because the Roman government had declared the need for a census, people were on the move, many traveling the roads of Judea in order to get to the right spot to be registered. The added numbers meant commerce began to grow in the sleepy environs of Bethlehem. The shopkeepers noticed a little more demand for their wares. The local taverns seemed to have more people on more nights. Roadside vendors sold more bread and fruit and produce than they had in a number of seasons. The local inns felt it too. They all seemed to do a brisk trade. It was not uncommon for the inns to be filled to capacity. Many nights sent the innkeepers scrambling for additional places for their customers to sleep. Even the stable built by Joash was used a couple times when the inn overflowed. It was the brisk business that once again brought Joash to the innkeeper's door.

The innkeeper was all about business. He had decided that if he had more room, he could house more guests, and with each guest came a little more profit. And so Joash was called upon to think through the design needed to add on to the inn. It was late in the afternoon when Joash arrived at the inn. The sun had just slipped below the roofline of the stable when he knocked on the door. While waiting for the innkeeper to answer, he noticed that the stable boy had opened the vent on the roof. With the half-doors and shutters opened across the front of the stable, Joash knew there was a nice breeze blowing through the stable, keeping things at a pleasant enough temperature. He was letting his mind wander a bit when he was suddenly startled by the presence of his old friend, the innkeeper, at the door. "Ah, Joash, my friend!" said the innkeeper. "It's good to see you again! Come in. Come in. Ruth is just about to put food on the table for our guests. I told her to set a place for just the two of us in the back so we can get down to business."

Joash followed his friend to the rear of the inn, where Ruth had indeed prepared a wonderful meal. The two men enjoyed a leisurely paced meal. They talked and laughed and discussed the news of the day. After the meal was cleared away, Joash unrolled a piece of parchment he had carried in a leather pouch, and the two men began to talk about the plans for the addition. As expected, Joash had done some preliminary sketches, complete with a list of materials, costs, and the number of days it would take to complete the project. The innkeeper, of course, wanted less cost and a quicker construction time, but in the back of his mind, he knew it was better to have Joash and his son take the time to do their usual good work. After a lengthy discussion the two men enjoyed a sweet cake that Ruth set before them. Joash scribbled down a few notes and carefully rolled up the parchment and put it in its place. The two men were bidding one another farewell when their conversation was interrupted by a sharp knock on the front door of the inn.

The innkeeper dutifully opened the door and asked the visitors to please step inside. He was surprised to discover it was a young couple traveling because of the census. That alone was not unusual. What *was* unusual was the fact that his wife was very pregnant and seemed a bit anxious. He could see the weariness etched across the face of both the man and the woman. "We've been traveling for days," reported the young man. "We've come from up north, and we desperately need a place to sleep for the night. My wife is very tired, and I fear that she could give birth soon, maybe in the next few days. Is there any way you can help us for the night? Our donkey is also tired and needs some rest. We will gladly pay for a night's rest."

The innkeeper started shaking his head. "I don't know how to tell you this, but we are already full. There is not an empty bed in the house. We've been at capacity since early afternoon."

"Is there anything you can do?" pleaded the young man. "We have no place to go, and the hour is getting late."

Though he was hesitant to do so, the innkeeper finally said, "Well, we do have a stable out back. We've used it a few times in the past. It's not like having a bed here in the inn, but at least there will be a roof over your head and protection from the night. There is plenty of fresh hay, and we can spread a few blankets and make you some sort of pallet. It's not much, but you are welcome to it if you think it might help."

The young husband almost broke the innkeeper's hand as he shook it gratefully. "We'll take it! I'm sure it will be fine. We can't thank you enough." For the first time since the conversation began, the innkeeper began to see a small hint of relief flash across the faces of the young couple. And then the husband said something odd: "I will pray for God to bless you in some special way for your act of kindness." The innkeeper just sort of nodded in response and called for Michael, the stable boy, to help the young couple find whatever they needed to get comfortable for the night.

As they began to make their way toward the stable, the innkeeper turned to Joash and said, "You just never know, do you?"

Joash replied, "You've done a good deed. Hopefully they will get some rest, and you will get your blessing." With those words, Joash turned and began the walk to his home, knowing that his wife would be worried that he had stayed so late.

As he walked along, he couldn't get his mind off the young couple he had met only a few minutes earlier. "Glad I'm not in their sandals," he thought to himself. He knew all too well what it was like to be a nervous father-to-be and have a very expectant wife while being miles away from home. His mind raced back over twenty years earlier when he had been in a similar spot. He and his young bride had traveled to Jerusalem just days before she was to deliver. He was working on a house for a landowner just outside the city and wanted his wife to see his handiwork. The trip was to be short, and she was still weeks away from giving birth. He thought the trip would help take their minds off of the stress and worry. They both thought they would be back long before little Timothy would be born. But Yahweh sometimes has a different plan, and his son was born in a canvas tent pitched in the middle of a pasture, not far from the city wall of Jerusalem.

The further Joash walked, the more the young couple filled his mind. Could he do more to help? Should he go back? Did they need food or blankets or maybe just some friendship? He felt the chill of the night air and wondered if the stable boy would remember to close the roof vent and shutter all the windows of the stable. He was within sight of his house when he decided that maybe he should return. He stepped into his house long enough to explain the situation to his wife. She loaded him up with a spare blanket, some bread, and a few candles. Off into the night he went, hoping to be of some help to the young husband and his sweet bride.

As he made his way, he noticed that the sky seemed unusually bright. He walked through the rough road without a single stumble. One star in particular seemed brighter than most and seemed to be hovering right over Bethlehem. For a moment he even thought he heard the sound of singing, like the voices of a chorus, way off in the distance. "Who would be up at this time of night?" he thought to himself. "Maybe I'm just hearing things." He quickened his pace toward the inn. When he rounded the corner of the inn and headed toward the stable, his mind couldn't process all that he was seeing. Rather than being cloaked in darkness, the stable seemed to be filled with light. Streaks of light spilled from the cracks in the shutters and from the gap in the front doors. He heard the sound of muffled voices as he drew near the door. He peeked through and discovered that the young couple was not alone. A group of shepherds stood near them. Some were bowing on the ground as though in the presence of something sacred. Others lifted their arms toward heaven with an expression of praise. He looked closer and discovered that the young woman was holding a baby in her arms, her face beaming with joy. He felt that same odd feeling he had felt several years earlier when he built the stable—like it was no ordinary spot, almost like it was sacred space. Something about the night made him feel that the stable had become a sanctuary and that the moment called for praise and celebration.

He had decided simply to step inside long enough to leave the blanket and bread. He startled one of the shepherds, who then motioned to him to come and kneel beside him. The young mother and father were softly speaking to the shepherds. They talked of angels and dreams and visions and God's unfolding plan. The leader of the shepherds spoke about the bright sky and the visit of the angels on the hillside and the heavenly chorus that had appeared. Joash's mind was reeling from all that he was hearing. The young couple talked of amazing things. Could it be true? Was it all real? Was the tiny child the promised messiah? Why would God visit the earth in the form of a baby, and why, among all the places on earth, would God appear in a stable?

After a few moments of what had been the purest worship he had ever experienced, Joash turned to slip his way out of the stable quietly. Something caught his attention. The light splashed across the back of the door, where he saw a message burned into the soft wood years earlier, words that he himself had written the day he finished the stable: "Honor God with the work of your hands and with the devotion of your heart."

Is it possible that God can still appear in any place where he is honored and where hearts are devoted to doing his work? It's not just a stable in Bethlehem that can welcome the savior of the world. He can also appear here in this place, in our time, even in us. Sometimes babies are born in stables. I hope this year he will be born in us.

Christmas Now...

CHAPTER 14

Christmas Grace

Luke 2:8-14

His name was Charles Edward Wall III, but everybody called him "Trey." Mostly, however, his teachers called him "Trouble." He was, by far, the most notorious fifth-grader at Riverside Elementary School. Of the four teachers who had taught him in the lower grades, two had retired and another had transferred after teaching Trey for a year. He was assigned to Mrs. Hamilton's class. She was a "tough old gal" and had weathered her share of unruly little boys. Trey would not be the first—or last—she would encounter. The principal, Mr. Carr, thought it best for Trey to be under her care. Mrs. Jones, the other fifth grade teacher, breathed a sigh of relief when the assignments were made over the summer. "Remind me to send a thank-you note to Mr. Carr," she thought to herself, "and a sympathy note to Mrs. Hamilton."

Trey was not really a bad kid, just a class clown. You know the type—always into mischief, always pushing the limits. He craved the attention that such a role afforded him. Sure, he got in trouble for his little pranks, but what's a little trip to the principal's office compared to the laughs he got from his classmates? It was his way of being accepted.

Life had played a cruel trick on Trey. He was being raised in a single-parent home. He had never met his father. His parents were just teenagers when Terri got pregnant. His father was not willing to accept the role of fatherhood at the age of nineteen, so somewhere around the third month of pregnancy, he just took off. Trey's mother hardly ever spoke of him, figuring that as Trey got older, she would let him in on more of the family secrets.

For now, all he knew was the love of his mother, who did all she could to pay the mortgage, manage the bills, and raise her son.

Terri had a good job. She worked in the dispatch office of the local UPS center. The pay was decent, and the hours were good. She worked Monday through Friday, from 8:00 a.m. until 5:00 p.m. She was glad that she and Trey could at least begin their day together. She hated the fact, however, that Trey was a latchkey kid in the afternoon, riding the bus home and using the key under the mat to let himself in. She also hated the fact that, because of her work, she could seldom attend events at the school during the day. She felt that Trey was growing up too fast and that she was powerless to slow down the process.

Trey had blonde hair and blue eyes. He wore baggy jeans most days, along with his favorite Adidas tennis shoes. He had a Miami Dolphins t-shirt that he was especially fond of wearing. His mother didn't really care for it, but what she didn't know was that he kept it in his backpack and changed into it on the bus nearly every morning. He would change back long before she got home in the afternoon. He reasoned, "What she doesn't know won't hurt her."

Trey was a pretty good student—not great student, but above average. He was a bright kid, who probably could have done much better if he had really applied himself. Grades were not his priority, though. Gaining acceptance in the fifth grade was, so the constant pranks and jokes were his way of being known and accepted by all. For a while, Mrs. Hamilton would call the house every time Trey got in trouble. Terri, tired of the almost daily message on the answering machine, finally called Mrs. Hamilton and offered the following advice: "I understand that Trey gets into a lot of trouble at school. He gets into a lot of trouble here at home as well. Let's do this—don't call me when he gets in trouble at school, and I won't call you when he gets in trouble at home!" The pact seemed to work.

To say that Trey tested Mrs. Hamilton would be an understatement. There was the day when Mrs. Hamilton had the class doing quiet work at their desks while she enjoyed a nice cup of morning coffee. She was called away to the office for a phone call. She told her class, "I will be right back. I expect you to behave for a moment. I expect ALL of you to behave." She shot Trey a look as she said those words.

As soon as she closed the door, Trey was out of his desk and fishing for something in his pocket. A moment later he said, "Ah, here he is, my little friend," and he pulled a rubber cockroach out of his pocket. He marched his way right up to Mrs. Hamilton's desk and deposited it into her coffee cup. "That should work," he proclaimed to his classmates. And it did! Mrs. Hamilton was quietly enjoying her next sip when suddenly the roach floated to the surface. She screamed and threw the cup from her hand. Coffee went all over the top of her desk. She glared at Trey, who had the most innocent little "*Who, me?*" look on his face. The rest of the day didn't go well for Trey, but the prank probably moved him well into "legend" status.

Then there was the day that Mrs. Hamilton was teaching geography. She was explaining some of the rearrangement of nations following World War II when she reached for the big pull-down map at the front of the classroom. Where she had expected to see Poland, she discovered that somehow Britney Spears' navel had become part of Europe. When the class spotted the pop star's poster, they exploded in laughter. Mrs. Hamilton didn't think it was all that funny. Trey quietly began collecting his work, sensing that he would soon be on his way to detention. He was right.

It was in early November that Trey's class was studying the works of William Shakespeare during English. For over a week, Mrs. Hamilton had played bits and pieces of some of the well-known works on the CD player. Trey was intrigued by the accents of the British players. He practiced for a couple days before he unloaded his next prank. One Thursday morning Mrs. Hamilton was calling the class roll like she did every morning. She called out, "Trey Wall? Trey Wall?" She looked up and saw him sitting in his desk just sort of waiting and anticipating her question. "Trey! Why won't you answer me?"

He spoke up in his best British voice: "I prefer that you call me 'Sir Charles Edward Wall the Third, of Nottingham.'" The class erupted in laughter.

Mrs. Hamilton didn't miss a beat. "Fine," she said. She reached over and flipped the switch for the intercom system that connected each classroom to the principal's office. "Mr. Carr, it seems that Sir Charles of Nottingham will be joining you for after-school detention."

"Very good, ma'am," Mr. Carr replied.

One of Trey's best deeds, at least in the eyes of his fellow students, but not in the eyes of Mrs. Hamilton, occurred in early December. On Friday the students were to be tested in math—long division, mostly, with a few fractions thrown in for good measure. Mrs. Hamilton had carefully prepared the students throughout the week. On Thursday she brought to class a stack of tests that were to be used the following day. As she always did, she placed the tests in her desk drawer and locked if for safe keeping, just in case someone would be tempted to take a peek.

Trey was intrigued by the locked drawer. "How funny it would be if she couldn't unlock the drawer! There would be no test tomorrow!" he thought to himself. That night when his mother got home from work, he told her he needed superglue for a school project. On Friday morning before class began, Trey glued the lock. At about 9:30, Mrs. Hamilton reached for her keys and tried the lock. The key would not even go in. Mrs. Hamilton called maintenance. They couldn't come until that afternoon. It took the maintenance crew about three hours to drill out the lock and open the desk. Thus, no Friday math test. Mission accomplished. Needless to say, on this occasion Mrs. Hamilton decided to call Trey's mom if for no other reason than to explain why Trey was being suspended for a week. Terri Wall was "delighted" to hear from Mrs. Hamilton. She expressed her joy in a special way to young Trey when he got home from school that afternoon.

The week before Christmas break found the students of Riverside Elementary busy with Christmas plays, choir presentations, and class parties. With each coming day the students got a little more excited, a little harder to control. Everyone except Trey. Mom's message for better behavior had been communicated well. Trey had been unusually quiet and well behaved for most of the week. Apparently, his Christmas gift hinged on whether or not Terri got another call from Mrs. Hamilton during the last week of class. Trey was determined that she would not.

The fifth grade Christmas party was to be held on Friday afternoon. It would be one of the highlights of the school year. Even though she was a bit strict, Mrs. Hamilton sure knew how to throw a party. Her class parties were the best in the whole school. There would be punch and ice cream, homemade cookies, and a tree to decorate. Mrs. Garren, the music teacher from down the hall, would come to lead the students in singing all the old Christmas favorites. The highlight of the party was always the exchange of "white elephant" gifts. Each child was to bring a carefully wrapped gag gift from home, not more than five dollars in value. Numbers would be drawn, and the students would open and trade and laugh the afternoon away.

Trey had selected the perfect gift—perfect by his standards, that is. At a shop in the mall, he was able to buy a novelty gift called "fake vomit." He told his friend Joey all about it. "Make sure you get my gift when it's your chance to open a present. It will be the one with the green wrapping paper and a silver bow. When the time is right, we can throw it on the floor and act like you're sick. It will be so funny! Mrs. Hamilton will have a heart attack."

All week long the excitement about the party grew. On Friday morning all the students came with gifts in hand, ready to spend the afternoon laughing, singing, and eating. Trey was really excited about the party. He didn't even wear his Dolphins shirt, but the green shirt with a collar that his mother had laid out for him that morning. He even exchanged his usual jeans for a pair of pressed khakis.

When lunch was over, the students went back to the classroom to get ready for the party. Mrs. Hamilton had them all get their things ready for the dismissal bell so the party could last right up until the end of the day. At precisely 1:05, Mrs. Hamilton announced that the students could gather the gifts they had brought and line up at the door. The party was always held down the hall in the school cafeteria. As always, they were to line up single file and in alphabetical order. So, as always, Trey Wall was at the end of the line.

"Students, you may now walk down the hall to the party, inside voices please." As they began to file out, she then directed a comment toward Trey. "Trey, could you come over to my desk for a moment?" He walked slowly, sensing that something was not quite right. "Trey, I'm sorry, but you will not be allowed to attend our party this afternoon. Mr. Carr and I agreed that you should not be rewarded for your recent poor behavior. You should be punished instead. You will remain here in the classroom, and I'll check back with you in a little while. In the meantime you are to erase the boards, and I want you to begin writing sentences: 'I will not misbehave in class.'"

Trey was devastated. "I can't go to the party? I brought a gift and everything." His voice quivered, and his eyes filled with tears.

"I'm sorry," Mrs. Hamilton said, "but you know the rules. Besides, it wouldn't be fair to the students who have behaved well all semester."

Word about Trey spread like wildfire up the line toward the cafeteria. "Trey can't come to the party! Mrs. Hamilton is making him stay behind." Joey was bummed out; he really thought the fake vomit bit would have been fun. Margaret, a snooty little redhead said, "Well, I, for one, am glad that he is not coming to the party. He would just do something stupid and get all of us in trouble."

The cafeteria had been wonderfully transformed. The students couldn't believe their eyes. Crepe paper had been strung from the ceiling, a tree had been placed in the corner, a long table with a red cloth sat right in the middle of the room with a big punch bowl surrounded by all kinds of cookies. Chairs had been arranged in a circle, and Mrs. Hamilton had labeled each chair with a student's nametag. They all found their place. Trey's chair was the only empty one.

The party was just getting underway when Mrs. Hamilton paused. "Class, something is just not quite right. I'll be back in a minute. Bobby, you can start the CD player. Mrs. Jones will poke her head in to check on you while I'm gone."

Mrs. Hamilton made her way back down to the classroom, where she watched Trey through the window in the door. The blackboards had been erased, and he had begun writing his sentences. The word "misbehave" had been consistently misspelled in every sentence. She just shook her head. She could tell he had been crying. His eyes and nose were red. His present sat on the top of his desk.

She opened the door. "Trey, I need you to do something else for me," she said.

He was startled by her voice. "Yes, ma'am. What is it?"

She paused before she said, "I want you to get your gift and come with me down the hall. There's a party going on, and you belong there." Then she reached down and gave him one of the biggest hugs he could ever remember getting.

Trey just stood there for a moment, mouth open, eyes wide with excitement. "You mean I get to go to the party? I thought you said that I had misbehaved too much."

"You have," she responded, "but I still want you to come to my party. It won't be the same without you." He was afraid that she was about to hug him again.

As they walked toward the cafeteria, Trey said, "Mrs. Hamilton, can I tell you something? You're my favorite teacher." He paused. "And I guess you should know something. The next time you erase the board, you'll need to know that I stuck chalk in the bottom of the erasers while you were at the party." He heard her mumble something under her breath. It sounded like she said, "Give me strength." He wondered if this would be a good time to mention the fake vomit.

And when evening had come, the owner of the vineyard said to his foreman, "Call the laborers and pay them their wages, beginning with the last group to the first." And when those hired about the eleventh hour came, they thought that they would receive more; and they also received each one a day's wage. And when they received it, they grumbled at the land-owner, saying, "These last men have worked only one hour, and you have made them equal to us who have borne the burden and the scorching heat of the day." But he answered and said to one of them, "Friend, I am doing you no wrong; did you not agree with me for a day's wage? Take what is yours and go your way, but I wish to give this last man the same as to you. Is it not lawful for me to do what I wish with what is my own?" (Matt 20:8-15a)

Christmas is all about grace. The gift of the Savior was not earned or deserved by any of us. The gift of Christmas is God's way of saying to every one of us, "I want you to come to my party; it won't be the same without you."

Trey walked into the cafeteria with a grin on his face and his present under his arm. He found the chair with his name on it. Mrs. Hamilton noticed his toe tapping with the music.

God invites all of us to his party. "Behold, I bring you good news of a great joy, which shall be for ALL the people. For unto you is born this day in the city of David, a savior, who is Christ the Lord."

CHAPTER 15

Randy's Tree

Matthew 1:18-23

Randy McSwain's childhood began like most in his small North Carolina town. He was born to loving parents who offered him their constant encouragement and strong Christian values. Family was important to the McSwains. Little Randy grew up knowing the security of a solid and stable environment. The McSwains owned a landscape business. Randy's dad, Tom, had started the business not long after college. Two years at a junior college studying agriculture and two years at Chapel Hill learning the ways of economics had prepared him well for this endeavor. He had met Lisa while in school. They had married the summer after graduation and moved to her hometown to start "McSwain's Landscaping." New industry in the area had provided a number of housing developments. Tom had aggressively sought and won some contracts and was well on his way to a successful business enterprise.

The McSwains bought land near the county line and built a very tasteful brick house that bordered seven acres of land on which the business was founded. They grew what you would expect in the Deep South. Trees were really their specialty, but along with the pines, the magnolias, the maples, and the sweet gums, they had a good variety of shrubs, mostly azaleas and boxwoods. They had some holly and some gardenias as well. They also had mulch and ground cover and several varieties of bordering plants and bedding flowers. The first few years they struggled, but by the time Randy came along, business was good, and Tom had already added a half a dozen workers, including Lisa's brother, Joey, who had a keen business mind and was good about developing new customers.

As soon as Randy was old enough to do so, he loved to walk the property with his dad. At first, Tom would throw Randy on his shoulders, and the two would go exploring together. When he got a little older, Randy decided that the family business was really his personal playground. He loved to play in the huge pile of sand that was near the mulch, and he spent countless hours watching the goldfish in a display "landscape pond" that his father had built. Hide-and-go-seek was also a favorite game between father and son. Randy would always run and hide among the young pine trees. Tom could always find Randy by his giggle when he went to hide. Randy was also fond of building forts out of the bales of hay that were stored under one of the sheds. In the hot months of summer, he loved running through the sprinklers that fed water to all of the young plants. Randy loved everything about his world. He loved the trees and the plants and his house. But most of all he loved his dad.

The two were inseparable. In fact, some of the workers got to calling Randy "Little Tom." They looked alike; they talked alike. Randy would even get his mom to dress him in clothes that looked like his dad's. He had a pair of khaki pants and a shirt with the company logo, just like his dad's, except the name "Randy" was embroidered on his shirt instead of "Tom." When he turned six, Randy started as a first-grader at Oakwood Elementary School. Every morning, he stood at the gate of the white picket fence and waited on the bus. He always called to his dad as the bus pulled up, "Don't worry; I'll be home this afternoon to give you a hand."

The McSwains also grew blue spruce trees on their property. When they grew big enough, Tom would allow a few to be sold as Christmas trees. He hated the thought of cutting trees, so he would always offer to replant the trees in the customer's yard after the season was over. Many people accepted his offer. That's what first put the thought in Randy's head. He wanted his own tree, and he wanted it planted outside his window. Tom gave in, of course, and early one May a tree was uprooted from the lot and carefully planted in the rich soil near the house. "This will be our special tree," Tom told his son. We'll watch it grow together. It will grow strong and tall just like you." It was really no more than a sapling at first, but Randy offered it the best of care. He watered it carefully. When told to do so, he fertilized it. Tom would help him to prune it carefully and to shape it as it grew taller so it would be the perfect Christmas tree.

The first Christmas it stood outside Randy's window, a single string of lights was more than enough to cover the tree. But by the third Christmas it was really beginning to take shape. Randy worried over "his" tree. He protected it from the cold of winter and the drought of summer. After every thunderstorm he checked to make sure it had survived. Sometime during the fourth year it had surpassed Tom in height. Something about the tree always brought joy to Randy. It was like a link to his father—strong, tall, and sturdy.

It was June of Randy's eleventh summer. Tom had been out working with some of the men when he seemed to have a little dizzy spell. He dismissed it at first, chalking it up to the Carolina summer heat. He downed some water and found some shade and seemed to feel a bit better. A couple weeks later it happened again, only this time it came on him at the breakfast table. He was so dizzy that he felt sick to his stomach. When it happened a third time, about a day later, Lisa insisted that he see a doctor. Tom was checked for inner ear problems and blood pressure issues. They even ran blood work to see if there were signs of diabetes. Still, Tom received no answers. The dizzy spells grew worse. It was finally a specialist who suggested some more elaborate tests be performed. Three separate tests confirmed the worst possible diagnosis. Tom was suffering from an aggressive type of cancer that was quickly overtaking his brain. The doctors concluded that it was inoperable and incurable. They gave him three months to live. He made it seven weeks.

Everything about Randy's world changed that summer. There was no longer any laughter. There was no spring in his step, no sparkle in his eyes. He didn't want to walk the property or drive the golf cart like he had done with his father. In fact, he spent a lot of days alone in his room, so many that his mother got worried and took him to a psychologist, who explained it was all "normal" for what he had been through. He insisted that the fog would slowly lift and that, in time, normal behavior would return. Lisa found Randy out by his tree one night, crying for his tall and sturdy father to return.

It took most of the fall, but slowly Randy began to live again. His grades started to improve slightly. He tried out for the basketball team and made it. He even began to venture out onto the property again. In her mind, Lisa wondered about their first Christmas without Tom. It would be unbearably hard for her, but she knew she would have to hold it together for Randy's sake. She thought a little change might do them some good, so she decided not to spend all of December at home, but instead she surprised Randy with a quick trip to Disney for a few days. They flew down on a Thursday and stayed through the weekend. It was good for them to be away. It was hard, but it was so desperately needed. It did her heart good to see some laughter and joy return to her son's life. She knew the joy would be temporary, that nothing about what had happened would change—the house would be just as empty and the hole in their lives just as big. But you take comfort when and where you can find it. And she was grateful for the momentary reprieve.

They had only been home for about ten minutes when Randy first discovered it. He tore through the house, running for the back door, screaming at the top of his lungs, "It's gone! Daddy's tree is gone!" Lisa ran out the door after him. The two rounded the corner of the house where the tree should have been. When they got to the spot, all that was left was a pile of sawdust where someone had obviously cut the tree off at ground level. For a moment both stood in horrific silence with a dozen questions racing through their minds—"Who could have done this? Why would someone steal a tree—and why *this* tree?" Randy felt like someone had just kicked him in the stomach. This very tree, one of the few tangible reminders of his father, was now gone, ripped away in a moment, just like his dad had been. It's odd how something as insignificant as a tree could hurt so much, but it did. He dropped to his knees and began to sob. His mother put her arms around him in a fleeting attempt to comfort her son, who at the time was inconsolable.

Within a few minutes all of the workers were rounded up and everyone questioned about the tree. "Can anyone tell me about our tree?" asked Lisa. "Did anyone see anything out of the ordinary?" No one had seen or heard a thing. Apparently, someone had spotted the tree from the street that ran in front of the house. It was the perfect shape for a Christmas tree, and seeing no lights on for a few days, they must have stopped, hopped the picket fence, and cut it with a handsaw. Uncle Joey looked closely at the yard by the street and noticed some tire marks that had been left in the grass. It's hard to believe that someone would have actually stolen a tree for Christmas, but the evidence certainly pointed that way.

After a day or so, Randy's anger turned to resolve. He was going to find *his* tree. Somewhere in their small town, someone was using a blue spruce to hang their ornaments. He would search until he found it, and he would bring it home where it belonged. Every afternoon as soon as the school bus stopped in front of the house, Randy would throw his books on the kitchen table, grab a glass a milk, and jump on his bike to race into town to continue his search. Trying to find one tree among hundreds of trees was a little daunting—like trying to find a needle in a haystack. But he just *knew* he could find it.

The convenience mart on the corner had a tree, a blue spruce, but it looked a little tall. Then there was the tree in the lobby of the library. It was also a spruce. The local supermarket had a tree just inside the door, near where the "greeter" stands. Another spruce, another maybe. The courthouse had a tree. The school had three. The four downtown churches all had trees. There was one in the lobby of the post office. The hospital had one at the front entrance, but it was too big. The fire hall had a tree with red ornaments. Another spruce. Even the local hardware store had a tree, theirs decorated with flashing lights and a star on top. Someone told him about the tree at the auto parts store. It was a tree all right, but a pine, not a spruce.

As Randy pedaled his way up Virginia Avenue, he counted seventeen trees in people's homes. And those were just the ones he could see! How would he check on all the trees? How would he ever find his father's? His mother had sanctioned his afternoon search attempts but made him promise to be home before dark. So each day he would look at as many trees as he could find, only to return home at the end of the day a little more dejected, a little more defeated.

He spent a week looking for the tree before he finally came to the conclusion that it was really gone. The tree had been taken, and it was not coming back. Mom, of course, had offered to plant another tree, in just the same spot. They could decorate it and even leave the lights on all winter if he wanted. But they both knew it just wouldn't be the same. It was really more than the tree he mourned. It was what the tree represented. It was a reminder of his father and all the joy they had shared. In his mind the connection had been made that as long as the tree stood growing in the yard, his father would always be close.

The days leading to Christmas had crept along as "slow as molasses," to use the southern term. School was out for the holidays. Lisa was determined to keep as many of the usual traditions of Christmas as she could. They put up a tree in the house with Uncle Joey's help. Brightly wrapped packages were placed underneath. Lisa had set out the usual decorations all around the house. The nativity scene was on the mantle, the wreath on the door, and the little porcelain snow village adorned the top of the dining room table. Christmas music played throughout the house, and the smell of gingerbread cookies and spiced tea always seemed to swirl around the kitchen. Several large poinsettias were placed strategically around the house, and Christmas card photos covered the front of the refrigerator.

The Christmas Eve service began at 7:00 p.m. The church was filled to capacity. The children's choir sang a couple carols while several students acted out the Christmas story. Randy was one of the wise men. He bowed at the appropriate time and offered his gift of gold to baby Jesus. The youth group did sign language to "O Holy Night." Mrs. Moyers sang her usual rendition of "Silent Night," and then the pastor offered a few words. He didn't say anything that Randy hadn't heard before. Mostly he talked about the angels, the shepherds, and the bed of hay. He finished by talking about the star that appeared over Bethlehem, the one that had led the wise men to the manger, a true sign of God's presence. He talked of how he liked to look up in the night sky on a clear night and see the millions of stars that filled the sky. The preacher said, "It reminds me that the God who put the star above the stable is the same God who watches us each night." Nice thought, but what really had the attention of Randy was the tree over by the piano. He looked at it long and hard before concluding that it was not the stolen tree.

Several hours later, Randy's mom checked on him one last time and turned out the light. From his bed he could see the night sky. It was a crisp, clear night, with a billion stars brightly shining. He remembered the preacher's words and thought about a God who was so big that he could be in a billion places, watching over all the people of earth.

Something in Randy's mind suddenly clicked. It dawned on him why he couldn't find his father's tree. Instead of being in one place, it was in a hundred places. His father's presence hadn't left him; in fact, it would find him in a thousand places. Every Christmas tree in town was a reminder that his father was still close, still loving him, still laughing with him. He thought about all the places he had been where the trees were placed and how, even in those places, he could sense his father. His father would be with him in spirit when he went to school and to church and to the library and to the supermarket. Dad's memory and influence would be at the gas station on the corner and at the entryway to the courthouse. The trees of Christmas would remind him of his father's love! He sat straight up in bed and thought of the trees on their landscape farm.

He ran to his mother's room, shouting excitedly, "How many trees do we have for sale? How many blue spruce trees?"

"Not many," she said, "maybe a dozen, maybe a few more. Why?"

"We have to plant more!" he shouted. There was a sparkle in his eyes that she had not seen in months. "The more we grow, the more we can sell," he continued. "Don't you see? As long as there are trees, I'll know Dad is close by." Randy's mother was not sure that she understood all that Randy was saying, but she was very sure that they would plant and sell all the trees they possibly could.

One of the gifts Randy opened the following morning was a wood-burning set. By noon he had almost finished his first creation, a sign burned into a flat piece of cedar that read, "McSwain's Landscaping and Christmas Tree Farm."

The Christmas season is filled with reminders. There are a billion stars in the night sky. There are decorated trees in millions of homes. There are evergreen wreaths on nearly every door. There are bright lights in yards, nativity scenes on lawns, and carols played on stations up and down the dial, all reminders of one thing—that Christmas is close, that *God* is close. In fact, God never leaves us or forsakes us. He loves us and forgives us and comforts us when we need it. I don't know what the past year has been like for you. Probably some pain, some heartache, maybe some joy. I do know this—that through it all, God was with you and will continue to be. That's the message of Christmas.

"His name shall be called Immanuel, which means, 'God with us'" (Matthew 1:18).

CHAPTER 16

Fallujah Rain

Isaiah 9:6; Luke 2:13-14

*This story is dedicated to all the men and women of our Armed Forces who
sometimes find themselves a long way from home at Christmas.*

It seemed like a good idea at the time—enlisting in the Army, that
is. But that moment, almost four years ago, seemed a million light years
away from where Mike Harris was now living. Mike was the only son of his
parents, Susan and Jim. The Harrises lived in Warner Robins, Georgia, just
a few miles south of Macon. Mike had been born and raised there in the
midst of southern hospitality and pride. His father was a graduate of the
University of Georgia and remained a loyal fan of the Bulldogs through the
years. He had met Susan during his senior year of college. He had majored
in business and, upon graduation, moved back to Warner Robins to follow
in his father's footsteps as an insurance agent. Susan graduated a year later,
and the two married in late December of the same year and settled into life
in Warner Robins.

Because of his father's love for football, young Mike was introduced
to the sport at an early age. He grew up playing first in the youth league at
the recreation center near their home. By the time he reached junior high,
Mike was playing for the school team and soon became a good player. In
fact, he played all the way through high school and was a member of a team
that played in the state finals one season. Warner Robins High School was
a huge school, with about 1,900 students enrolled each year. They were in
the biggest and, many felt, most competitive classification in the state. The
Demons, as they were known, were a team to fear and respect.

Mike's life was typical of many young men of that region. He loved to play football. He loved to fish and hunt. And he loved to work on his car, a '99 Mustang. On the outside the Harris family seemed happy and close-knit. And for the most part they were. But somewhere along his teenage years, Mike and his father began a stormy relationship. Maybe it was his physical size, or his defiant attitude, or the questionable crowd with which he ran, but toward his junior year, Mike and his dad seemed to drift apart. Occasionally they would travel to Athens on a fall Saturday to take in a Bulldogs game. Sometimes they went to a car show. Every once in a while the family took a few days of vacation, but mostly Jim stayed too busy with work, and Mike stayed too busy with the distractions of adolescence. It was not that they were enemies; they just weren't friends. They didn't often share the kinds of conversations that define the bond between a father and his son. Mostly it was small talk and casual conversations about petty things.

The distance between them grew wider and the frustration more intense as high school graduation approached. Out of obligation, Mike had applied and been accepted at the University of Georgia, but in the back of his mind, he had no intention of attending. In fact, one afternoon he announced to his father, "I'm not going anywhere for a while. I'm going to work, get an apartment, and hang out with my friends." The news did not sit well with the older Harris. Over the course of the summer, the tension grew worse, and the words were seasoned with greater anger. As fall approached there was no hint of going to school and, at least in the mind of his father, no hint of Mike doing anything worthwhile.

Mike got a job at the local supermarket as a stock clerk. He liked his supervisor and co-workers and was getting in a lot of hours. The money he earned easily fed all of his desires. There was money for dating, money for gas, and money for wasting. Soon his father decided that if his son wanted to be all grown up, he could start paying for some of his own bills. First it was the cell phone, then his car insurance. His dad even thought he should help out with the groceries. After all, he wasn't paying any rent to live at home. Finally, Mike got tired of all the "hassle at home," so he began to look for his own place. He found a couple roommates, and the three young men found a garage apartment. In October of that year, Mike moved out of the house and into his life of freedom.

The dream was short-lived. One of his roommates decided to move in with a girlfriend. The rent became too high for the second one, and he was forced to move back home. That left Mike with a poorly furnished apartment, an expensive rent, and a dad with an "I-told-you-so" attitude. Mike had grown weary with his job. His car no longer gave him the excitement and thrill it once had. His father was more distant than ever. And most of his high school buddies had gone off to college. That was when the lure of Army life began to trickle into his mind. "Not a bad idea," he thought. So on a bright, clear January morning, Mike walked into a recruitment center and enlisted, just like that. The papers were signed, and the ink had been dry for over a week before Mike told his parents. They were stunned—and worried. Mom cried. Dad slammed a door in frustration.

The brief couple weeks before induction passed very quickly. Reality set in for all the members of the Harris family. Hearts melted, and some deep wounds quickly mended, yet much of the distance between father and son was too great to overcome in such a brief time. Mike's dad helped him move his things back into the house. He offered a lot of advice and counsel. And when they drove him down to the processing center, Jim put a hand on his son's shoulder and told him he was proud of him. Mike hadn't heard those words in a long time. Mom kissed his cheek and started to cry.

The initial months of Army life were not easy. In fact, it was the biggest challenge Mike had ever faced in his life. He was homesick, tired, lonely, and scared. He was sent to Fort Benning for boot camp. At least he was close to home, and on long weekends he either drove up to see his parents or they came down to see him. He actually stayed at Benning for Advanced Infantry Training (AIT). And as is usually the case, he met a lot of new people, people just like him and people who were not like him at all. He grew close to his fellow recruits. One of them, a boy from Valdosta named Gene Whitehead, became his best buddy. They spent a lot of time together and liked a lot of the same things. They double-dated. They talked about football. They seemed to encourage each other and helped keep each other out of trouble. They shared stories and cookies from home and a thousand conversations. When basic and AIT were out of the way, both boys were assigned to Fort Bragg, where they became a part of the 82nd Airborne Division.

Time passed. They trained well and quickly advanced in rank. Gene moved up one rank to become E2, and Jim actually moved up two ranks to E3, also known as private first class. They, like many others, were being fast-tracked for duty in Iraq. The idea of going there was a mix of emotion. There was that exhilarating sense of "gung ho" mentality mixed with a deep sense of fear. They were smart enough to know that the war was real and that a lot of lives were being lost in the fighting.

They were assigned to Camp Fallujah, a large base just outside the city of Fallujah that had become so prominent in the fighting. Fallujah is located in the center of Iraq, only about fifty "clicks" due west of Baghdad. The town itself is built on the banks of the Euphrates River and has over 200,000 inhabitants. Mike and Gene were assigned to a platoon under the direction of Master Sergeant Jose Torres. Mostly they were charged with guarding the western perimeter of the base. So most of their days were spent in the relative security of the base, standing guard in a fortified bunker for eight hours at a time. Occasionally, they were assigned to escort a caravan of supplies that would roll into town from Baghdad. Mike and Gene's camouflage Humvee usually brought up the rear of the convoy on such missions.

It was in early September when Mike and Gene were assigned to provide escort to a food and supply shipment. The skies were overcast and cloudy that day with an unusual light rain falling in the early morning hours. As was the custom, Mike was driving, and Gene was riding shotgun as the convoy snaked its way through the center of Fallujah. They were within about two miles of the base when it happened. A dirty roadside bomb detonated about the time their Humvee passed. Though the armor plating did its job, a quarter-size piece of shrapnel made its way through Gene's open window and tore through his right jaw. In the confusion of the moment, instinctively Mike gunned the Humvee quickly away from the blast. It was when he turned to ask Gene if he was okay that he saw the blood pouring from Gene's nose and mouth.

He caught Gene as he slumped toward the dashboard. "Gene! Are you all right? Talk to me!" There was no response, no sound. Mike raced toward the base at breakneck speed. The rain was falling with greater intensity. He didn't even slow as he sped through the gate and on toward the EVAC hospital. He skidded to a stop and raced around the vehicle to grab Gene. When Mike picked him up to carry him in his arms, Gene's body was limp and already lifeless. Mike knew, but he didn't want to believe that Gene was already gone.

A sergeant major came running toward the Humvee. "What's the matter with you, boy? You could have killed someone the way you came driving onto base!" It was then that the sergeant saw the size of the wound and knew instantly what the outcome would be.

Out of neither defiance nor disrespect, but purely out of the depth of human pain and anguish, Mike yelled as he held Gene's limp body in his arms, "Why are we *here?*"

The sergeant, with water dripping from the brim of his hat and with a well-chewed cigar clenched tightly in his teeth, said, "We're here to offer peace. And sometimes bringing peace costs dearly."

Mike's commanding officer assigned a chaplain to help him with the loss of his best friend. Captain Jim White, a Baptist and a Georgia native, spent a lot of time with Mike over the course of the next few weeks. Chaplain White was forever patient, a man of deep faith, and for Mike a real gift of grace. Chaplain White gave Mike a copy of the New Testament, and the two of them agreed to study a few passages together. Mike had gone to Sunday school as a child, but ever since his teenage years, going to church had not been much of a priority. Like many, he had casually moved away from his faith. Chaplain White made the Scriptures come alive for Mike. He taught Mike how to pray and how to seek the heart of God. His newfound faith gave him strength and helped him cope with his loss. He became a regular at the Sunday worship service on base and even read Scripture when called upon to do so. Mike often thought to himself how odd that his faith grew not in the heart of the Bible Belt, where he had been raised, but in the midst of a war, where his faith had been challenged.

Christmas was rapidly approaching, and signs of the season began popping up all over the base. There was a Christmas tree set up in the mess tent. A couple of Humvees were decorated with a wreath on the front. Christmas cards from various groups back home were displayed in several spots. One disabled tank was decorated with strings of colored lights. It was hopeful and hard at the same time. It was good to be reminded of the joy of Christmas and the hope of real peace on earth, but at the same time every sign of the season made the soldiers miss family and friends all the more.

On Christmas Eve, Mike had been assigned to the far outpost on the western perimeter of the base. The western side of the base pointed toward friendlier territory, so night duty was relatively peaceful and calm. It was a clear night when Mike climbed to the outpost tower to pull his shift. He spoke briefly to the soldier he was replacing and settled in behind his M-16 with its night scope and infrared sights. From his vantage point, there were few lights in the distant horizon, mostly just the spectacular night sky with a million bright stars. Behind him were the lights from the base. He could see the tank with the Christmas lights, and occasionally he could hear the sound of Christmas carols that were being played over the PA system. At 2200 hours the base grew quiet, and Mike was left alone with his thoughts and his duty.

His watch beeped. He turned on his helmet light for a moment to see the dial. It was midnight. His mind raced back to Warner Robins and to his family and friends. He thought about what they would be doing and how the house would be decorated for the season. His mom always went overboard.

Every room had some sort of decorations—candles, wreaths, nativity scenes. She also went overboard with cooking. There was always something in the oven—chocolate chip cookies, pumpkin pie, a Christmas ham. His dad usually took some time off around the holidays. When he was young, they used to hunt together over the holidays. His dad was always upbeat during the season and always bought the best gifts. Mike's heart ached. Home was where he wanted to be.

His thoughts were interrupted by the rhythmic sound of boots walking across the gravel courtyard of the base. A soldier was approaching with a flashlight in his hand. Before he called out the required greeting, Mike had already recognized the gait. It was Jim White, the chaplain. "Captain White, what are you doing way out here at this time of night?" asked Mike.

"I have something for you," Jim replied. "It came yesterday, but I thought I'd hold on to it and bring it to you tonight. Looks like a Christmas package from home." Chaplain White climbed into the outpost and handed the shoebox to Mike.

Mike switched on his helmet light and read the box. "That's exactly what it is! It's from home." It was a sturdy box that had survived the trip with little wear and tear. It had been completely covered in duct tape, a sign that his dad had had a part in wrapping the contents.

Chaplain White told Mike that he would keep watch for a while so Mike could enjoy the contents of the box.

"Are you sure?" asked Mike.

"Yep, and don't make me remind you that I outrank you. I'm ordering you to sit down and enjoy a little Christmas!"

The box was an absolute treasure. A lot of thought had gone into what needed to be packed among its contents. There were two bags of his mother's homemade chocolate chip cookies, most of which had remained intact. Mike began on one, eating it just a small nibble at a time, not wanting to gobble down something so precious. It was wonderful. It tasted of home and holidays. Next, he pulled out a rolled up t-shirt. As soon as he unfurled it, he knew why his mom had sent it. In big letters across the front, it read, "Warner Robins High School. Home of the Fighting Demons. 2006 State Champs!"

"Well, what about that?" thought Mike. His mother had also packed a new pair of socks and a new pair of underwear. "Some things never change," he thought to himself, but he was gladdened by the usual gift. There were also some pictures, mostly from past Christmases, pictures of the tree and presents given and smiles exchanged. His mother had also sent a Christmas tree ornament wrapped in bubble wrap. He immediately recognized it as one of her collectable ornaments. It was a tiny manger scene that had been one of his favorites through the years. Even as a teenager it was always his duty to place it on the tree.

There was one other item left in the bottom of the box. It was small, about the size of a half-dollar, only thicker. It was wrapped completely in duct tape. "I don't know what this is, but it's definitely from Dad," he thought to himself. As he began to unwrap it, he knew exactly what it was, and he couldn't image that his dad would dare risk sending it all this way. It was his father's pocket watch, which had been given to him by his own father shortly before his death. It was probably the single most important keepsake that his father owned. Mike's dad had carried it for years; the golden watch was worn smooth on the outside from all the years of use. Attached to the watch was a note that read, "Mikey, you may have thought this was the most important thing in the world to me. It's not. You are. I just thought you needed to know. I want you and the watch to come home in one piece. Merry Christmas. I love you. Dad."

Tears streamed down Mike's face, making a small tapping noise as they hit the plastic of the bag in his lap. It took a few minutes for Mike to regain his composure. He wiped his eyes on his sleeve and took a few deep breaths. He climbed back into the outpost where his chaplain friend was carefully scanning the horizon.

"Everything okay at home?" Jim asked.

"Yeah, everything is good. Just wish I were there tonight. By the way, thanks for bringing the box."

"No problem."

The two men sat in silence for a few moments, looking over the horizon with its brilliant display of stars. In only the mystery that Christmas can bring, a shooting star shot across the night sky—oddly enough, in the direction of Bethlehem. "Wow, that's really something," said the chaplain, "a real Christmas star. Let's pray it's a sign of Christmas peace, real peace, lasting peace."

"Yes, sir," said Private Harris. "Peace between nations, peace between fathers and sons, and peace between God and men."

Offering peace is never easy. It is costly. God forged peace with men on the anvil of Christ's sacrifice. The peace that will bring nations together and will cause families and friends to be reconciled and will gladden our hearts with the joy of grace and forgiveness is not found in the guns of war, nor in the coercion of angry words, nor in the intellect of the human mind. The peace we desire and need is found only in the manger of Bethlehem, only in Jesus Christ. When Isaiah wrote about the coming messiah, he offered these simple words: "For a child will be born to us, a son will be given to us; and the government will rest on His shoulders; and His name will be called Wonderful Counselor, Mighty God, Eternal Father, Prince of Peace" (Isa 9:6).

Let us praise the Prince of Peace as we celebrate his birth this Christmas and as we welcome him as Lord of our lives.

CHAPTER 17

When Is Daddy Coming Home?

John 1:14

Bill Montgomery was a thirty-eight-year-old accountant for a large firm in the city. He lived with his wife, Margaret, and their three children in the residential community of Riverside. Elizabeth was the oldest of the three children at twelve. Ann was nine, and their son, Blair, was just seven. Bill had been with the accounting firm ever since college graduation. He had done well and was well liked by all. He lived in a nice house in a nice neighborhood, and he drove a late model car with leather seats and a sunroof. Bill was a little paunchy around the middle, too much time behind the desk and too little time at the gym, not overweight by any means, just the spread of middle age. Bill enjoyed his life. He worked hard at his job. He was dedicated and disciplined. He tried hard to balance work and church and time with the kids. He was very organized. His life was always planned, deliberate, and thought out. He was a keeper of lists and seemed to be forever tied to his planner to keep him on track.

The office had been slammed through much of December. Bill had felt the strain of the season. Like most of the others in the firm, Bill had worked around the clock, but starting the morning of Christmas Eve, he was off for the next ten days. It would be a good break before the beginning of tax season. As he drove home from the city, he felt his whole body relax at the thought of a quiet Christmas at home with his family. He caught himself thinking about the traditions in the Montgomery home. Christmas Eve was always a huge family occasion. His parents would arrive after dinner. Margaret would serve coffee and dessert, and then the whole bunch would gather around the piano for the singing of Christmas carols. After the carols the children would get to pick out one of the presents under the tree and open it, sort of a prelude to Christmas morning. Then, once the kids had on their pajamas, the family would load up and drive through the little town of Riverside to look at all the Christmas lights. Bill loved the thought of it all. The fireplace would crackle with a warm fire. The tree would sparkle with a thousand lights. The smell of the Christmas ham would waft its way through the house. Bill looked forward to just being in his recliner and taking it all in.

When Bill awoke on the morning of Christmas Eve, a steady downpour was falling all over Riverside. From a quick glance out the window, Bill could tell it had been raining most of the night. There were puddles on the street and a few places in the yard where the water was starting to pool. Bill didn't care. "It's Christmas," he thought. "There's no way the rain is going to dampen my spirits." Having said that, he put on his Santa hat and made his way downstairs to join his wife at the breakfast table for coffee. He was almost as giddy as the children. He checked his watch. "This time tomorrow, and we'll be opening the presents!" he said to Margaret. "I hope you spent lots of money on my present," he joked.

Bill was rather proud of himself this year. Here it was Christmas Eve, and all of his shopping was done and wrapped. Granted, he had spent a lot of late nights on the Internet searching through all the popular sites. But everything that had been ordered had arrived. It was all the right stuff, the right colors, the right sizes, and hopefully the right fit. The only present that he was a little unsure of was a remote-control car he bought for his son from an auction site.

It was during a long and savory sip of coffee that Bill's wife reminded him of a couple things yet to be done before the family gathering that night. He was to pick up a fruit basket that had been ordered from a local fruit market. He was to go by the grocery store to buy some pie shells, and he was to go by the florist to pick up the centerpiece for the table. "And," she added, "don't forget that the piano tuner will be by at 1:00. I can't meet him; I'll be delivering presents with the kids, so make sure you're here to let him in."

"Not a problem," he proclaimed. "I have a list, and I've mapped out my day. I have plenty of time to get it all done." With that, Bill made his way upstairs to shower and dress and get ready for his assault on the final Christmas list.

When Bill pushed the garage door opener button, he was once again reminded of the pouring rain outside. "Better take my raincoat," he thought. He walked back into the house to grab his trusty raincoat that he had worn for years. Grabbing his cell phone off the kitchen table, Bill dropped it into his coat pocket and headed out to his appointed rounds. As he slipped his car out of the garage, the rain was beating hard against his windshield.

First, Bill stopped to pick up the floral centerpiece for their Christmas dinner table. When he pulled up to the shop, there were, of course, no open spaces anywhere close to the door. "Great," he thought, "my shoes will be soaked in a second." He looked down at his cordovan penny loafers and wondered why in the world he hadn't chosen a different pair.

Clutching his coat tightly around him, Bill ran for the door. As he stepped inside, Mr. Bailey called to him, "Merry Christmas, Bill! You know, you look a little damp."

"Thanks a lot," Bill replied. "I can't believe this is my first stop, and already I'm soaked." Mr. Bailey went to the walk-in cooler in the back of the shop and returned with the centerpiece for their table. It was a work of art. It had red roses and white carnations. There were pieces of evergreen and holly with red berries. A green ribbon was woven throughout the flowers, and a dark green candle stood tall in the middle.

"I'll help you to the car," said Mr. Bailey, "I've got a huge umbrella that should keep us both dry." Bill decided that the trunk would be the best place for the flowers to ride. When he opened the trunk, he grimaced. Sitting just where he had placed it a couple weeks earlier was the package to Margaret's parents that he was to have dropped off at the shipping store. He had forgotten all about it. What would he tell Margaret? Maybe she didn't need to know. He figured he'd drive straight over and ship it overnight. Maybe, with some luck, her parents would get the package a day or two after Christmas. He'd blame it on the busy season and tell his wife that he'd send an angry letter to the company for ruining their Christmas.

When Bill closed the door of his car, he didn't realize that not all of his coat had gotten in with him. As he sped through town, his trusty old raincoat was flapping in the breeze, including the pocket that contained his cell phone. It was at a red light that the rain-drenched pocket gave up its contents. The phone spilled out onto the roadway, and when Bill drove away from the intersection, he ran over it with his rear tire. "I wonder what I just ran over?" he thought to himself. "Probably just a pothole." His mind got sidetracked to a discussion of why the city didn't do a better job of filling the potholes, so he never thought twice about what that bump really was.

The grocery store was packed, as you might imagine. Too many people were trying to get their last-minute shopping done. Of course, there were no parking spots anywhere close. Bill parked about a hundred yards from the front door and made a mad dash for the entrance. As he sloshed his way along, his feet got wetter, his hair was flattened by the moisture, and now his slacks were feeling the effects. From the knees down, his pants were soaked. He stood dripping in the refrigerator section of the store, staring at the pie shells. "Graham cracker or those kind that unfold?" he wondered. He knew he had seen his wife use both. He knew that she had probably told him earlier which ones to get. He also knew that this choice was too important to be left to chance. "I'll just call her and see which ones she wants." He reached into his pocket to grab the phone. It wasn't there. "Now I wonder where that phone could be?" He fumbled around through all his pockets and decided that he must have left it in the car. Little did he know that he had left it on 4th and Broadway. He decided that the best thing to do was simply to buy both kinds. "I'll be safe either way."

As he ran back to the car, little did Bill know that his day was only about to get worse. Next stop—the shipping store. It was noon when Bill pulled up to the place, which was doing great business. Normally, the line would have trailed out the door, but people were crowding in so that no one would have to stand in the pouring rain. Bill grabbed the package from the trunk and made a mad dash for the door. Somewhere along the way, the heel of his penny loafer had held all the rain it could hold, and off it flew just as Bill attempted to hurdle the large puddle in front of the store. When he landed, one foot went one way and the other in the opposite direction. Bill hit the ground hard and slid face-first into the glass door. The package tumbled out of his reach, and his nose started to bleed. Not wanting to lose their place in line, the people on the inside just stood and watched as Bill gathered himself and his package and finally made his way inside.

After waiting for nearly thirty minutes, Bill finally got to the front of the line. His nose was swollen and red, his shirt was bloodied, his shoe was ruined, and to top it all off, the clerk said, "I'm sorry, sir, but I can't read the address. Looks like it got wet or something." Bill thought about the penalty for strangling the worker. "You'll need to go to the table in the back and affix a new label. Next!"

If Bill had been home at the time, he would have heard the piano tuner ringing the bell. As it was, the doorbell seemed to just echo through the empty house. Finally, after waiting for fifteen minutes for someone to come home, Mike, the piano tuner, wrote a note saying he'd drop by sometime after the holidays. Nice.

What happened next is a little hard to believe. Bill was heading for the next stop, McCrory's Fruit Market. In the back of his mind, he remembered that Margaret had told him that Mr. McCrory was closing early, around

3:00 or so. "Well, at least I've got plenty of time to get the fruit basket. I mean, what could happen between here and McCrory's?" Bill was stopped at a light next to the bank. On the top of the bank, some four stories above the street, was Santa's sled and his team of reindeer, which had been a part of the seasonal decorations for longer than Bill could remember. In fact, part of the Christmas Eve ritual with the kids would be a drive past the bank to check on Santa. It was usually the last stop before heading home for the night. As he waited at the light, Bill thought to himself, "I sure hope they've got old Santa tied securely. I'd hate for the old boy to get blown off the roof in all this wind and rain."

As if his thoughts had willed it to happen, in the blink of an eye, a sudden gust had lifted the sleigh with all the reindeer attached and sent it streaking for the ground. All Bill could do was watch in horror through his sunroof as Saint Nick and company landed on his car. Gratefully, the back end of the car caught most of the impact. The trunk was smashed, the back window shattered, and the hood dented and scratched. "I've just been hit by Santa Claus," thought Bill.

When the 911 dispatcher got the first call from an eyewitness, she had to ask twice: "You're telling me that some guy just got clobbered by Santa Claus and the reindeer? Sounds like you've had one too many eggnogs."

As you can imagine, it took the police quite a while to sort it all out. Once they determined that Bill was unhurt, although the blood on the shirt from the incident at the shipping store was a bit misleading, everyone seemed to relax. The car was still drivable, just not nearly the pristine automotive machine it had been a few hours earlier. The bank president apologized a dozen times and promised to send a case of steaks to the house. Bill looked at his watch when he limped his car away from the curb. It was 4:17 p.m., and it was getting dark.

At home, Margaret was both angry and worried. Where was Bill? Why had he not called? And why wouldn't he answer his phone? She had left him half a dozen voicemail messages, each revealing a growing sense of anger. She had found the note from the piano tuner and couldn't imagine what had kept Bill from meeting him. "I'll piano him!" she mumbled under her breath. She told the kids, "He better get home soon, and he better have a good explanation, and he better have all the stuff I sent him to get!"

All afternoon, the kids kept asking, "When is Daddy getting home?" They, too, had begun to worry. Ann started to cry. "Doesn't Daddy know it's Christmas Eve? We need him to be here."

McCrory's was long closed by the time Bill drove by. He figured Mr. McCrory was long gone, but he had held out the hope that someone would still be there. No such luck. His only option was to stop at the gas station near his home and hope for the best. They carried a few produce items; maybe they had something left. They did—two oranges and one grapefruit. And of course, for some unexplained reason, Bill's credit card didn't work, and he had to count coins from his ashtray just to pay for the fruit.

"Mom, when is Daddy coming home?" the kids asked for the millionth time. By now, Margaret was frantic. It was after 6:00 p.m. She had moved from anger to real fear. Her mind raced through a dozen scary possibilities. She was just about to call the police when she saw the headlights pull into the driveway. It was Bill's car, or at least it looked like his car. Bill's garage door opener had somehow been lost in the melee with Santa, so he had to stop in the driveway and unload the car in the rain. Of course the magnificent flower centerpiece had been crushed in the accident. The fruit basket was nonexistent. The pie shells had lost their shape. When Margaret opened the door, there stood Bill with a swollen nose, blood on his shirt, a torn overcoat, wet pants, holding two crumpled roses, an orange, and a very dented graham cracker pie crust. In an instant she realized things had not gone well. But he was home, and at that moment, that was all that mattered. His presence alone seemed to melt away the anxiety and fear and anguish of the day.

Tears rolled down Margaret's cheeks as she cried out, "I'm so glad you're home!" She hugged his neck, not caring that her dress was getting soaked. She did wonder why a big plastic Santa was strapped to what was left of his car. In the background she could hear the kids banging away on a very out-of-tune piano. Elizabeth was playing "Joy to the World."

There is a certain security that you feel as a child when your father is at home, and a certain insecurity you feel when he is away. A house that seems dark and scary and lonely and empty suddenly is transformed when your daddy comes walking in. I spoke with a friend this week who told me how, even as a grown married adult, he always slept better whenever he visited home because he knew his father was in the house. There is something about the presence of the father—and the Father—that gives a whole new feeling to the house. There is a sense of security, a sense of calm, a sense of peace.

What must the world have been like before the coming of Christ? Imagine the fear, the anxiety, the loneliness, the darkness, the hopelessness. And then the Father came home. As Gospel writer John states, "The Word became flesh and dwelt among us." Everything changes with the coming of Christ. There is peace and hope and grace and love. We are not alone any longer; the Father has come.

CHAPTER 18

Christmas Feast

Luke 2:15-20

"Go, therefore, to the main highways, and as many as you find there, invite to the wedding feast."—Matthew 22:9

Mattie Lou Akin had been planning Christmas dinner for nearly a year. In fact, at last year's dinner she had made several mental notes, and even jotted a few down, about ideas for the following year. For Mattie Lou there was no meal more important during the entire year. And this year's meal would be legendary. She always planned Christmas dinner to the nth degree. No portion of the meal was left to chance. She planned the menu, the table decorations, and even the smells she wanted swirling through the air while the meal was being served. She even stressed over which CD to play quietly in the background while everyone was eating. Kenny G was her favorite.

Of course she would use the good china. She had over a dozen place settings of the holiday pattern. It was reserved for this one day. She even required that her family dress appropriately for the dinner. Her husband and son were to wear a tie and sport coat. She and her daughter would always wear a skirt. The family used to balk at the idea, but years of fighting the same battle had caused them all to cave in. Her husband, Jim, kept a quiet protest going year after year, always wearing the same tie. Intentionally, he would spill something on it, which he never cleaned away, and so the tie carried a history of the last four or five years of the Christmas feast. He could tell it drove Mattie Lou crazy, but she was not going to give him the satisfaction of mentioning it.

There were always eight people who gathered for the meal. The four members of the Akin family would, of course, be present. In addition, Mattie Lou's parents, Katie and John Baker, would drive up from Florida. They had retired to Naples about a dozen years ago. Florida suited them well, and for most of the year they stayed in the warmth of the Florida sunshine. Even though Charlotte, North Carolina, was not terribly cold at Christmas, Mattie Lou's father always complained his way through the two-week visit. Mostly he complained about the cold. "Don't you folks ever turn on the heat around here? It's freezing!" The thermostat was always set on seventy-two degrees; he just didn't trust it. One year he insisted on building a fire in the fireplace, even though the high on Christmas Day was going to reach into the sixties. Her parents drove to Charlotte in their RV and insisted on staying in it during the visit. "We've got everything we need," her father would say. "We've got a shower, a TV, a bed, and plenty of heat!" If the truth be told, Mattie and her husband didn't mind the fact that her parents retreated to their home-away-from-home each night around 8:30 p.m.

The other two places at the table were set for the Baggetts. Laura and Steve had been friends with the Akins for many years. Steve and Jim had served together in the Army, when both were fresh out of college. They had served one tour of duty together in Vietnam and had remained close through the years. They would often vacation together. When all the kids were young, they would rent a house over at Myrtle Beach every summer for a couple weeks. It was always a lot of fun, and the two families enjoyed one another's company. The Baggett children were a little older, and both were now married, so it was just Laura and Steve who made the annual pilgrimage to Charlotte. They lived in Asheville, about 250 miles away. They would always drive over during the day on Christmas Eve and spend the night, maybe two, before heading home.

As they headed into the home stretch, Jim always tried to steer clear of Mattie Lou as she cleaned and decorated the house. He was the errand boy. He was constantly dispatched for the "little things"—a roll of duct tape, more glue sticks, another spool of ribbon, twelve more feet of garland, silver polish, replacement bulbs. It was endless, but he had learned the hard way to just go with the flow. His only real duty as far as the meal was concerned was that of buying the Christmas ham. That part was easy.

There was a little butcher shop not far from their home. For the past seven or eight years, Bob's Meat Shoppe had been the source of the ham. Jim would call and order the ham, and on Christmas Eve it would be delivered to the house, complete with cranberry glaze to be applied while it baked. All Jim had to remember was to order the ham a few weeks in advance.

It promised to be a perfect meal. Everything had been carefully planned and well coordinated. What could possibly go wrong? A lot. Mattie Lou's perfect Christmas feast began unraveling by mid-October. It all started with her teenage daughter, Karen. Karen was a proud member of the Kennedy High School Marching Band. She was in the color guard. Every Friday night, when the band took the field at halftime, Karen and the other members of the guard would dance their way through the music of the show, a tribute to the music of Billy Joel. It was in October that the final word had been received saying the Kennedy High School Marching Band had been invited to participate in the Tournament of Roses Parade in Pasadena. The trip would be a long one, completely crossing the nation. The band director announced the trip would leave the week of Christmas and return January 3. Mattie Lou had mixed emotions. She was grateful that her daughter would enjoy such an experience, but suddenly she saw her table of eight reduced to seven. "Oh well," she thought, "it's just this one year. We'll still have a great Christmas, and the dinner will still be a huge success."

Did I mention Rob? He was the Akins' son, a junior in college. He called in early December to drive the second stake into his mother's heart. It seems that his college sweetheart, Lindsey, was going to spend the holidays with her family on the slopes of Vail, Colorado. It was their annual ski trip. Lindsey's dad had done well in the carpet business, very well. Apparently, over Thanksgiving break, Lindsey had convinced her father that it would be "really neat" if Rob could join the family for Christmas. By the time Rob called home to ask permission, he was already holding the airline ticket in his hand that Lindsey's dad had sent. The ticket was in the same box with the new ski jacket. Suddenly, the table would be set for six. "I guess we'll get a taste of the empty nest," said Mattie Lou to her husband. "At least the Baggetts will be here."

Christmas week dawned with much hope and promise. The house had been decorated tastefully from top to bottom. The table had been set, the china had been washed, and the dog had been groomed, complete with a little red and green bow. Christmas was only two days away when Jim got a call from work saying the Jennings deal was in serious trouble. Jim was ordered by his boss to jump a plane and head to Minneapolis to fix the problem. "Don't worry, dear," he said to his wife. "I'll be home by noon tomorrow, long before your folks and the Baggetts arrive." With that, he gave her a kiss and headed to the airport.

It was somewhere 35,000 feet over West Virginia when he suddenly remembered that he had forgotten the only thing he was supposed to remember—the Christmas ham. With sweat breaking out on his brow, he placed a call from the airplane's phone to Bob's Meat Shoppe. "I'm sorry, Mr. Akin, but I just sold my last ham."

Jim thought it best to reach for an airsick bag. "Well, what do you have?"

"To be honest, not much is left; we've been hit hard, and it's Christmas, you know."

"Yes, I do know it's Christmas. I don't care what you send; just do what you can, and deliver it to my house late tomorrow afternoon."

"Sure, Mr. Akin. I'll take care of it."

For the next thirty minutes, Jim pondered the question of whether or not he should call Mattie Lou and apprise her of the situation. He decided to just let the cards fall where they would. "At least she won't yell at me with company in the house."

It was late afternoon when Mattie Lou's parents called from Florida. "We're not coming," said her father. "I've been watching the weather forecast all morning, and they are talking about possible snow as far south as the Carolinas."

"Dad, it's fifty-seven degrees here today. I seriously doubt that snow is going to block the Florida Turnpike anytime soon!" Mattie Lou countered.

Her dad continued, "Besides, your mother's bursitis is acting up again. It never gives her any problem unless a cold snap is coming through. I think we better stay put." In the background she could hear her mother reporting that she had already turned up the thermostat and unpacked the electric blankets.

Mattie Lou knew it would be pointless to argue with her hardheaded father. When she hung up the phone, she thought to herself, "Well, it will just be the Baggetts and us. It might not be all bad. It will give us time to catch up." The table would now be set for only four.

Jim called early on Christmas Eve morning from Minneapolis. "My flight is overbooked," he said. "I've got to catch a later flight. Don't worry; they're checking on it now. I'll be home by late afternoon."

It was just past noon when the phone rang. The caller ID read, "Asheville, NC." It was the Baggetts. Laura's mother had fallen during the night at the nursing home near their house. They were in the ER waiting for x-rays. "They think she may have broken a hip," Laura said, her voice quivering with emotion.

"I'm so sorry," said Mattie Lou.

"Needless to say, we won't be coming," said Laura. "Maybe we can get together later, around New Year's." When she hung up, Mattie Lou didn't know whether to laugh or cry. The huge feast was now down to two.

"At least Jim will be home in a few hours," she consoled herself.

Jim called around 2:00 p.m. "So far, no luck," he reported. "The flights are all jam-packed. I may be able to fly to Chicago and then to Atlanta and then to Charlotte. Don't worry; I'll get there."

The doorbell rang about 4:00 p.m. When Mattie Lou peeked out the front window, she saw the little white truck from Bob's Meat Shoppe. "At least we'll have a great meal," she said to herself.

When she opened the door, she was met by Tim, the delivery boy. "Here's your rack of ribs and your five-pound tube of ground beef. Just sign here."

Mattie Lou stammered, "There must be some mistake." "You're supposed to deliver a ham."

Tim fumbled with his paperwork. "I'm sorry, Mrs. Akin. That's what the order says. Besides, it's all I have left in the truck."

Mattie Lou called the meat shop as soon as Tim drove away. All she got was the answering machine saying they were now closed for Christmas but would be opened again on the 27th. She just stared at the meat now defrosting on her kitchen cabinet, wondering where in the world her beautiful ham and cranberry glaze had gone.

Jim called at 8:45. "Honey, I'm in St. Louis. Everything is booked solid. The airline said they'll get me home sometime tomorrow afternoon. I'm so sorry."

Mattie Lou let down her guard for the first time and began to cry. "At least you were going to be here, and we were going to have a wonderful day, all to ourselves. Guess what? Even the ham isn't coming. Bob's messed up the order and sent ribs and ground beef. Can you believe it?"

Jim was not about to play his hand. "You don't need to even call them, honey. I'll go over there when I get home and give 'em a piece of my mind." Jim wondered in the back of his mind if lying on Christmas Eve counted double.

Suddenly, the table was set for one. Mattie Lou looked at her dog, Oscar. "Looks like it's you and me, kid." Before heading upstairs for the night, she took one last long look at the beautiful table and dreamed of what should have been.

It was almost eleven when Mattie Lou was startled awake by the telephone next to her bed. It was Father Patrick, the parish priest. "Mattie Lou, I hate to call so late, but I figured you of all people would be up late getting ready for Christmas dinner. I have a huge problem, and I need your help." Mattie Lou wondered what kind of help she could possibly offer Father Patrick. He began to explain the situation. Every Christmas, the church opened its fellowship hall and served lunch for anyone who wanted to come. Usually the crowd consisted of a few elderly members who didn't want to be alone, several homeless people, and a few other misfits who needed some place to be on Christmas. "Mattie, I'm expecting a couple dozen people tomorrow for lunch. It's our way of sharing the Christmas spirit. I'm afraid that Mrs. Ayers is home sick with the flu and won't be able to cook. I don't know what else to do. I was wondering if maybe you could spare a couple hours in the morning."

Before he could even finish his question, she blurted out, "Yes! Yes. Count on me. I'd love to help." The thought of having a place to be and people to be with gave Mattie Lou a ray of sunshine on a very dark day. "What do you need for me to do?" she asked.

"Well, I was hoping you could come lend a hand with the cooking. I'm pretty lost in the kitchen. And if it isn't too much to ask, I was wondering if you could maybe bring a dish or two. Mrs. Ayers has most of the stuff at her house, still frozen."

Mattie Lou's mind began racing at the possibilities. She thought of all the food that was filling her refrigerator. "Not to worry," she told Father Patrick. "I've got sweet potato casserole, corn pudding, green beans, and even a couple pies I can bring."

"That's too generous," he protested.

"Not at all," she replied. "Believe me, I have plenty to spare." Then she asked, "What about meat? What are you planning to serve?"

Father Patrick sheepishly responded, "I'm afraid we're in bad shape. I have a turkey, but it won't be enough to go around."

"I've got just the answer. How does meatloaf sound to you?" asked Mattie Lou. "I have plenty of ground beef."

"Sounds great," said Father Patrick.

Taking charge of the conversation and the meal, Mattie Lou then said, "Meet me in the morning at 7:00 at the church. It will be a Christmas feast to remember."

Father Patrick couldn't believe his eyes when he got to the church. Mattie Lou had been there long before he arrived. There were linen tablecloths on the long fellowship hall tables. There was Christmas china at each place setting. The tables were decorated with beautiful garland and candles. A Christmas tree had even appeared, fully decorated, in the corner. And the smells coming from the kitchen were out of this world. Mattie Lou was in the kitchen finishing the meatloaf. Her apron was covered in flour, and her hair was falling out of its bow. She had on a beautiful sweater and wool skirt. "Merry Christmas, Father," she called.

"Merry Christmas, Mattie Lou," he said with utter amazement.

Around noon the orphans of Christmas started to gather. The Peacock sisters drove over from the nursing home. Linton, the church yardman, came shuffling in. A couple poor families showed up with their children. Two members of the youth group dropped by. An odd assortment of single adults and senior adults also gathered. All told, about eighteen people had come for the free lunch. Father Patrick read from Luke 2. One of the Peacock sisters banged out a couple Christmas carols on the piano. Mattie Lou was called upon to offer the blessing. She simply thanked God for the joy of being loved and needed. She thanked God for the richness they all possessed in Christ. And she also thanked God for the Christmas feast they were all about to enjoy.

When Jim finally got home around 4:30 p.m., he found Mattie Lou asleep in the recliner. He noticed a huge pile of dirty dishes stacked up in the sink waiting to be washed. "Must have been some feast," he thought to himself. "I wonder who came to dinner."

He found a plate covered with foil in the refrigerator with a note that read, "Glad you're home; hope you enjoy the leftover meatloaf."

"Who cooks meatloaf on Christmas?" he thought to himself.

Sometimes the best celebrations are the unexpected ones. And whether you know it or not, you've been invited to the marriage feast of the Lamb. It's a celebration you don't want to miss. I invite you to put on your party dress and come to the feast.

"For unto you is born this day in the city of David, a savior, who is Christ the Lord" (Lk 2:11 KJV).

CHAPTER 19

Secret Santa

Matthew 2:1-12

Jorge Sanchez and his wife, Maria, had three young children: Juan, their only son, who was ten years old and in the fourth grade; Elena, a six-year-old first-grader; and Rosita, who had just turned four. They had immigrated to the United States three years earlier from Juarez, Mexico, with the help of family, in order to give the children the opportunity for a better life. The moment came for immigration. The proper documents were signed, the politicians paid off, and the family resettled. At first Jorge worked the fields of South Georgia as a migrant worker picking tomatoes. He soon realized that the constant moving of migrant work was too much for his family to endure. Mostly due to a broken-down car, the family chose to settle in the South Georgia town of Sunnyside.

Sunnyside was a small town that knew little of other cultures or races. In fact, aside from a dozen or so African-American families, there were no other ethnicities represented in the community, except for an Irish family whose father was employed at the local supermarket. Suffice it to say that the Sanchez family stuck out in any crowd. They were also mostly avoided. Even though they had been in the community for over three years, they had few friends and very few neighbors. People in the town referred to them as "those people." The older two children were in the local elementary school. They were often teased at school for their clothing and for their lack of English skills. Juan was quickly learning the language, yet there were many things he still didn't understand. He tried to make friends, but found little acceptance. And although his soccer skills were better than most, he didn't even try out for the school team. He knew his parents couldn't afford to buy soccer shoes and pay for uniforms.

The Sanchezes even had trouble finding a place to worship. Both Jorge and Maria had shared a Catholic upbringing. Unfortunately, the small town had few Catholics. The only Catholic church in the area was about thirty minutes away. The family attended special events from time to time but struggled to have the means to go on a weekly basis. They visited several local Protestant churches but never felt very welcomed. The culture was different. The language barrier was a problem. The attitudes toward them were "standoffish" at best. It's not that they were treated rudely; they were just not embraced with open arms. It's funny how in the midst of the Bible Belt, so many failed to live by or even read the Bible. Leviticus 19:33-34 speaks to the deliberate welcome that Christians are to give those who are strangers in the land: "When a stranger resides with you in your land, you shall not do him wrong. The stranger who resides with you shall be to you as the native among you, and you shall love him as yourself; for you were aliens in the land of Egypt."

Jorge found work at a local tire store. He knew how to change tires, replace brake pads, and lube the chassis. He worked extremely hard, putting in a lot of long hours. He seldom took a break for lunch. Sometimes he brought a small paper sack with him, filled with some leftovers from Maria's supper the night before. But even on those days, he paused only a few minutes to eat. He was never late. In fact, he was early each morning. He walked almost three miles from their apartment each morning, rain or shine. Though his clothes were old and frayed in a few places, they were always clean and pressed.

His boss was fair, but he was not the kind of man given to befriending a stranger. He was a local. His family had been in the little town for several generations. He knew everyone and was known by everyone. Though he was a member of the Baptist church, there wasn't a lot of religion in him. He went to the races on Sundays and drank a little on Saturday. Either out of ignorance or intolerance, or maybe both, he never bothered to learn Jorge's name. He called him "Taco" and would joke about "Mrs. Taco and the three little burritos." At least he paid Jorge a decent wage and sometimes gave him a ride home in his pick-up when the weather was stormy or cold.

The month of December was a busy one at the elementary school. There were Christmas pageants and parties and school programs. In Elena's class the students made Christmas lists for Santa. They were told to put five things on the list that they wanted to have for Christmas. The lists were laminated, glued to construction paper, and posted around the room. It was fun seeing the lists along the walls. Most of the children had some really big wishes. Elena was a little more realistic. She did ask for a Barbie doll and for some new shoes, as well as a few other gifts. At the end of school, just before the break, the students were allowed to take their lists home. Elena told her brother and sister about the lists they had made, and the three of them decided they should make a list at home for Santa, with each child adding a few things to the page.

For several days they scanned the junk mail that came to the house and looked at the flyers that came in the paper. They listed big things and small things, wonderful things, expensive things, impossible things. Their mother tried to reign in their zeal. "Santa cannot bring you all of those things! He must give to many children. You must not ask for so much." In her mind she knew that each child would be lucky to get just one gift.

Little Rosita, who had no concept of money and its value, would protest, "But, Momma, Santa doesn't need any money. He makes all the toys himself! He will make our wishes come true."

Money was always tight around the Sanchez house. Maria worked a few days each week cleaning houses for others. But even after combining her money with Jorge's, they barely had enough to pay the rent and put a few groceries on the table. Their apartment was small, with only two bedrooms and one bathroom. Jorge and Maria slept in one bedroom, and the two girls shared the other. Juan slept on an old sofa in the large living area. The sofa had been purchased at a yard sale, along with a few other pieces of furniture. Most of it was in bad shape, but Maria worked hard making it look as nice as she could. The small kitchen was sparse but very clean. The pipes rattled, and the refrigerator hummed a bit too loudly, but at least the Sanchez family had a roof over their heads.

Maria was trying very hard to learn English in order to help her children understand the language. On the days she cleaned houses, she would turn on the television and listen as she worked, trying to learn phrases and words. She encouraged her children to speak as much English as possible around the house. She would use as many words as she knew to use. However, when she lost her patience or became angry, suddenly she would resort to a bunch of quickly spoken words entirely in Spanish. If Momma was speaking only in Spanish, her children knew she was angry.

About three blocks down from the Sanchez apartment was the entrance to a rather nice subdivision called Pine Forest. The third house down on the left was a well-kept, two-story brick house owned by Mr. Ben

Powell. Ben lived alone in the big house with a six-year-old pug, Stumpy, that he had inherited from his daughter. Ben had retired about seven years earlier, at the age of sixty-five, from a local factory that produced and shipped small, single-serve pecan pies all over the Southeast. Ben had worked at the plant for years. At first he ran one of the packaging lines but later moved into more "white collar" work as a personnel supervisor. He worked his way up the organization until he became the assistant plant manager. He could have worked until he was seventy, but he chose early retirement so he and his wife could spend their "golden years" seeing the world. They had plans to travel to faraway places. Most of those plans were never realized, however, because Ben's wife died within a year of his retirement. She had long battled blood pressure problems, really for most of her adult life. While shopping one day at the local grocery store, she suddenly collapsed to the floor, the victim of a sudden and massive heart attack. The paramedics arrived on the scene quickly, but there was nothing they could do.

Ben had to adjust to life on his own. He learned to cook a few things. He could microwave frozen dinners and bake a few pizzas. He also figured out how to use the washer and dryer, although he continued to send his dress shirts to the cleaners to be pressed. Mostly, he took his meals at the local diner on the corner of 4th and Main. He and Stumpy would walk to the diner every morning, where he would drink a cup or two of coffee, eat a Danish, and read the paper. Stumpy was known to all the usual patrons and accepted as one of the regulars. He would sit at Ben's feet and never make a sound. Margaret, the diner's morning waitress, felt sorry for the two of them, and she developed a habit of cooking a fried egg and a piece of bacon for Stumpy. She would set it at his feet, and he would lick her hand in gratitude.

Ben and his wife had raised a daughter named Kathy. Kathy was grown and married with kids of her own. She and her husband lived in Birmingham with their two children, Jake and Angie. Ben made the five-hour drive several times throughout the year. He attended t-ball games, soccer matches, and kindergarten graduations. And, of course, he would make the trek during the holidays to spend a few days after Christmas with the kids. Some years, they came to his house; this year, however, was different. Kathy's husband worked at a steel company that had enjoyed a successful year. He had received quite a bonus—a family ski trip to Colorado. They were to leave the day after Christmas and return a week later. Kathy had called her father to describe how hectic things would be prior to Christmas. Between all the school stuff and church stuff, it would be hard to plan time for a visit. It was decided that Ben would go to Birmingham sometime in late January, after the mad pace of the holidays settled down. Worried that her dad would be all alone on Christmas, Kathy made a point of calling some of his close friends around town just to let them know. Several, in fact, had already called, inviting him to spend Christmas Day with their families. He told them that he would have to think about it but that he would call soon.

Ben tried to keep the family Christmas traditions alive and well in his home. When his wife was alive, she decorated every room with garland, wreaths, and candles. She would also set out four or five nativity sets, along with a miniature snow village that she always placed in the big bay window on the front of the house. The first few years following her death, he tried to do a lot, but the memories were painful. He gradually pulled back on most of it. He still put a wreath on the door and continued to place the snow village in the bay window. He also put a red and green bow on Stumpy's collar, but that was about it. Especially this year; it seemed pointless. No one was coming, so why bother? He would set it all up just to take it all down again in a few weeks.

Ben and his wife used to shop for his daughter and the grandkids. He would complain his way up and down the mall, but on the inside he loved doing it. He didn't mind the crowds or the congestion. He liked the activity of it all—the people, the sounds, the carols playing on the radio. He missed it—he really did—and he struggled to know what to buy. Kathy was good about offering suggestions of what to get, where to buy, and what color would be popular. This year, because of the ski trip, he was really in a quandary over what to buy. Kathy sent him a catalogue with certain pages well marked. She attached a list to the front cover with every product number, the sizes, and the colors. She even wrote down the phone number. All he had to do was make one call, which he did. His entire Christmas shopping was completed in one afternoon from his kitchen table. It was shipped directly to Kathy's house, wrapped and ready to go. No trip to the mall, no crowds, no gifts to wrap, no stress, and no fun. He had told Kathy that he was "delighted" with her suggestion about gift buying, for making it all so easy, but on the inside he felt as though some of his joy had been stolen and that he had been robbed of getting out and mingling among the people of his town.

It was about ten days before Christmas when Ben noticed one evening that a bulb had burned out in one of the snow village houses. The next morning, he ventured out to get a replacement bulb, along with a few other things that he needed around the house. It dawned on him as he drove that it was Saturday, one of the two remaining before Christmas. The parking lot was full. He drove around for over thirty minutes to find a place. The crowds were intolerable. The lines were long, and the shopping carts were scarce. There were short-tempered people everywhere. Ben was greeted at the door by the ringing of the Salvation Army bell and by an old friend who was employed as a part-time greeter. Once inside, he was sucked into the vortex of crazy shoppers, whining kids, and falling prices. He found the needed bulbs, picked up some toiletries, and even placed a red velvet cake in his cart. Just for the heck of it, he ventured into the children's department, just to get a taste of kids and Christmas. He was glad to see toy cars were still being sold and that bikes and board games were not totally eclipsed by all the new electronic gadgets.

He rounded the end of the aisle when he heard the angry voice of what sounded like an exasperated mother with several tired, weary, and disappointed kids. He peered around to catch a glimpse of Maria Sanchez and her three children. Though he had never met her, he recognized her. He and Stumpy walked by her apartment every morning on their way to the diner. They had never spoken but had exchanged a wave or a nod. She was obviously upset. She was speaking Spanish. Ben was not a Spanish scholar, so he couldn't make out all that she was saying, but he knew enough to know that she was not happy! "Dame esa lista!" she shouted. "No hay ningun dinero!" Something about a list and money—that was all he could gather. He saw her snatch a piece of paper from her daughter's hand, wad it up, and throw it on the floor. She stomped off, dragging both girls, leaving one little shell-shocked boy standing in the aisle.

Ben approached the boy softly. "Excuse me, son. Is something wrong?"

In broken English Juan replied, "My momma is very upset. There is no money for presents." Juan then turned and ran to catch up with her. Ben walked over and picked up the crumpled piece of paper. In a child's handwriting was written a Christmas wish list. The three names were written, Juan, Elena, and Rosita, and beside each name were their Christmas wishes. Juan wanted a videogame system. Elena wanted a toy pony. Rosita wanted a Barbie.

Ben took the list, folded it, and put it in his pocket. At the checkout he showed the list to one of the clerks. "That's quite a list," he said, "expensive and hard to find. We haven't had some of those things in weeks. Good luck finding your grandkids those presents."

"They're not my grandkids," Ben said instinctively. He paused before continuing, "What I mean to say is that these are not the *only* things my grandkids are hoping to get; this is just part of the list." He didn't know why he felt like he needed to offer any explanation or excuse. But suddenly a thought washed over him: "Why not consider them as my grandkids? They live in my neighborhood. They are a part of my town. They surely want these things, but can't afford them, and I've got money. I was going to make a donation to the Salvation Army anyway, so why not give some children a real Christmas surprise?" The very thought energized him like a new pacemaker battery! He was giddy by the time he walked to his car. His mind was racing. His spirit was soaring. It was as if the act of gift giving chased away all of his Christmas sadness.

As soon as he got to the house, he immediately called his daughter and asked for her opinion. He didn't tell her all that he was up to, but simply said that he was helping his Sunday school class with a project. He wanted a list of good gifts for two small girls and a young boy. He also called a local teacher he knew and asked the same questions. By suppertime he had a list that would make any child excited on Christmas morn. On Sunday afternoon he began his assault on the list. The clerk was right; some of the things were extremely hard to find. He spent the whole next week on a mission, like a knight on a noble quest. He shopped, he bought, he wrapped, he ordered. He even drove all the way to Atlanta to buy the game console that a store had agreed to hold for him. He loved moving among the crowds. He whistled with the music. He ate junk food and bought Christmas candy. He even had his picture made with Santa at the mall!

Christmas Eve finally arrived. He had everything ready for the big night. He had arranged for a friend to invite the Sanchez family to attend a Christmas Eve service. They were stunned and excited to be included. They were picked up at 5:30 p.m. from their apartment for the 6:00 p.m. service. At precisely 5:45 p.m., Ben and Stumpy began making their way down the street with a wheelbarrow full of presents. When they got to the house, Ben quickly began his work, with Stumpy carefully guarding the premises. Ben took the presents and carefully arranged them on the front porch. Each gift had been labeled. He then began stringing lights all around the porch and ran the extension cord around the side of the house. He took duct tape and placed a huge sign across the front of the apartment, which he unrolled from a cardboard tube. He had it made by a local print shop. It read, "Feliz Navidad."

His friend called his cell phone to tell him the Sanchezes were on the way home from church. Ben hid the wheelbarrow in some tall bushes and grabbed Stumpy. They hid on the side of the apartment behind a trashcan. The car arrived. His friend let them off right on cue and drove away. As they neared the porch, Ben plugged in the extension cord. The porch exploded with light. Suddenly, the Sanchez family saw the sign, the presents, and the labels with their names! The kids screamed with delight, and the parents just stood there with eyes and mouths wide open. Lots of questions, but no answers. Just wonder, amazement, and joy.

Ben and Stumpy watched the family through a window as they began opening all the presents. Tears ran down Ben's face as he watched the joy and excitement the gifts had brought. He didn't know who had the better Christmas—the ones receiving the gifts or the one who had given them.

There are two things that I hope and pray we will never forget about Christmas. First, I hope we will realize, again and again, the sheer surprise of it all. Why God would send his only Son to earth is so swirled in mystery and wonder and love that it's hard to comprehend. It's not anything that humanity would have ever expected or deserved. One morning, a precious baby just appeared on the world's doorstep, and the planet has never been the same. What a great surprise. What a great gift.

I also hope we will never forget the joy of the Giver. Because of love, God offered his Son. Wrapped up in the swaddling clothes of human flesh, God presented him to us. How he must have watched over us with such joy as he saw his precious children open the greatest gift they could ever receive. Mary's boy was indeed heaven's joy. How much the Father must love Christmas. How much he must love *us*.

CHAPTER 20

Homeless for Christmas

1 John 3:17

"But whoever has the world's goods, and beholds his brother in need and closes his heart against him, how does the love of God abide in him?"—1 John 3:17

Steve Wilson didn't grow up homeless or even poor. It just sort of happened that day. Steve grew up in the Deep South, not far from Jackson, Mississippi. His father had been killed in a car wreck when Steve was just a kid. His mother, who possessed a lot of spunk and determination, had carried off the task of being a single parent very well. She worked full time managing a department store and was good at keeping up with the family finances. She saw to it that her son had everything he needed and many of the things he wanted. She made sure he was active in the youth group at church, and she insisted that he continue in scouting, which he did, eventually earning the rank of Eagle Scout. He did well in school with his grades and was never in much trouble with any of his teachers. He graduated among the top in his class and headed off to Mississippi State to study horticulture. He had dreams of working in the landscaping business that suited his love of working outdoors. In fact, while in high school, he had worked part time for a landscaping business and had always enjoyed the tasks of planting, pruning, and planning the arrangement of various gardens and yard treatments.

His college career was rather uneventful. He pledged a fraternity, dated several girls, went to the home football games, and worked hard at his studies. Most of his summers were spent back at home, living with his mom and working summer jobs. It was in the spring of his junior year that everything about his life changed with a single phone call. A neighbor of his mother called to tell him that his mother had just been taken to the hospital by ambulance, the victim of a massive stroke. By the time he arrived in Jackson, she was struggling in intensive care. For two days he kept a constant vigil by her bed, joined by dozens of friends, church members, and neighbors. The doctors had not been optimistic. Key indicators offered little hope. On March 17 at 11:27 a.m., she was gone. Steve found himself twenty-one and orphaned.

With the help of some distant kin, neighbors, and friends, Steve made his way through the funeral and back to school. His professors were told of the situation, and they were very helpful in providing him the necessary time to catch up with his studies. The following summer was hard. Steve chose not to return to the empty house in Jackson but kept his student apartment in Starkville and attended summer school. By the end of the summer, it had become increasingly difficult for Steve to keep up the house and pay the utilities. Under the advice of several long-time banking friends, the decision was made to sell the house and place the money in various accounts to ensure that Steve could continue his education and draw out money for living expenses, books, etc. The house sold forty-two days later, and all of his family's worldly possessions were placed in a self-storage unit for safe keeping.

During his senior year, Steve faced many struggles, especially the holidays, but he seemed to weather it well with the help of fraternity brothers and school counselors. He graduated with honors in the spring and began working full time with a local landscaping company. Days turned into weeks, then months, then years. Fueled by an entrepreneurial spirit, Steve soon began thinking of starting his own business. He had dreamed of it on many occasions. He would call the company "Steve's Trees," and he would specialize in patios, ornamental gardens, and general yard maintenance and irrigation. A lot of capital was needed to get the new business off the ground. Steve reached deeply into the remainder of his savings accounts and risked it all on his new endeavor.

Within months the business was off and running. First, a few mowers, some weed eaters, and yard tools, along with a truck and trailer, comprised the whole enterprise. Next came the hiring of a few workers and another couple vehicles. Steve developed a logo, which he put on his equipment, and even invested in local ads. He did well. "Steve's Trees" was known throughout the city. His client base grew rapidly, and with his attention to detail and good service, he stayed very busy. He took risks, and he got into debt, but he always returned to his mantra: "It takes money to make money." By the time he reached his early thirties, the business seemed stable, the economy good, and his personal life was looking up. All who knew Steve felt that his life was headed in a positive direction. He bought a house, he owned a dog, and he enjoyed his hobbies, which included season tickets for Mississippi State football games and vacations at the beach.

It all fell apart a few years ago when one small event let to several catastrophic events. One of his work crews was working in an upscale neighborhood on the east side of Jackson. It seems that one of his men inadvertently forgot to set the parking brake on the truck while unloading a large mower. When the weight shifted on the trailer, suddenly the truck lurched forward, rolled down the steep driveway, across the front yard, and crashed into the front of the home. With the impact of the crash, a gas line ruptured under the house, quickly filling the house with explosive gas. When the gas hit the pilot light on the stove, the entire home exploded in a terrific fireball. The workers ran in all directions. Alarms sounded, and flames started to leap through the roof. In just a matter of seconds, the house was fully engulfed in flames. Two different fire stations responded to the call, to no avail. The multimillion-dollar mansion burned to the ground.

By the grace of God, no one had been at home when the fire occurred. And although there was no loss of life, the loss of property, furnishings, and family heirlooms was enormous. It took only a few days for the lawyers to get involved. Steve Wilson was called to task on a number of things. The depositions were unmerciful: "Did you keep adequate maintenance records on your vehicles, and when was the last time the truck in question was inspected? Did you provide training, and have you given proper supervision to those operating said vehicle? Did you know that the driver is an illegal alien in our country and did not have proper documentation at the time of his employment?" On and on it went. It was clear that the family and its lawyers were out for blood.

Steve quickly discovered that the liability insurance he had purchased was woefully inadequate. He also discovered that the attorney fees and court costs were going to take nearly every penny he possessed. When the case finally went before the judge, a huge award was given to the plaintiffs. The bank foreclosed on Steve's home. The cars and trucks were repossessed and sold at an auction. Even the family furniture was sold on the courthouse lawn. At the age of thirty-six, Steve found himself once again orphaned by his world. There was no house, no money, no family, and no hope for a bright future. He was left with his long-haired Chihuahua, Chester, and one worn-out utility van that had mistakenly been left off the reporting of any possessions. He quickly painted over the "Steve's Trees" logo on the side.

The old van became both a work truck and a shelter. Steve made the rounds with his old clients. Many were sympathetic to his plight, but without equipment what could he really do? Because of the foreclosures, the banks wouldn't even talk to him about a loan. He even leaned on the generosity of friends, but that wore thin. It didn't take long for the realities of homelessness to set in. Staying clean and staying fed became daily challenges. Although the van provided some relatively safe shelter from the elements, it was burning hot on late summer nights and freezing cold once late fall turned into winter. What little money Steve could earn from odd jobs, he spent on gas and meager amounts of food. Chester was his constant companion and only friend. It was stunning to Steve how quickly friendships dissipate in the face of need. Having Chester was both a blessing and a curse. The dog was good company, a faithful and loyal companion. But Steve was unable to take Chester with him into a shelter for the night. He had tried once, but when Chester started barking in the middle of the night. Steve was told, "Get rid of the dog, and you can stay here." That just wasn't an option.

When he did go to a soup kitchen, or when he could scrape up enough for a warm meal, Steve always hid food in his pockets for Chester. Chester seemed to know that times were hard, and he would always wag his tail and lick Steve's hands to show his gratitude at even the smallest morsel. As time went along, Steve noticed that Chester seemed to get a little more "scroungy" each day. He could only imagine how bad he must have looked. One real challenge was that of parking the van. More than a few times had Steve been awakened by a police officer in the middle of the night, telling him to move along. And so there began a constant moving around town from night to night. It was hard to find a safe spot; it was even harder to find a place to shower or wash his clothes on a regular basis. Steve found himself praying the simple prayers of the homeless—that the nights would be warm, the weather dry, and the gift of good food prevalent.

There were a few places that Steve tended to frequent when he was not out seeking employment. Several local soup kitchens and shelters knew him well. He found that if he disciplined himself, he could usually make one meal stretch into at least two for himself and Chester. Most of the people at the soup kitchen were nice and seemed friendly enough. Some even talked to Steve like he was a person of worth and dignity. Steve appreciated those who regularly gave their time. But as the holidays grew near, Steve found himself a little resentful of some of the volunteers he encountered. He could tell that some of them were wealthy folks who would do a little benevolent work one day a year to piously pat themselves on the back. Some even took pictures of themselves as though helping the homeless was nothing more than a good photo op. It was as if by volunteering to work with the poor and the down-and-out for a few hours, they could soothe their conscience as they flew off to some Colorado resort to spend insane amounts of money.

Christmas Eve began with a cold, damp morning. The clouds were gray and threatening. Steve knew the day would be difficult. He tried not to think of how his life used to be. He tried not to think about his home or his once successful business and how differently he had spent Christmas Eves when days were better. But still the thoughts would come. He remembered collecting food for the needy. He remembered putting money in the Salvation Army bucket. He thought of the friends for whom he used to shop and spend lavishly. He even thought about those teenage years when his mom used to bake, decorate, and drag him off to church. His eyes grew misty more than once, and little Chester would stare at him and cock his head over to one side, the way only a dog can do.

The large shelter downtown had planned a big turkey and dressing meal for the homeless. When Steve arrived shortly after noon, the place was overflowing with folks just like himself, folks glad for the great meal but who longed to be any place else. Late in the afternoon, Steve took Chester for a long walk. The two of them walked past a number of brightly decorated shops and stopped several times to admire the lights of a tree or storefront window. It was well past 4:00, and darkness had begun to settle in when they returned to the van. Steve fired up the engine to warm it up a little. He turned on a radio station and listened to Christmas songs until both he and Chester drifted off into a light sleep.

They were both startled into consciousness by a sharp tap on the driver's window. Chester went berserk and started barking loudly. Steve instinctively reached for an axe handle that he kept down by the driver's seat. When he wiped away the condensation on the window, he was surprised to discover that it was neither a policeman nor an angry storeowner telling him to get off the property. Instead, it was a well-dressed gentleman in a cap, a chauffeur who had just emerged from a huge black limo.

"Are you Steve Wilson?" shouted the driver.

"Who wants to know?" was the quick response.

"That's not important. Are you Steve or not?"

Steve could not imagine who would have known his name or where to find him. "I'm Steve. What do you want?" he said gruffly.

"I've been told to bring you with me and to also bring your dog."

"Bring me with you? Bring me where? Who knows about me and my dog?"

"Look, buddy, I'm just the middle man. I got a call telling me to bring you to a certain address. That's it. That's all I know. Are you coming or not?"

Steve sat behind the wheel of his van in a perplexed swirl of thought. Who? What? And why? His time on the street had taught him to be a little skeptical. He rolled down the window just enough to get a little better look. Then he said, "I am not getting in the car with you, but I will follow you." "That way," he thought to himself, "at least I'll have some protection."

They drove for about twenty minutes to a part of town in which Steve had not been for quite a while. It was upscale, with wide streets, beautiful lawns, and big houses. Every house was gloriously decorated. The limo finally pulled into the circular drive at 113 Concord Lane. As soon as he turned off the motor, a short little gray-haired woman came bounding out of the house. She looked to be in her early eighties but was still spry as she quickly negotiated the steps from the porch to the driveway. "Well, come along quickly now, Mr. Wilson! And bring your dog. There is not much time to get ready." She turned and walked back into the house, confident that Steve and Chester would follow.

Steve looked at the limo driver, who just shrugged his shoulders, as if to say, "I don't have a clue."

"Come on! Come on!" she shouted as Steve, with Chester in his arms, walked up to the front door. In the light, something about the lady seemed familiar. He recognized the face, but from where? "There's no time to explain it all now," she said. "We'll be late for church." She told Steve to go up the stairs and take the first door on the left. "There are towels and washcloths and anything you might need. You will also find a suit of clothes lying across the bed. Leave your dog with me; he'll be fine." Chester gave Steve another one of those crooked dog looks. She took Chester in her arms and walked hurriedly toward the back of the house. "Now, go, and be snappy!"

All he could get out in response was a quiet "Yes, ma'am."

It was the best shower he had known in weeks. The soap was fragrant, the shampoo was soothing, and the razor for his face was sharp. And the towels—he had forgotten such softness. By the time he had dressed and made his way to the bottom of the stairs, there she stood, purse on her arm, gloves on her hands, and Chester at her feet. At least it looked sort of like Chester. He had been shampooed and dried and even had on a new collar with a red and green bow. "You look positively dashing," she said. "Now grab the dog, and let's get to church." They walked out to the driveway and got into a luxurious late-model Cadillac. She drove, of course.

"Ma'am, I don't even know your name. Who are you, and what is all of this about, anyway?"

"It's about Christmas," she said. "I've decided to put my faith into action." That was really about all she said on the way to church. The three of them—the lady, Steve, and Chester—sat on a pew near the back of the church.

"Won't they get mad about a dog in church?" whispered Steve.

"They won't get mad at me." she explained, "Who do you think paid for the new carpet and the new steps out front!" She winked and shot Steve a slight grin.

The service was short and simple. Some children acted out the manger scene. The pastor offered a brief meditation. Communion was offered, and the service ended with a rousing rendition of "Silent Night, Holy Night." As they walked back to the car, it finally hit Steve how he knew her. "You're one of the ladies from the soup kitchen, aren't you? You are one of the regular volunteers!"

"Yes," she replied, "and you are also one of the regulars. I've been watching you for a long time. I kinda figured that you needed me and that I needed you." She went on to explain how she was starting to have a little trouble keeping up with the yard and shrubs since her husband died a few years back. "I miss having someone around the house. I need to have some-one to care for, and I figured you and Chester could use a little help. I've asked around, and I know all about your lawsuit and family and everything."

Steve was stunned. "You want me to work in your yard? Is that what this is all about?"

"It's more than that, young man. I want you to come and stay in my house. Lord knows I've got more than enough room. I want you to have a decent place to live and to have people in your life who will care for you. I want to see you get on your feet again. I just figured I could help make that happen."

"Let me get this straight. You want me and my dog to come and live in your house? You want to help me get back on my feet? Why would you do such a thing? We're strangers."

She simply answered, "Because I believe in you. I know that you are better than your surroundings and situation allow you to be." As he sat in stunned silence, a carol played on the radio. The words penetrated his heart and mind like never before: "How silently, how silently, the wondrous gift is given! So God imparts to human hearts the blessings of his heaven. No ear may hear his coming, but in this world of sin, where meek souls will receive him still, the dear Christ enters in."

His thoughts were interrupted by her feisty little voice. "So what about it? Is it a deal?"

"Sure," he said. "A guy would be crazy not to accept such an invitation."

On that first Christmas Eve, Holy God offered hurting humanity an invitation to enjoy a whole new life. We were strangers, separated from God. We lived with no hope, no promise, and no future. And yet the child of Christmas came, and new life was offered. Paul said, "While we were yet sinners, Christ died for us" (Rom 5:8). Why would Holy God do such a thing? Because he believes in us. He knows that we are better than our surroundings and situations allow us to be. We are invited to new life in Christ. So what about it? Is it a deal or not?

CHAPTER 21

Sarah Henderson: A Broken Child

Luke 2:8-20

The figures for the nativity set had been in the family for four generations. Sarah's great-grandfather had brought them back from the war in France, where he had bought them in a little shop in Paris, about two blocks from the great cathedral of Notre Dame. At least, that's the way the family legend told the story. When purchased, the storeowner had carefully wrapped each piece in newspaper and placed them in a small wooden box to protect them for the trip to America. Her great-grandfather had carefully nurtured them all the way home, first on a train, then on a ship, and then another train. He successfully brought the treasure home without a single mishap or broken piece. When Sarah and her mother unwrapped them for use, they were still as vibrant with color as they had been over eighty Christmases earlier.

Each piece was made of porcelain, each handcrafted and painted, signed on the bottom by the artist. There were eight figures in all, with a cow and two lambs making up the complete set. The set contained figurines of the baby Jesus in the manger, with Mary, Joseph, three wise men, and two shepherds. For eleven months of the year, they remained stored in the same little wooden box that had brought them home from France. Someone in the family through the years had lined the box with a soft purple fabric. Pieces of the newspaper that had once wrapped each figurine had been shellacked to the bottom of the lid. One small scrap contained a date, February 19, 1918. Another scrap bore the name of the daily paper, *Le Parisian*. Sarah's

grandmother had made little cloth bags that gathered at the top with a draw-
string to hold each piece. The bags were made of a soft golden cloth. Her
grandmother always thought the color went so well with the purple lining.

The stable had been a later addition. Sarah's father remembered when
his dad had crafted it in his woodworking shop behind the old family farm-
house. It stood about two feet tall and contained a little fence that enclosed
an animal's stall, and it had a little ladder that led to a loft above where a care-
taker might sleep. The front was opened so that each figurine could be easily
seen. Unlike the figurines, it had not stood the test of time quite as well, so it
had been reworked a few times during the years. Still, when set in place, the
whole scene was gorgeous.

The nativity set was always placed on the middle of the dining room
table. For most of the year, a silver tea service sat in its place, but for the
month of December, the silver service was upstaged by the beautiful set.
With a crimson cloth beneath it, the set dominated the entire room. Sarah's
mother even hung a golden star from the chandelier above it. Setting it in
place was always the first order of business as the decorating of the house
began each year. This year marked a special occasion, at least in the mind of
six-year-old Sarah. This was to be the first year that Sarah would be named
the keeper of the manger scene, a Henderson family tradition. This would be
the first year that she would get to set up the scene, deciding for herself the
exact position of each piece.

Sarah Henderson was a radiant young girl with curly red hair and
blue eyes. She looked as though she had stepped out of a Norman Rockwell
painting. She was polite and kind, always well dressed by her mother. She was
halfway through her first-grade year, with Mrs. Warren as her teacher, and
she was doing very well. She had approached the season with great anticipation. Hardly a day had passed since last Christmas that she did not think
about the manger scene and the promise made by her mother that this year
would be her year to finally get to help with the set.

The Hendersons lived in a huge Victorian house in the middle of the
historic section of town. It was built in the mid-1800s and had gone through
several renovations. Though very old, the house had never looked better. A
recent coat of paint, along with a newly poured front sidewalk, made it one
of the most attractive homes in the area. The Hendersons had taken a lot of
pride in doing much of the renovation work themselves. They had lived in
the house for a dozen years and had continued with at least one new project
each year.

Harry Henderson, Sarah's father, was in the banking business. He had made vice president by the age of thirty, and now that he was in his early forties, he was a sure lock for the president's office when Mr. Hamilton would one day retire. Harry was well respected and well known throughout the community. In addition to being very involved in the local Baptist church, he was also on the board of the local YMCA and was a member of the Rotary Club. He did a lot to give the bank a good name in the community. He established a scholarship fund that helped make college a little more affordable for many of the local kids. He was also a patron of the local sports teams. A sign hung on the left-field fence each baseball season, advertising the hometown bank. His wife, Kathy, Sarah's mother, was a stay-at-home mom who served on the local PTO board and was a teacher in the fourth-grade Sunday school class at church.

Decorating the house for Christmas began the weekend after Thanksgiving. As always, the nativity set was the first item to be addressed. Harry had climbed to the attic to get the wooden stable. The little box that contained the figurines was kept in the hall closet, just off the front foyer, near the grandfather clock. The dining room table was quickly cleared. The silver service was placed on the sideboard, near the big red poinsettia, an annual gift from Mr. Hamilton. The crimson cloth was spread across the table, and the miniature stable was softly placed upon it. The wooden box was finally opened. The purple cloth and the golden bags made Sarah think that a wonderful treasure chest was being opened once again.

One by one, her mother carefully unwrapped each piece. She smiled as she held each one, remembering previous Christmases. She could not help but notice how brilliant the colors seemed to always be, how perfectly unchanged the whole scene seemed to stay, year after year. As each piece was unwrapped, she carefully handed it to Sarah, who cradled it in her hands with the greatest of care. Then, after a moment of reflection, she would place the figurines in just the right place—Joseph first, then Mary, then the wise men and shepherds and all of the animals. She placed the baby Jesus over to the side until all the others were in the right spots. Then, and only then, did she carefully arrange the porcelain manger with the Christ child in it. She stepped back in order to take it all in for a moment. "Look, Mother," she said. "It's perfect. Everything is in its place."

"You have done a wonderful job, Sarah," said her mother. "Your grandfather will be so proud of you when he comes for Christmas."

That year, the first-grade class presented a Christmas play just before the holiday break. Sarah had been given the part of an angel. She and seven others were to make up the heavenly chorus. Her mother, along with several others, had made all the angel costumes. Each child would wear a white robe with wings sewn onto the back. A gold belt would be worn around the waist, and a golden halo would sit on each head. Sarah had rehearsed her lines a thousand times: "Glory to God in the highest, and on earth peace, goodwill toward men." On the second day of play practice, Sarah raised her hand to offer a little help to Mrs. Warren, her teacher. "Mrs. Warren, the shepherds are standing in the wrong place. They are supposed to be standing on the right side of the manger."

"And how do you know this, Sarah?" asked Mrs. Warren.

"That's what my daddy told me," she said. "He should know; he's a deacon at the Baptist church."

Mrs. Warren responded, "Well, I'm a Presbyterian, and we do things a little differently at our church. Thank you for your help, but I think we will let the shepherds stand right where they are."

"Yes, ma'am."

Each afternoon, as Sarah arrived home from school, she would run to the dining room to check the nativity set. After all, it was her job this year. She would carefully eye each piece, pausing to make a small adjustment here and there. She would sometimes look at the shepherds and think, "Poor old Mrs. Warren; she just doesn't know."

Sarah's mother loved to decorate with candles. There were several in the dining room. Sarah would beg her mother to light them at night when it was dark outside. She would then turn out all the lights and stare at the manger scene. She loved the way it looked when it was illumined just by the candles. She would often think about the Christmas story, retracing each part in her mind. She loved to play the part of the angel and sing to the shepherds, "Glory to God in the highest, and on earth peace, goodwill toward men."

Christmas Eve was always a special time at the Henderson house. The bank always closed at noon, so Harry would rush home from work to be with his family. Granddaddy Ed would always arrive in the late afternoon. Sarah's mother would spend much of the afternoon putting together the various dishes and desserts for the next day's dinner. Harry's contribution was the cooking of the turkey, a task he greatly enjoyed and one in which he took great pride. He would season and stuff it on Christmas Eve with his own special recipe. He would cook the bird as part of his Christmas morning routine. The family would always attend the Christmas Eve service at church. Sarah loved the service each year. She especially enjoyed the candle-lighting part of the service. This year would also be her first year to hold a candle. The service was a wonderful celebration of the season, with lots of beautiful music and warm hugs from many friends. After the service the Hendersons stopped over at the Woods' home. This, too, was a Christmas tradition. Each year, the families would get together for a chili and grilled cheese supper.

It was close to 9:00 p.m. by the time they arrived at home. Sarah's mother disappeared to the bedroom to finish wrapping a few presents. Sarah joined her father in the den to help with the wrapping of her mother's presents. After the gifts were placed under the tree and snacks left out for Santa's reindeer, Sarah was sent off to bed. Before retiring for the night, she went to the dining room to take one last glance at the nativity scene. She again watched by candlelight and only left for bed at her father's insistence.

Like a lot of little girls, Sarah had trouble falling asleep on Christmas Eve. A thousand different thoughts raced through her head. She thought of all the wonderful presents she had seen under the tree and wondered what surprises would await her the next morning. Her mother stopped by her room to kiss her goodnight and put on a Christmas CD of soft music to help Sarah go to sleep.

The house was soon quiet, and Sarah heard the grandfather clock chime the hour. She counted to eleven. "It will soon be Christmas!" she thought to herself. She thought again about the manger scene on the dining room table below. She wondered if it was okay. She quietly got out of bed and slipped on her pink bunny slippers. Walking on her tiptoes, she soon reached the stairs and made her way down to the foyer and then into the dining room. There it sat in all its glory. Only a lamp in the living room was on, giving her just enough light to take it all in. She took a moment to adjust several of the characters to ensure that they were in just the right spot.

She then picked up the baby Jesus figurine. She held it in her hands and examined it closely. Just then, the grandfather clock, a few feet behind her, chimed the quarter-hour. The sudden noise in the midst of the quiet night startled her. And when it did, the porcelain figure slipped from her hands and fell to the table below. It landed upside down. When Sarah reached to pick it up, she noticed that one of the arms and several pieces of the manger had broken off. The family heirloom that had survived over eighty Christmas seasons was now shattered, and it was her fault. What would her parents think? She would never get to touch it again, she told herself. Tears began to stream down her face. She sat there in the dark dining room, sobbing all to herself. The manger scene, now forever ruined, sat on the table just before her.

Her father had heard the sound of the crash from his bedroom. Thinking that perhaps a burglar had broken into the house, he grabbed the only thing he could find in that moment, the plunger from the hall bathroom. He crept down the dark stairs, plunger held high above his head, waiting to plunge the unsuspecting robber into oblivion.

He heard the sounds of Sarah's crying. "Sarah?" he called. "Is that you?"

"Yes, Daddy," she said.

"What are you doing down here all alone, and why are you crying?"

"Oh, Daddy, I wanted to come down and see the manger scene again, and I was holding baby Jesus, and the clock scared me, and I dropped the baby. Now it's broken, and I know you're mad, and I know I can't touch it anymore." She wept bitterly.

Harry saw the tears in his daughter's eyes and heard the anguish in her voice. He picked her up and held her, stroking her curly red hair and wiping away the tears. "It's okay, Sarah," he said. "It's okay."

"But it's broken, Daddy. Baby Jesus is broken. And it's all my fault."

He studied the pieces for a moment. "I think a little super glue might fix this," he offered.

"No it won't," she protested. "It will never look the same again."

He looked straight into her eyes. "Sarah, I know how you feel. I know what it feels like to break something very valuable."

"How could you know, Daddy? No one has ever broken a piece of the set before. It was perfect until now."

"Sarah, I want you to pick up Joseph and take a very close look at him. Look at his hand."

Sarah slowly picked up the figurine of Joseph. "I don't see anything, Daddy."

"Look closer."

It was then that she saw it for the very first time. There was a small crack around the wrist. Someone had glued the hand back into place.

"I did that, Sarah, when I was about twelve years old. I was throwing a ball in the house, and I hit Joseph and broke his hand off. It scared me to death. Your grandmother found out, and I got in big trouble for throwing a ball in the house, but she helped me glue it back in place. That was a long time ago, but I still remember what it felt like when I broke Joseph's hand."

Harry went into the kitchen and came back with a little tube of super glue. Together, they began to glue each piece back into place. When they finished, it looked perfect; it would be hard to notice that it had ever been broken. He handed it to Sarah to put it back in place.

"Here, Sarah, you put it in the right place. After all, you're the keeper of the nativity set this year."

The clock began to chime midnight. "Listen; it's Christmas, Daddy! Merry Christmas!"

"Merry Christmas, Sarah!"

Sometimes it takes someone who has experienced brokenness to fully understand and appreciate our brokenness. Christmas is all about identity. The Christmas story is a reminder that God loved us enough that he would choose to send his only begotten Son into a broken world. Dressed in the clothes of humanity, Christ experienced our world. He knows what it is like to be broken, to be lonely, to be cold, to be sleepy, to be fearful, to be hungry, to be angry, to grieve, to laugh, to feel betrayed, to know pain, to experience anguish, to know the love of good friends. Christmas reminds us that our God knows what it is like to be us. He identifies with us in each moment of our lives. And because of his love for us, he also knows what it takes to make us whole again when we are broken. It takes the love of our Father, who says, "I know, my Son. I know. I love you. I forgive you. I offer you my peace."

Christmas is all about identity.

"And the Word became flesh and dwelt among us" (Jn 1:14).

CHAPTER 22

The Crunch of Christmas

Matthew 2:7-11

"And they presented him with gifts of gold, frankincense, and myrrh."

Bob Howell and his wife, Carla, had been happily married for a number of years. Having grown up in the Deep South, both had been raised with solid family values, a strong faith, and a dedication to both God and country. Bob and Carla had been blessed with the gift of two daughters, Amanda, who was twelve, and Stephanie, who was ten. They lived on the south side of Birmingham in a well-to-do neighborhood. A quick drive through the streets of the subdivision would reveal that most in the area were doing well. Many of the families had landscape companies to manage the yard, and there were few cars parked in the driveways that were more than two or three years old. Bob and Carla were not "crazy rich," by any stretch of the imagination, but they did live comfortably, with little financial stress. They enjoyed nice vacations every summer and winter, and Bob was a member of a local country club, where he played a round of golf nearly every week. The girls were involved in a number of school activities as well as extracurricular involvements. They took piano lessons and tennis lessons and swam competitively with a local swim club.

Bob had graduated with a business degree from college. With that education joined to a keen mind, he had done well for himself. He was in middle management with a steel fabrication company that supplied steel to construction firms all across the South. Through the years the business had done well, and Bob and his co-workers enjoyed the fruits of their labors. The future seemed bright and the job secure.

When the economy began to stumble and when stock prices began to fall, Bob's company hardly seemed to notice. There were many orders to fill, and prices were holding steady. The business seemed to chug right along. No one was able to see just beyond the horizon at the uncertainties that lay ahead. In fact, it took months for the economic downturn to trickle down to their business. But all across the South, things were slowing down. Companies were not turning the profits they once did. Money for new initiatives and expansion seemed to dry up. Contracts for new buildings, roads, and bridges became few and far between. Construction companies felt it first, then the engineers and the architects, and then the suppliers of materials. It was becoming apparent to those who worked in the top offices of Bob's company that cutbacks and layoffs were coming. The official word from on high was, "We're going to be okay," but unofficially the corridor talk among the executives was rather bleak. Difficult decisions were coming.

It was early on a Monday morning in mid-October that Bob was summoned to the office of the president. He didn't think much about the call. He and the president of the company had been friends for years, and Bob was often in his office to talk about things like manufacturing outputs, worker complaints, and even SEC football. When Bob reached the office, he could tell the mood was rather somber. The president closed the door behind Bob and said, "Won't you be seated? I'm afraid I've got some bad news to share with you." In the next few minutes the president painted a rather bleak picture of the company's solvency. The orders for new steel had simply dried up. There were several government contracts still in place, but for the most part things were grinding to a halt. Finally, the rumors of cutbacks and hard times became rather personal. "Bob, our company can't afford to operate as it always has. The decision has been made to cut out all of our middle management personnel. Your position and that of four others are going to be eliminated by the end of the year. I'm sorry, but we just have no other choice. We are going to pay you through the end of the year and then partial health benefits for the first quarter, and of course you will have access to your retirement fund, and you will keep the stock options." The boss went on to talk about his willingness to be a reference and how he would help any way that he could. Bob sat in silence, not really hearing anything else that was being said. His head was spinning from all that he had just heard. "I know that's a lot to process," said the president. "Why don't you take the rest of the day off to collect your thoughts, and we can talk more in the morning."

Bob spent the rest of the day driving around town while headed no place in particular. He went through the whole range of emotions. At times he was angry, then depressed, then worried, then shocked, then angry all over again. He had no idea how to share the news with his wife. He had always been the provider. And now he faced the prospect of no job. How could he have let her down? How could he have let down his girls? They were all counting on him. How were they going to face the new year? How would he pay the mortgage? How would they pay the bills? Who was hiring? How long would it take to find a new job? He drove around until it was dark. When he finally got home, Carla had supper on the table. "Thanks, but I already ate," he told her. The truth was that he had not eaten since breakfast, but somehow the events of the day had taken away his appetite. He told her that he had some work to do from the office. He went straight to his study and closed the door, where he remained until after midnight.

The next morning, he awoke, showered, ate breakfast, and kissed his wife and daughters goodbye, the way he had done for years. As he drove to work, he tried to clear his thoughts. Unknowingly, he was slipping into a denial that would last for weeks. He decided not to tell Carla, at least not yet. He was also not going to tell his daughters, his friends, or even the folks at their church. He would think of some solution and fix the problem before he would ever tell anyone about the job loss. His plans were to let his life go on as though nothing were wrong. "We'll be just fine," he kept telling himself.

But things weren't fine. He had spoken with a dozen colleagues and even some old college friends to explore the job market. He told all of them the same lie: "I have a friend I work with who is losing his job. I'm trying to help him find a place to settle. Got any ideas?"

Over and over, he heard the same refrain: "Things are just bad right now. No one is hiring. I'll let you know if I hear about anything your friend might be interested in."

The days turned to weeks. It was already Thanksgiving, and Bob had no real answer. He simply kept up a false front and a brave resolve. No one, not even Carla, noticed the toll the stress was taking on his health and spirit. Bob was losing weight, and the circles under his eyes grew darker by the day. There was no joy in his life, only stress and worry. When Carla occasionally asked if everything was okay, he would reply, "Everything's fine, sweetheart. We're just really busy at work these days, and I'm having to do a lot. Not to worry."

A defining moment came one afternoon when Bob ducked into a coffee shop for a cup of coffee. Christmas music was playing, and decorations were all around the store. Though it was already early December, for the first time it really dawned on him that Christmas was just around the corner. His mind started racing. He thought of how he and his wife tended to go a little overboard with presents each year. They always bought expensive gifts—and lots of them. The girls always asked for the latest things, and they usually got them. Bob always gave his wife jewelry and a new dress or two. Suddenly, it all came crashing in. "I can't afford Christmas! We have to save all we can. We have to cut back." He thought of all the expectations and all the gifts to buy. How could he let everyone down, especially at Christmas? A sudden panic overtook his thoughts. His stomach knotted up as though he had been punched.

Bob was finally jolted back to consciousness when the young girl behind the counter said for the third time, "Sir, are you going to order something or not?"

At that moment, even a cup of coffee seemed too extravagant. He turned and walked back to his car without saying a word to her or to anyone else.

The next few days around the house were intolerable. The financial stress and the sense of failure kept Bob on the edge. He started questioning every expenditure, even the simple, everyday things. "Why are you going to the store again? Do you really need to buy something for *all* your Bible study group? And don't take that suit to the cleaners; it still looks fine. And while I'm at it, I don't see any reason to buy gift cards for the mailman or the paperboy; they both have done a sorry job this year."

Carla, of course, noticed the stress. She finally brought it up. "What's wrong, Bob? You're just not acting like yourself. You are snapping at every little thing I do."

He responded curtly, "I'll snap whenever I feel like snapping!" And with that he slammed the door on his way out. He was in a downward spiral that seemingly had no end.

To add insult to injury, that morning when he arrived at his office, he had a voicemail message from Pastor Rick. He pushed the play button and heard the familiar voice of his pastor. "Bob, I was just working on the Christmas Eve service. I was wondering if you could give a short testimony during the service, right after the children's nativity scene. I need you to speak on the theme 'Christmas blessings.' Think about it, and let me know. Thanks."

Bob could no longer carry the weight of his secrets. A few days later, according to what had become his recent habit, he drove to a local fast-food place for a quick lunch and then ate by himself in the parking lot of his business. The weight of it all hit him like a ton of bricks, and he found himself sobbing uncontrollably in his car. In the providence of God's timing, a friend from his church, Tom, happened to walk by. Tom was actually on his way up to visit him. Every year, Tom would drop by at Christmas to say hello. He always brought a box of chocolates for Carla, a poinsettia for Bob's desk, and some collectable ornaments for the girls. In the madness of his situation, Bob never even thought once about his annual visit. Tom spotted Bob sitting in his car and walked over to tap on the glass. Bob had not seen him approaching the car. He was startled and turned to look. It was then that Tom saw the tears streaming down his face, and Bob knew he would have to offer an explanation.

Bob rolled down the window and tried to pass it off. "Tom, what a surprise! It's good to see you."

Tom immediately knew something was very wrong. He noticed the gaunt look and the untidy car. The two had been friends way too long for any pretense. "Bob, what's wrong? Is it Carla? Are the girls okay?"

Bob felt some kind of stronghold suddenly burst on the inside. "Get in," Bob said, "this could take a while."

Tom sat in the passenger seat as Bob began to let weeks of stress and strain come pouring out. Like a dam bursting under too much pressure, Bob's emotions came spilling out. He told Tom everything. He told him about the job loss and the financial pressure. He told him about losing weight and trying to hide it all from his wife. "I've let them down," he said, tears streaming down his face. "I have no answer, no job prospects, no hope. We'll probably have to sell the house. Carla will think I'm a failure. I can't even afford Christmas! They'd all be better off if I were dead."

Tom tried to offer some wisdom and some solid advice. He told Bob that he really did need to talk to Carla and that she would understand. He also told Bob that he should talk to Pastor Rick. "You can't carry all this by yourself. You've got people in your life who care about you, and they will help you get through it, but you have to let them know what's going on." Bob nodded several times and knew that his friend was right. Tom went on to say, "You know, maybe you're focusing on the wrong stuff. It's not about what you *don't* have; it's about what you *do* have. You have a great family and lots of support. Promise me that you'll start talking this out." After a few more brief moments of conversation, the two men shook hands and said their farewells. Both left the conversation knowing they had work to do.

Tom knew he had to find some ways to help his friend—*really* help. He knew that his friend needed more than just some words of encouragement. And so he set his mind to thinking of things to do that could really make a difference. He made a list of some people he needed to call. He was determined not to let his friend founder for very long.

Bob had *his* work cut out as well. He called his secretary to say that he was heading home and that he would see her in the morning. He cranked his car and drove to his house and to the difficult conversation he needed to have with his wife. When he got home, she was startled to see him. "Why are you home this time of day?" she asked. "Is something wrong? Are the girls okay?"

"They're fine, and there is no emergency, but I do need to tell you a few things."

They sat together on a sofa in the den while he spilled his guts for the second time that day. Carla sat and listened with shock and pain and maybe a little frustration. How could she have not seen it coming? Why didn't he tell her weeks ago? She thought about all the things she *could* say like, "Why didn't you tell me? How could you keep this from me? What were you thinking?" But instead of harsh words, she chose the path of grace. She immediately began to heal the wounds in his life with her demeanor, warm smile, and genuine love. She had always been the pragmatist in the family, and her nature shifted into high gear. "So we'll just cut back this year. No big deal. I've been concerned over the past few years about how many gifts we buy anyway. It will do us some good to spend a little less." She went on to describe how she wanted it to be more of a simple family Christmas this year and how she was looking forward to the simple pleasures of just spending time together over the holidays. Bob was chagrined and marveled again at what he had done to deserve such a special wife.

That night, he called his pastor and quickly brought him into the loop as well. Pastor Rick had some good words of counsel and promised to pray and do anything he could. They, too, had been friends for a long time, and Bob knew there was great sincerity and love in his words. "I still need you to speak on Christmas Eve. Just talk about whatever the Lord lays on your heart," said Pastor Rick.

There was a long pause. "I'm not so sure," Bob said, "but I'll give it some more thought."

Christmas Eve found Bob and his family walking into church for the annual service. Bob was keeping his promise to give a word of testimony, but he still didn't know exactly what to say. Tom caught him in the foyer and took him off to the side for a moment. "I hope you don't mind, but I took the liberty of calling one of my friends who is a headhunter; he helps people find new places to work. I told him about your experience and your background, and he was hopeful. In fact, he has set up three interviews for you for the week after Christmas. Two seem promising." Bob didn't know what to say. He just grabbed his friend and gave him a huge bear hug.

The children had just finished their Christmas play, complete with bathrobed shepherds and aluminum-foil-crowned wise men, when Bob made his way to the lectern. He cleared his throat and offered his best. "I was reminded," he said, "when I saw the wise men a moment ago, about the three gifts given to the Christ child: gold, frankincense, and myrrh. I also have received three gifts this Christmas, gifts that I think may be better than those of the magi. This Christmas, I have been reminded of the greater gifts in my life. I have a family who loves me always, friends who encourage me faithfully, and a church that supports me constantly. I may have fewer gifts under the tree come tomorrow morning, but it's going to be a great Christmas." And then he offered one other insight. "You know, a few weeks ago, I was so worried, thinking I couldn't afford Christmas. And then it dawned on me that it's not about what I can or can't buy; it's about what's already been given to me by the child in the manger."

As the service drew to a close, Bob thought the candles somehow seemed brighter, the carols more inspiring, and the world more hopeful.

So maybe this hasn't been the best year for some of you. Some of you are really struggling. I know, because we've talked. And maybe there won't be as many presents under the tree as there are some other years. Let me simply remind you that it's not about what you can afford. It's about what you already have in Christ. So enjoy the greater gifts.

CHAPTER 23

Wrapping Paper

Luke 2:17-20

Tom Collier stepped out of his warm and crowded house to face a stiff, brisk December breeze. He headed down the driveway to the front curb to make his fourth trash trip of the day. In each hand he held a large black plastic bag of Christmas wrapping remnants. The rather large pile at the street testified to the overindulgent Christmas the Collier family had just experienced. At the curb was a large assortment of cardboard boxes, foam containers, flimsy and torn gift boxes, and piles and piles of wadded-up wrapping paper, along with a few colorful bows.

Going into the season, Tom and his wife, Jane, had agreed that this Christmas would be different. They were going to cut back and spend less. But you know how the season tends to take off. Once again, they had overspent, overextended, and overbought. As Tom added to the ever-growing pile of trash, he wondered how many gifts given this year would even be remembered by next December.

The house had been filled with a steady stream of family and friends all throughout the holidays. Like many families, the opening of Christmas presents had spanned several days, as another group of family members would straggle in and out of town. Jane's sister and her kids had spent most of the week leading up to Christmas at the Collier home. Tom's parents, along with his brother and his family, had arrived the day after Christmas and were still hanging around. There had been lavish meals, decadent desserts, and too many calorie-laden cookies. There had also been endless games played at all hours of the night by the various members of the family. They had viewed the movie *Elf* numerous times, and *The Christmas Story* had played nonstop on Christmas Day. Tom was convinced that if they ever did a remake, he could play the part of Ralphie, as every word of dialogue could quickly come to mind. Tom's teenage daughter, Alice, had insisted on nonstop Christmas music throughout the season. The various CDs had been played so much that Tom thought surely the voices on the CDs would have grown hoarse by now.

As he stepped outside, the sudden rush of cold air was refreshing to Tom, maybe even exhilarating. He rather enjoyed the brief respite that his trip to the curb would afford him. The house was still full of guests, still reeking of Christmas candles, and still cluttered with air mattresses and sleeping bags. The refrigerator was bursting at the seams with leftovers, and the kitchen counters were a disaster. To be honest, Tom was ready for it all to be over. It had been fun and stressful all at the same time. He was ready for life to get back to normal. He winced as he thought about all the things still left to do to put away Christmas. Taking down the tree would be no small task. The ornaments had to be carefully packed away, and the Christmas china still had to be hand-washed and tucked away in the attic for another year. There was also the job of taking down all the lights that Jane insisted needed to be placed in the front trees and along the roofline of the house. "I'll be glad when Christmas is over and done," Tom thought.

Standing in the street, Tom attempted to stuff one last bag into his already stuffed city-approved trash container. As you might guess, the side of the bag split open, spilling most of its contents out into the street. The breeze quickly sent hundreds of foam peanuts scampering down the street. Wads of tissue and wrapping paper began their seemingly choreographed dance down the street as well. Tom quickly assessed the situation and decided to just let the foam peanuts go, but he resolved to make a valiant effort to retrieve as much of the paper as he could. He was able to quickly gather the larger pieces, but a few of the scraps kept teasing him as they danced away from his outstretched arms. Finally, he corralled all that he could see. He stuffed everything into the trash container and slammed down the lid. "Good riddance," he shouted. And in his mind he thought, "And good riddance to all that's left of Christmas! I don't want to even think about Christmas again until next December."

As he turned to walk back toward the house, he spotted one last piece of wrapping paper blowing around the front yard. It was the paper that Jane had used to wrap all of Alice's presents. Jane always insisted on wrapping every gift, thinking there was joy in opening presents that would be extended for a while if each gift were individually wrapped. The paper that Jane had selected for this year was a foil wrapping paper, mostly shiny silver with green Christmas trees and red and white candy canes carefully patterned across the paper. Jane thought the silver foil paper added just the right sparkle under the tree.

Tom walked over to grasp the last sole survivor of Christmas wrapping paper escapees. As he stooped to pick it up, the breeze suddenly moved it just beyond his outstretched hand. And so it started—a sort of cat-and-mouse chase down the street. Tom would get close, only to have the scrap of paper escape by just the tiniest of margins. For Tom it became a determined quest, and he was *not* going to be defeated. In the back of his mind, he wondered what the neighbors might have thought had they taken in the scene. Tom had been so intent on corralling the scrap of paper that he was a little surprised to discover that he had pursued it for nearly a block. The breeze seemed to pick up a little momentum as Tom watched the scrap tumble further and further away. He finally gave in to defeat and waved off his prey, saying, "To heck with it!"

As he turned to make his way back toward the house, the winter wind had stiffened considerably and carried a little bite. He realized that his sweater and slippers were no match for the cold. He finally closed the front door behind him, glad to have survived the battle of the Christmas trash. Jane had heard him come in and yelled from the kitchen, "Tom, I've got another bag of trash here in the kitchen. Do you mind being a dear and carrying it out to the trash for me?"

Tom mumbled something under his breath that sounded like, "Why don't you take that trash bag and…" but then let the thought go.

It was early spring when Tom first noticed a very busy robin building a nest in the large sycamore tree just outside the bedroom window. He was fascinated by the meticulous care that the mother robin had taken to carefully construct her nest of twigs and leaves and whatever else she could find. He noticed the nest again a few days later. She seemed to have built quite a sturdy nest, although his view was partially obscured by the budding leaves that were pushing their way out of the end of every tender branch. A couple weeks later, an early spring thunderstorm rocked the tree pretty severely. Tom looked out and found some comfort in discovering that the small nest had survived the storm. It was then that something caught his eye that he had not seen before. The mother robin had used some bits of paper scraps when building the nest. There was a shiny piece of foil paper that almost looked like the wrapping paper Jane had used so abundantly at Christmas. Tom thought about the scrap that got away and said to himself, "Surely not.

What are the odds of that happening? Where would the momma bird have even found it?" He quickly dismissed the thought and the memory of the Christmas wrapping paper.

At the end of May, Bill Davis, a long-time co-worker of Tom's at the office, was celebrating his retirement. After forty years of life as an accountant, Bill was finally calling it quits. The office staff had planned to send him off in grand style. On his last day, a catered meal was provided, and everyone brought gifts to extend their well wishes to Bill, whose future plans included travel, more time with the grandkids, and finally reading all those books he had never finished.

The table was filled with parting gifts, given by each member of the staff. Just as the party was starting, Margaret, who was always a little scatterbrained and unorganized, came running in at the last minute. "I'm sorry I'm late," she explained, "but I had trouble finding any wrapping paper at my house. All I could find was some leftover Christmas paper. Sorry, Bill. I hope you don't mind!"

Bill was gracious, as always. "I don't mind at all. Who's going to argue with such a beautiful gift?"

Tom was a little stunned to see the gift that Margaret had pulled from her rather large purse. It was the same exact wrapping paper that had filled his home last December. "What a coincidence," he thought. "That crazy paper keeps showing up. It's like the spirit of Christmas just won't go away."

It was late July when Tom, Jane, and Alice returned from a week-long vacation at the beach. The car was a total wreck after a week of ice coolers, beach chairs, and fast food. It looked to Tom as though they had brought most of the beach home with them in their car. There was sand everywhere—in the seats, on the floorboards, and in the trunk. Being a little zealous about car care, Tom immediately began cleaning the car as soon as the suitcases were unloaded. He meticulously scrubbed the highway bugs off the windshield and grill. He washed the car and scrubbed the tires. Once the exterior was pristine again, he took on the work of cleaning out the interior trash. He took out the floor mats and pressure-washed the dirt away. Then he brought out the vacuum and tried to suck up every little grain of sand. It was while cleaning out the trunk that Tom got a little surprise. He was lifting up the mat that covers the spare tire when he noticed that a scrap of paper had found its way wedged between the spare and the jack. When he pulled it out, he discovered that it was a piece of Christmas wrapping paper—shiny foil with green trees and candy canes. He thought, "How could this scrap of paper have gotten into the trunk? I know I've cleaned out this trunk since last Christmas, haven't I?" Still, he wondered at how Christmas paper could appear in late July. It all seemed a little too coincidental.

It was on a Friday night in late October that the Collier family loaded up the car to head to the local high school football game. The freshman cheerleading squad had been invited by the varsity squad to help cheer at the big game against the crosstown rivals. Ever since making the freshman squad, Alice had all but worshiped the junior and senior girls on the varsity squad. The night was clear, the winds calm—it was going to be a perfect night for football. Tom and Jane had gotten to the stadium early to stake out a good seat in the stands from which they could watch their daughter cheer. They had been in their seats for the better part of an hour when the first smells of the concession stand came wafting across the crowd. Tom immediately picked up the scent of grilled hotdogs. Knowing that it was still twenty minutes before kickoff, he told Jane that he was starving and that he was headed off for a hotdog and coke.

"Just make sure you are back in time to run the video camera," said Jane. "We have to make sure to catch the moment when the team runs through the big banner. Alice is going to help hold the sign."

"Not to worry," Tom responded. "I'll be back in a minute." And with that, Tom raced off to the concession stand in search of a juicy dog and an ice-cold coke.

A few minutes later, he climbed his way back into the stands with his prized possessions in each hand. He slipped momentarily as he made his final long stride to his seat. Once seated, he looked down at his shoe to see what may have caused him to slip. It seems that a piece of paper was stuck to the bottom of his shoe—a piece of shiny foil wrapping paper with green trees and candy canes.

"How in the world?" thought Tom. But his thoughts were interrupted as the marching band burst onto the field with the snare drums beating and the trombones blaring.

After the game, Tom and Jane headed home. Jane was tired and went upstairs to get ready for bed. Tom had settled into his recliner, with a book in his hand, enjoying the solitude of a quiet moment. He told Jane that he would stay up and wait for Alice to get home. One of the other parents was going to take a bunch of the girls to a pizza place for an after-game treat. Tom didn't know if any boys were included, and he really didn't want to know. The other parent had promised to have Alice home by 11:00.

Just as he was about to crack open his book, he noticed the daily newspaper that was still rolled up, waiting to be read, just a few feet from the recliner. He decided to give it a quick scan before getting into his book. In the lifestyle section he came across a big colorful ad that read, "Early Pre-Christmas Sale."

"Pre-Christmas sale?" he thought to himself. "We haven't even had Thanksgiving yet. Who thinks about Christmas in October?"

Then he remembered for the first time his latest sighting of the Christmas wrapping paper at the ballgame earlier that evening. "That was really weird—a little too weird," he mused. "Why does that crazy wrapping paper find a way of continuing to show up in my life? I can't seem to get away from it! It's like someone is trying to remind me about Christmas all year long. Surely a few days of devotion in late December is more than enough." He thought about how soon the season would once again be upon him. He thought about the tree, the lights, the endless trips to the mall, and how stressful things would be yet again.

And then, suddenly, late on a Friday night in October, ten months after he had bid good riddance to Christmas, the real miracle of the season started unfolding in his heart and mind. He remembered how quickly and forcibly he wanted to put the season away last December. He remembered how he had wanted to pack away the Christmas spirit with all the ornaments, decorations, and Christmas china. And yet, in its own way, Christmas had found a way to show up all year. Maybe there was a message, a spirit, a joy, a gospel that Tom somehow had missed. Maybe Christmas is not intended to be a seasonal celebration, but a life-altering event. Maybe Christmas, or at least the spirit of Christmas, should be evident in the heart of every believer, every season. Maybe a little kindness, a little sharing, a little joy, a little compassion, a little hope could go a long way in changing the world. Maybe instead of shunning the season, it ought to be embraced, observed with passion, and lived out continually. And there, in the gentle grace of the moment in the recliner, Tom vowed never to complain about the Christmas season ever again, but instead to do his best to keep the spirit alive throughout the year.

About a week after Thanksgiving, Jane was anxious to start the run-up to Christmas, having already purchased most of the gifts. She was particularly anxious about wrapping the gifts. She talked Tom into stopping at the supermarket on the way home from church one Sunday afternoon. "I want to be sure to get plenty of paper. You know how I hate running out," she said. And then she added, "I've got to be sure to get a different paper from last year. I don't guess by any stretch of the imagination that you remember last year's wrapping paper do you?"

Tom answered quietly, "It was a shiny silver paper with green Christmas trees and red and white candy canes."

Jane was stunned. "How could you possibly remember that?"

Something about experiencing the first Christmas changed the lives of the shepherds forever. They went back glorifying and praising God and telling the story to anyone who would listen. And all those who heard were amazed. It really should affect us in the same way. Once we have experienced the real story of Christmas, our lives should never be the same. Sure, it's easy to get caught up in the stress and strain, the frenetic speed of the season, and wish it all away too soon. But what if we chose to do something different with the story? What if we determined to keep it alive all year? What if we extended grace, offered forgiveness, shared freely, and lived passionately? What if we determined that Christmas is not a seasonal celebration, but the start of a whole new life? What if we lived this entire year as though the story of Jesus really matters? What if?

CHAPTER 24

Wayfaring Stranger

Luke 2:1-7

Bill Emery was a traveling salesman. He sold commercial kitchen equipment for a company based out of Dayton, Ohio. He was responsible for a three-state region, including Ohio, Kentucky, and Indiana. He actually lived about an hour south of Dayton in the little town of Norwood, Ohio. Located in the southwest corner of the state, Norwood provided Bill with a home base that was strategically close to his entire region. Bill and his wife, Donna, had three children: Tracy, who was a middle-schooler; Kathy, who was in second grade; and Derek, who was in kindergarten. They lived in a nice home that was located at the end of a private lane, about a mile from the main part of town. Donna was a stay-at-home mom who busied herself with the kids' activities and who was involved with a women's shelter in Norwood.

As Christmas approached, the three kids got more excited by the day. The older two had both starred in school plays, and all three had sung in the Christmas program at church. Now that the holidays had begun, the three reached new levels of excitement. They decorated the tree, wrote letters to Santa, and helped Donna make several batches of Christmas cookies. Each of them had also taken the time to write out their Christmas wish list. Tracy had the most extensive and expensive list. She wanted the latest cell phone, a lot of clothes, and some makeup, because "all the girls were wearing it." Kathy had a much shorter list, but one that was filled with a couple hard-to-get items, including a pair of concert tickets to see her favorite pop star. Derek wanted the typical little boy stuff: a bike, some Legos, and a couple robot toys—and maybe a private plane to fly around in.

It had been a lean year in the commercial kitchen equipment business. The downturn in the economy had many restaurants deferring new equipment purchases until next year. Many were trying to limp along with the old stuff until things got better, all of which meant that Bill's commissions were way down. There just wasn't as much to go around this year. Still, Bill knew that he was better off than others. They would be okay. They weren't struggling like some families. They were just going to have to scale back a little this year. Even with the smaller salary, Bill was still a very generous soul. His family had adopted a needy family from their church and provided them with plenty for a great Christmas meal and a few presents for the kids. Bill also volunteered at a local food bank. He had personally walked through four neighborhoods rounding up food donations.

As he read the wish lists from his children, he winced and rubbed the back of his neck. "I hope they won't be too disappointed," he said to Donna. "They are certainly not going to get everything on their lists."

"I'm sure they will be excited to get whatever is under the tree on Christmas morning," Donna said.

"I hope so," thought Bill. He hoped, at least in the back of his mind, that his children would grow up unselfish, to be mindful of others and generous with whatever blessings they would know, to be grateful for every gift, no matter how great or small.

Bill's company was closed the week following Christmas, so the boss had encouraged all the salesmen to work as hard as they could, right up to Christmas Eve. Bill was out early on Christmas Eve morning. He drove a couple hours west into Indiana to make a few calls. Even though he didn't make any sales, he enjoyed spending a few moments with familiar clients and wishing them a merry Christmas. It was just after 2 p.m. when Bill pointed his car back east, back toward Norwood, back toward home. With still more than a hundred miles to drive, Bill noticed the clouds turning gray. Soon, a heavy snow started to fall. The grassy median turned white almost instantly. Bill knew the roads would get treacherous after nightfall, so he kept up a good pace as he headed home. By the time he neared the outskirts of Norwood, a good five inches of snow had fallen. He was glad to be almost home and glad that his Jeep had four-wheel drive.

He spotted her about a hundred yards ahead of him. A car was broken down on the shoulder of the road. A woman was stumbling in the snow, trying to make her way around to the front of the car to raise the hood. She looked to be in her sixties and very much in need of help. A little thought surfaced in his mind for just a moment: "Someone will stop and help her.

She's probably already called someone on her cell phone. Maybe the police are on the way."

But by the time he pulled next to her, those thoughts were gone, and his benevolent spirit had kicked in. He rolled down the window and said, "You look like you need some help. Are you okay?"

She replied, "It's my car; it just quit on me. I have plenty of gas, but it just died for some reason."

"Maybe I can help," said Bill. He pulled over in front of her car and walked his way through the snow to where she was standing. He got the key from her and tried to start the engine. It turned over, but wouldn't fire off. He checked the gas gauge and looked under the hood to make sure the spark plug wires were connected, but nothing he tried seemed to make any progress.

"Do you live close?" he asked before he noticed the Georgia plates.

"Afraid not," she said. "I was trying to get back home for Christmas. I've been visiting an aunt of mine in Columbus. I didn't count on this snow-storm."

Bill said to her, "Listen, there is a gas station about a mile up the road. A good friend of mine runs it. Maybe he can help. I have a chain in my car. Let's try to pull it to the station. There is no way we can find a tow truck on Christmas Eve." The lady looked a little apprehensive but finally agreed to let Bill pull her toward the station.

Things didn't look very promising as they pulled into the gas station. All the lights were out, and a sign on the door simply read, "Went home early for Christmas. Will open at noon on Christmas Day."

"Shoot! We're out of luck," said Bill. "The place is closed until tomor-row. There is no way we are going to find a mechanic tonight. I'm afraid you're stuck."

The elderly lady looked a bit out of sorts. "I don't know what to do. Is there a motel close by where I can spend the night?"

"There's one about a mile from here. I can drive you and see if they have a room."

"That's really nice of you," said the woman. "By the way, my name is Clara, Clara Williams. I appreciate all your help. Surely you have a family waiting for you at home."

"Well, I do," said Bill, "but it's still early. I don't live too far from here. I will be home soon."

The two of them rode together in Bill's Jeep. When they got to the motel, the parking lot was full. It seemed like a lot of travelers were riding out the storm. Bill went in and spoke to the clerk for a few minutes. He came back out and told Clara, "I'm afraid I have bad news. They're all booked up. Not a single room left."

Clara spoke up, "Listen, I have troubled you more than enough. I've got some blankets in my car and some coffee in a thermos. I'll just make a night of it in my car and get some help in the morning. Maybe the storm will clear by then."

Bill looked at her incredulously. "There is no way on God's green earth that I am about to let you spend the night in your car. You'll freeze to death! You're going home with me. I'll call my wife, and she can make you a place on the couch. I'll bring you back to your car in the morning."

"I couldn't put you out," said Clara. "It's Christmas Eve. You need to be home with your family. It's a special night. You sure don't need some old strange woman in your home."

"I am not going to leave you stranded. You're going home with me; it's settled." And with that Bill reached for his cell phone to call Donna and pointed his car toward home.

Clara could only hear one side of the conversation between Bill and Donna. She thought she heard the words, "Have you lost your mind?" and "Maybe *you* can sleep on the couch."

When he got off the phone, Clara asked, "Is everything okay?"

"Sure," said Bill. "Donna is very excited to have you as our guest tonight."

When they got home, Bill was greeted by his three children, who came running out to meet him. He hugged their necks and introduced them to his new friend, Ms. Clara. As they entered the house, their nostrils were greeted by the smell of a wonderful Christmas feast. Donna had cooked a ham with green beans and sweet potatoes. Bill noticed that she had set six places around the table. Hopefully, she was warming up to the idea of having a stranger in the house for Christmas. The meal was delicious. And as it turned out, Clara was a delightful guest. She had traveled extensively during her lifetime, and she fascinated the children with tales of faraway places and unusual sights.

After supper she took Donna off to the side. "You are certainly a special woman to treat a stranger with such courtesy. Thank you for allowing me to spend the night. I will be forever grateful."

Donna replied, "It's nice having you here. I'm glad that we could help. I'm sorry that you can't be with your family."

"I don't really have much of a family," said Clara. "I never married, and most of my people are long gone. It's actually really nice to be around children at Christmas time."

"Well, we are glad you're here. I hope you don't mind a bunch of excited kids on Christmas morning."

"It will be great," said a very grateful Clara.

One of the Christmas traditions in the Emery household was a reading of the Christmas story just before the kids went off to bed. As they gathered near the tree in front of a roaring fire, Clara asked if she might tell the Christmas story. Bill said, "Sure, why not?" and he handed her the Bible.

She waved it off. "Don't need it," she said. I know this story very well." And she began to share the most wonderful telling of the Christmas story that the children had ever heard. She described the exquisite colors of the wise men's robes. She talked about the shape of the shepherd's hook. She told about the manger and the light that glowed from the face of the infant Christ. She talked about the sweet face of Mary and the flecks of gray in Joseph's beard. To hear her describe the scene, you would have thought that she had been present on that first Christmas night.

When the story was over, the sleepy-eyed children were told to get ready for bed. They kissed their parents goodnight, and little Derek even dared to give Ms. Clara a hug. The house grew quiet. The snow had stopped falling outside. The moon cast a beautiful glow on the unspoiled snow in the front yard. It had been a good night. And Clara's presence had only added to the evening.

The morning sun was brilliant as it bounced off the white snow. Kathy was the first to awaken, and she quickly awakened Tracy and Derek. Within seconds the trio was bouncing up and down on their parents' bed. "Get up! It's Christmas! It's time to go open the presents!"

"Let's be quiet for a moment," whispered Donna. "Ms. Clara might not be awake yet. You three are going to scare her to death!"

Bill was the first to make his way down the steps to peek at the tree with all the presents beneath. There seemed to be a lot more than he remembered. When we went to awaken Ms. Clara, he didn't find her. The sheets were all carefully folded, and the pillow was placed at the end of the couch. She wasn't in the kitchen, the bathroom, or the den. In fact, she was nowhere to be found. Soon, the kids joined in the search. They looked in every crevice and corner, but she was just not there. She had apparently slipped out as soon as it was daylight. "I'll go search for her in a few minutes. I'm sure she walked back to her car. Probably waiting for Joe to open up the station."

Donna started gently pulling on Bill's arm. "Uh, Bill, did you put out some extra presents last night? There seem to be a few extra that I don't know about."

"I didn't put any out. You don't think Clara brought some gifts, do you? She didn't even have a bag."

Before they could get finished with their thoughts, the three children had started tearing into their gifts. Tracy raced over and hugged her mom and dad, "A phone! I can't believe you guys bought me one!" Kathy screamed when she opened a box that contained two front-row tickets to the concert. And Derek went ballistic when he spied not one, but two robot toys.

Donna looked at Bill. "Did you...?"

"No, did you?"

"Then who?"

There was no other answer—it had to be Clara. But how could she have known? How could she have found those gifts?

Bill cranked up the Jeep and headed for the gas station. He was surprised that he didn't find any footprints in the snow. "She didn't just fly back to her car did she?" he thought to himself. When he got to the station, Joe was just opening up. But Clara's car was not where they had left it.

"Joe, did you help an old woman with her car this morning?"

"No, I just got here myself. Look at the snow on the parking lot. No car has been here all day," said Joe.

Bill drove home and tried to make sense of it all. The kids were playing outside in the snow as he pulled into the driveway. "Look, Daddy. We are making snow angels, just like the big one in the front yard."

Bill looked at the angel print in the front yard. "Who made that big angel?" he asked.

Tracy responded, "Mom said you must have before you went to town. It's too big for one of us."

Derek chimed in, "I know! Maybe Ms. Clara made it."

"Maybe she did," said Bill. "Maybe she did."

I hope we never get too old to forget the wonder of Christmas. I hope that it will always have a little mystery, a little unexpected grace, and maybe a little beating of an angel's wings. I hope the story will still bring us hope, peace, and joy, even when we are very old.

Okay, so maybe Clara wasn't real, and maybe no one got concert tickets. But the part about the wise men's robes and the shepherd's hook and the child in the manger—that's as real as it gets.

CHAPTER 25

Christmas Gloves

Luke 2:8-16

It had been a tough year for George Baker and his family. George was a salesman who worked mostly on commission for a local floor covering company. Because of the slow economy, people were deferring home-improvement projects until better days, which meant for George that money was tighter than usual. Even in good years, he barely stayed afloat in terms of keeping the bills paid. This year had been a real struggle, though. He and his wife, Mary, spent a lot of sleepless nights worrying about their finances. Their house needed some attention. His car had over 175,000 miles and was literally falling apart. Every time George turned the key, he wondered if it would start. The radio only worked about half the time. The defroster was having some issues, and the driver's door handle was broken, which meant he always had to open the back door and reach around to open the front door from the inside. He knew he was driving on borrowed time. His children were young and blissfully unaware of the financial strain on the family. His son, Joey, was turning ten, and his daughter, Susie, was just six. For them the coming of Christmas meant decorating the house, eating Christmas cookies, dreaming of Christmas morning, and practicing for the children's pageant at church.

George began to feel the holiday pressure by mid-November. He not only worried about the usual expenses, but the thought of Christmas nearly sent him over the edge. Would there be enough money for Christmas presents? Could the family afford a nice tree and a few special treats for the holiday? Could he buy Mary something nice? The stress drove him to productive action. He decided that he would pick up an extra job during

December and try to save a little cash. He hated the thought of burning the candle at both ends and missing some family time around the holidays, but at least they would have what they needed—and some of what they wanted—for Christmas.

Seasonal jobs were hard to find. The Bakers weren't the only ones struggling to make a little extra. Each morning, George scanned the want-ads while drinking his coffee. On his lunch break, he always scanned the bulletin board at work and even called a few temp agencies. After nearly two weeks of unsuccessful attempts at finding a second job, George finally got a callback from one place where he had left his name and number. Of all places, the Salvation Army called and offered him a job as a bell ringer out front of a local store. All he would have to do was ring the bell and thank people who dropped their coins into the red bucket. Because he could only work nights, he was offered the 6:00–10:00 shift, four nights a week. The manager said George could probably work a few more shifts as well, especially if he was willing to work on weekends and even on Christmas Eve. "Anything is better than nothing," he reasoned to himself, and he agreed to take the job. It only paid minimum wage, but at least it was a job that he could work into his schedule. Starting the first week of December, George began selling flooring by day and ringing a bell by night.

The routine was pretty simple. He got off from his regular job at 4:30. He would dash home, eat a quick bite, and then layer up in preparation for standing four hours in the cold. Mary tried to encourage him as he headed out each evening. She always packed a little snack in a brown paper sack and would fill a thermos with hot coffee to help ward off the cold. On his first night of work, Mary had given him a small present to open on the way out the door. "I was going to give these to you at Christmas, but I thought you might need them now." He opened the gift to discover a beautiful pair of leather gloves with fur lining. "I hope they will keep you warm," she said, and she kissed him on the cheek on his way out.

Though he seemed to grow a little more tired with each passing day, there were some things about the job that he liked. He enjoyed the constant interaction with people. Even if they didn't always drop in a few coins, most at least said "hello" or offered a kind smile. He was amazed at people's generosity. Though it was not his job to count or deposit the money that went into the red bucket, he was impressed that each night the bucket seemed to slowly fill. "There are still a lot of good people around," he would often tell Mary when he called her on his break. Occasionally, people would stop to chat for a moment. Sometimes people actually brought him a cup of coffee or hot chocolate.

The weeks of standing in the cold on his feet began to take a toll on George's health. He noticed that his feet started to swell a little by the end of each night. His back ached now and then from all the standing. He also developed a pretty good set of the sniffles that kept his nose running and his eyes watering. Usually, by the time he made the fifteen-minute drive home, he was spent and ready to fall into bed. The whole business brought him both satisfaction and frustration. He was grateful for the work and the extra money, but angered that he was spending so little time with the kids. He was also getting increasingly frustrated by the things in his life that made such a task necessary. He hated the pressure that life was placing upon him. Why couldn't he catch a break? Why did business at the store have to be so lousy? Why did the kids need braces? Why couldn't he drive a better car? Why couldn't his family go on a vacation like other families? And what about his house—did the faucets really have to leak and the furnace have to clank all the time? As the nights grew longer, so his frustration with life grew more intense as well.

The flooring store was closed on Christmas Eve, so George was able to work an extra shift for the Salvation Army from 3:00–9:00 p.m. He spent the morning with his kids, who were on Christmas Eve overload. They were hyper, happy, and hopeful. They were going to help Mary with some of the baking for Christmas dinner. They were also excited about the Christmas Eve service and playing their parts in the pageant. The weatherman was predicting snow, and they were excited about the prospect of a white Christmas. All morning long, Christmas music played on the radio in their home. The smells of wonderful food drifted throughout the house, and the laughter of the children was contagious. George was weary from his exhausting month of work, but grateful for just one more night.

Around 2:30 p.m., George layered up one more time, grabbed his thermos and his gloves, and headed out of the house. Mary called to him, "Be sure to come straight home. Don't forget the Christmas Eve service starts at 11:00. We can't be late. The kids have to be there early, you know."

"I remember," he called back over his shoulder as he walked toward the car. "I'll be home in plenty of time."

As the afternoon slowly became evening, the temperature began to drop, and soon the skies were filled with dark gray, heavy-laden clouds. The first few snowflakes began to fall around 7:00 p.m. At first, the flakes melted as soon as they hit the ground, but after a while, they began to stick, and soon a dusting of snow began to blanket much of the parking lot. By 8:00, most of the shoppers were heading home. The store would close at 9:00, and George's long December of bell ringing would also come to a close. He counted only a handful of folks entering and leaving the store in the last hour. Right at 9:00, the main lights in the store were turned off, and the last customers and most of the employees scurried to their cars. The snow had let up, but there was a pesky slush on the streets that had many driving very cautiously out of the parking lot. By the time George locked up the collection bucket and stepped outside, he was all alone in the parking lot. He quickly walked to his car with the anticipation of getting on the road in just a moment or two.

When he got in and turned the key, nothing happened. The dashboard lights dimmed, and the starter made an ominous clicking sound. His month-long fear of a dead battery finally came to fruition. "Why now? And why tonight of all nights?" he asked himself. He got out and walked back toward the front of the store. Luckily, Fred, the night watchman, was still locking up. Fred had a set of jumper cables and promised to head that way as soon as the store was secured. About fifteen minutes later, they attached the cables, and George's car slowly came to life. He wished his friend a merry Christmas and started the drive home. He called Mary to tell her that he was running late. She seemed annoyed but glad that he was on the way.

"Drive carefully. I will see you in a few minutes," she said.

The windshield was fogged up, and the defroster was taking a Christmas holiday. George tried in vain to wipe the windshield with his gloves. Luckily, he found some napkins in the floorboard and was able to make at least a small opening through which he could see the road.

What he couldn't see, however, were the slick surfaces of the roadway. About five miles later, on a very deserted stretch of highway, the well-worn tires of his car lost their grip on the road. George tried to steer into the skid but quickly lost all control. The car spun end to end and ran off the roadway, careening into the guardrail. The conscious thought George had was remembering the sound of the right side of his car as it scraped its way along the metallic guardrail. He blacked out for a moment, maybe two; he didn't really remember. He woke up with a splitting headache and the sensation of something warm oozing down his face. It was blood. He had apparently struck his head on the wheel and possible broken his nose. "Great, a trip to the ER. How much will that cost on a Christmas Eve?" he wondered. He cursed under his breath and wondered what else could possibly go wrong.

Something about the collision had hammered the driver's door, making it impossible to open. The entire passenger's side was smashed against the rail. Finally, after contorting himself in a number of ways, he was able to climb into the back seat and open the left rear door. He stumbled onto the slick pavement and immediately fell to the ground. He was still a bit light-headed and had lost a little of his balance. He reached into his pocket for his cell phone. When he flipped it open, he noticed the usually well-lit screen was dark. "Great, no cell phone. Now what do I do?" he thought to himself. He waited by the car for about five minutes without seeing a single car. "I guess folks are mostly home for Christmas by now." He wrapped his coat a little tighter and pulled down his hat a little further and started walking down the deserted road, knowing that an all-night gas station was up ahead. After only a few steps, his feet were completely soaked from the wet slush.

With each step a little more of George's Christmas joy seemed to slip away. "Great," he thought to himself, "I spend a whole month trying to get ahead, and now my dumb car is probably totaled, and it will take all I've earned to just get the thing towed." He thought about Mary and how she would now be in full panic mode. And what about the cell phone—was it going to need to be replaced as well? He began to curse his misfortune, his crummy job, his worthless car, and his never-can-make-ends-meet life. By the time he walked to the gas station, he had worked up a pretty good frustra-tion with anything and everybody.

The young gum-chewing kid behind the counter said, "Hey, buddy, you look pretty rough. You okay?"

"No, I'm not okay!" George shouted. I've wrecked my car, my phone is broken, my wife is going to be mad, and I just spent the last month working like a dog, and for what? Heartache! Besides that, I think I broke my nose."

The attendant looked at him cautiously and said, "Maybe you need to just chill for a minute."

"Don't tell me what I need!" shouted George. "Just show me where I can make a call."

The kid pointed to the pay phone out front. George found a few coins in his pocket and called Mary. She was worried, stressed, and then frustrated. "I'll barely have time to get myself and the kids to church on time, and now I have to drive all the way out there because you can't drive in the snow?"

"Just come get me!" George yelled, and with that, he slammed down the phone.

He went back inside to wait until she arrived. With too much time to think about it all, and with too much frustration and a little cash in his pocket, he gave in to temptation. He had not had any alcohol since his son was born ten years earlier. He didn't think it was the kind of example to set, so he had walked away from it. But tonight he was so frustrated and confused and still hurting from the broken nose that he decided to numb the pain with a few beers. He had downed three tall cans by the time Mary arrived with the kids. She couldn't believe what she encountered. She made both kids sit in the back of the minivan and watch a movie while they drove home, hoping they wouldn't wonder about their father's strange behavior. Tears filled her eyes, and her voice cracked. He told her it was no big deal and to just get over it. By the time they pulled in the driveway, they were having an argument the likes of which the kids had never witnessed. The caustic conversation continued once inside. Mary was so angered and disappointed. Both spewed a few venomous words. She brewed him some coffee and told him he'd better drink it quickly. They *were* going to church, and he *was* going to get it together. He snapped back by saying how pointless the service would be. Pastor Tom would drone on for too long. Mrs. Jones' solo would be off pitch—again. And while he was on the subject, why didn't *his* kid get to play the part of Joseph this year? "Are we not important enough to have a good part?" he asked. "How many times can you be a stinkin' shepherd, anyway?"

The service turned out to be a disaster, and Mary regretted that she had made George come along. His eyes were red, his hair was disheveled, and he slept his way through the evening message. He refused to stand and hold a candle at the end of the service. At least by the time they got home, he started to act a little more like himself. Much of the anger and frustration was gone. He gave the kids a hug and a kiss and sent them off to bed. He tried to apologize to Mary, but she didn't want to hear it and went off to bed.

It was well past 1:00 a.m. when George decided to take a walk in the neighborhood to clear his mind and figure out how he was ever going to pull off a decent Christmas morning. About five houses down from his own, the Millers had put up their usual gaudy plastic nativity scene in the front yard. The lights were still burning brightly, and George stopped for a moment to take it all in. For the first time during the whole season, the real story of Christmas started to flood his mind. He thought momentarily about the Christ child and the manger. He remembered the angel's message and the shepherds who were first in all the world to hear of the Savior's birth. As silly as it felt to do so, he found himself suddenly kneeling in his neighbor's yard. He took off his gloves and folded his hands in prayer. He prayed for God's forgiveness for his bad behavior and for his selfish thoughts. He prayed for his family to still love him, for his kids to forget what they had seen and heard, and for Mary to find it in her heart to make things right again. He prayed for a Christmas miracle.

He was startled by the sound of knocking and the sensation of a bright light shining in his face. He recognized the voice. It was Fred, the night watchman. He was shining a flashlight through the car window. "George, wake up, and open the hood. Sorry it took so long to get out here. You must have fallen asleep for a moment. We need to get you on your way. I'm sure Mary's waiting for you to get home so you guys can head to the service at church tonight."

George tried to shake the cobwebs from his head. "What? What did you say?"

"Wake up, George, before you freeze to death. I have my jumper cables right here."

George felt a little bewildered. He was having trouble processing everything. He didn't know whether to laugh or cry or thank Jesus. Was it all a dream? Had he never left the parking lot? Was there no wreck after all? Where were Mary and the kids? He jumped out of the car and raced around it, looking for signs of a crash.

"What's wrong?" asked Fred. "Whatcha looking for?"

"I'm just looking at my beautiful old car, that's all. Hey, look! I'm not bleeding! Say, what time is it?"

"It's about 9:30 p.m., George. What time did you think it was?"

"Fred, swear to me, it's still Christmas Eve, right? And it's only 9:30. Please tell me that's true!"

"Of course, it's true, George! I think the cold air has made you a little crazy!"

George gave Fred a huge and unexpected bear hug. "Merry Christmas, Fred! Let's get the car started. I have to get home and pick up Mary and the kids. We can't be too late; they're in the play tonight! Plus, I don't want to miss Mrs. Jones' solo or what Pastor Tom is going to say tonight. After all, it's Christmas Eve!" Fred looked at him like he was a little nuts.

The service was the best Christmas Eve service George had ever attended. The music was glorious, the decorations were spectacular, and the message was most meaningful. It was late when they finally got home and got the kids wrestled into bed. Mary was tired and went to bed soon after the kids went to sleep. George couldn't rest. His mind was racing a thousand miles an hour. "Maybe a walk will relax me," he thought. As he walked outside, the once cloudy skies had given way to a bright, crisp, star-filled night. He walked down the street and paused for a moment in front of the Millers' plastic nativity scene, where his dream had taken him so much earlier in the night. He paused and reflected on all his true blessings. As he was about to walk away, something caught his eye. He looked down and saw his new gloves, the ones Mary had given him as an early Christmas present, lying on the ground. "That's odd," he thought. "How did my gloves get here?"

Christmas is always full of miracles. Which one will claim you this year?

www.ingramcontent.com/pod-product-compliance
Lightning Source LLC
Chambersburg PA
CBHW051526050726
47503CB00014B/1941